### "I have a feeling I've invaded a private party."

Drake's gaze wandered from the Scotch in his glass to the classically beautiful redhead by his side. "Actually, it's more of an Irish wake."

"For Jacques?"

Anyone who entered the Sundance Inn had known Jacques. It was a hideaway reserved for family and longtime friends.

"I've never seen you around before," Drake commented. "Where did you know Jacques?"

"Aspen," she said quietly. "It was a long time ago. This is my first visit to the Sundance."

"Well  I probably won't see you again. This inn has been left to me and to some blond bimbo who'll probably have condos by next year. I've never even laid eyes on her."

Stephanie sighed and braced herself as she extended her hand. "Yes, I've heard all about that," she said. "Because, you see, the bimbo is now a redhead."

Dear Reader,

When two people fall in love, the world is suddenly new and exciting, and it's that same excitement we bring to you in Silhouette Intimate Moments. These are stories with scope, with grandeur. The characters lead the lives we all dream of, and everything they do reflects the wonder of being in love.

Longer and more sensuous than most romances, Silhouette Intimate Moments novels take you away from everyday life and let you share the magic of love. Adventure, glamour, drama, even suspense— these are the passwords that let you into a world where love has a power beyond the ordinary, where the best authors in the field today create stories of love and commitment that will stay with you always.

In coming months look for novels by your favorite authors: Maura Seger, Parris Afton Bonds, Linda Howard and Nora Roberts, to name just a few. And whenever you buy books, look for all the Silhouette Intimate Moments, love stories *for* today's women *by* today's women.

Leslie J. Wainger
Senior Editor
Silhouette Books

# Kathleen Korbel

# Edge of the World

*Silhouette Intimate Moments*

Published by Silhouette Books New York

**America's Publisher of Contemporary Romance**

SILHOUETTE BOOKS
300 East 42nd St., New York, N.Y. 10017

Copyright © 1988 by Eileen Dreyer

ISBN: 0-373-07222-8

First Silhouette Books printing January 1988

America's Publisher of Contemporary Romance

Printed in the U.S.A.

**Books by Kathleen Korbel**

Silhouette Desire

*Playing the Game* #286
*A Prince of a Guy* #389

Silhouette Intimate Moments

*A Stranger's Smile* #163
*Worth Any Risk* #191
*Edge of the World* #222

---

## *KATHLEEN KORBEL*

blames her writing on an Irish heritage that gave her the desire and a supportive husband who gave her the ultimatum, ''Do something productive or knock it off.'' An R.N. from St. Louis, she also counts traveling and music as addictions and is working on yet another career in screen writing.

To Pierre for his generosity
and Joy for her patience
while we talked skiing and film

# Chapter 1

By the time Drake McDonald spotted the redhead, he was very drunk. Drake wasn't the kind of man who usually spent his evenings hitched to a bar rail. In fact, he hadn't had two drinks back-to-back since he'd won his last World Cup Championship. But tonight seemed perfect to both celebrate bad news and commemorate a friend. So Drake had set about toasting the future, knowing as he did that all it held was disappointment and loss.

"She gets here tomorrow, huh?" the bartender asked as he prepared another round of very old Scotch, straight up.

Drake nodded lamely, his attention on the ring his last drink had left on the countertop. A countertop of polished mahogany, saved from a saloon in Holy Cross City and transported from the old ghost town to Telluride with the care afforded newborn infants. The bar was a work of art, handcarved with scrollwork, its edges worn by over a century of supporting bent elbows. Drake remembered the day it had arrived at the Sundance Inn. Tomorrow it would be someone else's responsibility.

"Her flight gets in around noon, from what I hear. She was too busy in Hollywood to get here before this." Just the tone of his voice conveyed judgment and sentencing. His eyes were unforgiving. "My audience is set for about one."

"Jacques never mentioned all this to you?"

"Not me." He threw back another drink, the Scotch losing its bite with familiarity. "First inkling I got was when I heard the will read, just like everybody else. Jacques did like his little surprises."

Drake paused a moment, his eyes focusing beyond the amber fluid. He wasn't so much angry, he decided, as disappointed. Jacques Lavalle had been his coach, his mentor. He'd been the rare kind of man who carved out his place in the world and held it simply by the force of his character and love for life. Jacques had built the Sundance Inn with the same love, the enthusiasm that only a great passion for his work could sustain, creating in it a place unique in almost all the world.

"And then—" Drake sighed, finishing the thought aloud "—he throws it all at the feet of some blond bimbo named Cissy." Another gulp of Scotch slid down his throat. "With a C."

The bartender refilled Drake's glass with an unenthusiastic shake of the head. "Well, at least he didn't leave the whole thing to her. You said half."

"After March." Drake couldn't bring himself to call it "the end of the season" since there wouldn't be a season this year. "Who knows what havoc she can wreak by then? I can't believe he gave her total control until the spring."

"Until you win your World Cup..." Sammy's hopeful smile faltered suddenly with the slip. "The Olympics," he amended quickly, knowing that this was one of the problems that was propelling the Scotch. "You've never met her before?"

Drake shook his head. "Jacques has talked about her, but she's made it a point to stay as far away from the slopes as she can. Just the person to take over a ski resort."

"I hear she drives a Jag."

Drake didn't even bother to conceal the bitter humor in his smile. "Nobody ever accused Jacques of having simple tastes."

"Think she knows anything about skiing?"

"The difference between a ski pole and the North Pole. Beyond that, I don't hold out much hope."

"That doesn't sound like a very popular lady," he heard someone say behind him.

Drake managed to swing his head around. The voice addressing him slipped right in under his skin, a soft, husky voice, the kind men dream about. When he caught sight of its owner, all he could think of was that she was certainly worthy of it.

Tall, just shy of statuesque, she had elegant curves and an impeccable carriage. Even before he saw her face, Drake thought of royalty. Breeding, the kind you couldn't fake. She was blinding Sammy with a soft smile and a request for Kir as she slid her classy frame onto the next bar stool.

"I couldn't help but overhear," she began, turning her attention to Drake and then smiling again. "Well, no, that's not true. I was eavesdropping. You're Drake McDonald, aren't you?"

She wasn't classically beautiful. Her features were just a little too squared off for that, her eyes a little too large, with a mesmerizing, hooded look to them as if she were always assessing you while half asleep. And they were dark, a chocolate brown that seemed to absorb the light around them. Drake was hooked the minute they caught hold of him—even before his gaze crept to the mass of red-gold hair that framed her face.

Oh, lady, Drake thought with a silent groan. Why did you have to show up tonight?

"Guilty," he finally admitted, not at all surprised at her recognition. He'd been televised almost all over the world, even though it was usually in spandex and goggles.

Lauren Bacall or Stephanie Powers, Drake thought absently. This lady had that same smoky voice, the kind that taught you to whistle and tickled your senses. And he seemed no more immune to it than anybody else.

"I thought so," she nodded, extending a slim hand. "Stephanie."

Drake managed a slow blink, his hand caught at his side. "What?"

His first muddled thought was that she'd been reading his mind.

She smiled, tilting her head just a little. "My name. I was going to say it's a pleasure to meet you. Maybe that's a little too complicated just now."

His lips curled in response. "I apologize. You caught me in an unfortunate stupor."

Taking her hand, Drake quashed the impulse to kiss it. That had been more Jacques's style.

"I should be the one to apologize," she demurred, evidently not too interested in regaining her freedom. "I have the feeling I invaded a private party."

Drake absently shook his head, his eyes wandering back to the Scotch in his glass. "An Irish wake."

"For Jacques?"

It wasn't a presumptuous question. Anyone who entered Sundance knew Jacques. It was a hideaway reserved for family, for longtime friends who wanted a place to be comfortable. Jacques had been the father figure. It had been his gift.

Drake nodded. "I've never seen you around before." He didn't think he needed to add that he would have remembered. "Where do you know Jacques from?"

"Oh, Aspen," she answered quietly, her own loss briefly reflected in those elegant brown eyes. "It was a long time ago."

"Then you haven't been here before?"

"No. This is my first trip."

The frustration bubbled up again, the anger directed at Jacques's other heir and, irrationally enough, at Jacques himself. Drake didn't mind sharing the Sundance. He minded the idea of possibly losing it before he had a chance to do anything to prevent it.

"Well, it's too bad," he answered finally. "Because after this I probably won't see you here again."

She sipped at her drink, her gaze taking in his tousled head. "Why? Aren't you going to be here anymore?"

Drake's answer came in the form of a derisive laugh. "Here isn't going to be here anymore. By this time next year it'll probably be brand-new condos with cedar siding and skylights. And hot tubs." Drake emptied his glass once more and let it be refilled. Stephanie didn't seem to notice.

"Ah—" she nodded sagely "—the bimbo."

Drake shrugged, his eyes sweeping the haphazard array of pictures and awards that made up the room's decorations. His picture was on the wall, too, laughing, his arm around Jacques the day he'd won his own first gold medal. It had been a long time ago.

"You're not giving her much of a chance," Stephanie said gently.

"Neither will any of the sharks that swim these waters," he snapped, realizing that he was getting surly. He knew it was time to go because he didn't care what he was saying anymore. And this lady was too attractive to insult. "Telluride has become big business, and Jacques held out as long as he could. I'm just not sure his friend Cissy will be as lucky."

Without giving in to the temptation to seek the comfort of those incredible brown eyes, Drake got himself off the bar stool and turned for the door. "It was nice meeting you. Some other time, maybe."

And he left.

Behind him, Stephanie watched his erratic retreat. Once he was well out of the bar she turned to Sammy, who was watching, too.

"Does he do that often?"

Sammy shook his head, his eyes still on the main room where the front door could be heard slamming. "Not in the eight years I've been here."

When Drake showed up the next afternoon for his appointment with his new partner, he didn't look so great. He was cold sober by then but suffering from the hangover of the century. Just to be contrary, he decided not to clean up after his practice session. Clad in a well-worn gray sweat suit, he knocked on the door to Jacques's office for the first

time since the door had been installed and waited to be asked
in.

The new partner in the Sundance Inn smiled to herself as
she settled into a comfortable leather chair. That knock
sounded threatening.

"Door's open!" she called and braced herself for the on-
coming storm.

Drake's first impression upon throwing open the door was
of sunlight glinting off precious metal. Red-gold, an elegant mane of it, and enormous brown eyes. He stopped
dead in his tracks.

"The bimbo," Stephanie informed him with barely suppressed humor, "is a redhead."

First he gaped. Then he smoldered. And then he slammed
the door so hard that Stephanie was sure it was going to
drop right off its hinges.

He was really incredible looking, Stephanie decided. Even
sweaty and unshaven, which she supposed was an image
presented just for the bimbo. No, she amended, *especially*
sweaty and unshaven.

He was dark, his cheeks windburned and baked by the
sun, his face lean and dramatically chiseled, all sharp angles and shadows. It made his clear gray eyes stand out like
lights. Stephanie would have killed to see him backlit, maybe
in three-quarter lighting, shot in black and white. What a
great face he had for film! He had a smoldering intensity
that would transform those features into dynamite on a
screen.

His hair was dark, wild brown, tossed back to be out of
the way, his beard dark enough even when shaven. And that
glisten of perspiration. It reeked of sensuality. God, she
thought in an unforgettable instant, he is devastating. He's
so sleek and strong, like a whip. So graceful in a totally
masculine way, and completely unaware of it. So dangerous.

Down and dirty, one of her friends used to say, was the
best. Now Stephanie finally understood what she'd meant.
It would have been a disappointment to see Drake all shaved
and groomed.

But that was beside the point. Stephanie was never one to let sexual attraction distract her. Even an attraction that crackled at her like a brewing lightning storm. She had a purpose here, and even Drake McDonald wasn't going to distract her.

"I hope you don't expect an apology," he challenged her, dropping his frame into the chair across the desk. A customary position for him to be in, his posture told her. It must really have hurt him to lose Jacques.

"Not in the least." Stephanie smiled evenly, getting to her feet and walking to the window. She wouldn't have admitted that that storm had moved in just a little too close for comfort. "You're absolutely correct. I don't know the first thing about skiing—except that you can't balance with the North Pole." Reaching the warmth of the sunlight, she turned back to him. "What's more, I have absolutely no intention of learning."

That didn't endear her to him in the least. His jaw started to work to keep him from cursing. "Then why even bother to show up?"

"Because Jacques asked me to."

Drake couldn't take his eyes from her. He wasn't sure whether she'd moved over into the sunlight on purpose, but it was sure as hell a distraction. In the sunlight she became fire and air, her skin translucent, her hair brilliant. She wore tailored slacks and a heavy sweater of intense hues, mostly peacock blue. The gemstone colors played against that hair, her skin and the soft earth tone of her eyes.

"So, what did you have in mind for the next few months—Cissy, isn't it?"

It wasn't the sarcastic edge to his voice that made Stephanie straighten. Cissy was a name she hadn't been called in a long time. Just the sound of it brought back memories that she didn't want to deal with right now. "Cissy is just a nickname," she answered, then turned her question around. "What about Drake? Another nickname?"

"No."

She nodded. "An interesting choice. Were you named after the hotel," she asked, her eyes flashing with dry humor, "or the duck?"

Stephanie saw him pause. Then a slow smile touched his eyes, churning up a potent sensuality he knew damn well he had. "The pirate," he answered and Stephanie knew that Jacques had been right. They'd work well together, if only Drake would give her a chance.

Letting her arms fall to her sides, Stephanie smiled back. "No one ever called me Cissy but Jacques. I'd appreciate it if you'd call me Stephanie. Stephanie Fleming."

She tried to ease back to the desk again to reassure her own control. With typical pragmatism, she assessed the increase in friction the closer she got to her visitor. It would amuse her later, she thought.

"No offense," Drake was saying, dragging a hand through his tumbled hair, the pounding at his temples tightening his features. "But why you?"

"Why not me?" Stephanie countered.

Drake's eyes were a lot more intense than the offhand shrug he offered. "You don't know anything about skiing, and this is a ski lodge. You don't want to know anything about it. Why should you care enough to fight for it?"

"Because I loved Jacques." There would be no backing down at all here, not if Stephanie wanted to accomplish what Jacques wanted. Damn him for not at least warning her that he was going to demand so much. Damn him for dying on her when she was off in Bulgaria where telegrams got lost with all the rest of the capitalist luxuries.

The fleeting shadows in Drake's eyes recalled his assumptions of the previous evening. Conclusions reached about a relationship that would have provoked Jacques to leave even half a treasure to an outsider. Stephanie bridled at the injustice of Drake's attitude.

"Jacques was a friend of my father's," she explained, wondering why she was going to the trouble. "They were in the '48 Olympics together."

"Fleming?"

"Edward Fleming. He wasn't on the Canadian team with Jacques. He was an American. They grew close when they were all skiing the U.S. races before going over. I'm sure Jacques told you about it. It was the year he lost the Canadian national championship to Jalbert."

For the first time she got a grin out of Drake. "Repeatedly. He never did forgive Pierre for not leaving at least one title out of the four for him."

Stephanie nodded. "And when Pierre broke his leg just before the Olympics began, they all partied in his hospital room. For months, from the accounts I heard."

"Your father was part of that crowd?" Drake asked, now completely interested.

Stephanie couldn't help but smile, aching to share something of Jacques. She hadn't seen him much over the years; their different life-styles had precluded that. They had corresponded faithfully, and she missed him. But now was not the time.

"My father kept Jacques from being shot by a jealous husband, from all accounts."

Drake ran that hand through his hair again. He was calculating, assessing. "So just what is it you do in Hollywood that makes you the right choice to take over the Sundance?"

A barrier down. "I'm an editor."

"Book?"

"Film. It's what I was doing when I got word about Jacques. I was in Bulgaria, and the news didn't catch up to me until a week ago."

"And you really want to take out the time to run a ski lodge for the winter?"

"No."

Drake jerked his head up, his nostrils flaring a little as his distrust erupted again. Stephanie imagined he could already hear the bulldozers.

"According to the information I got," she said, "Jacques wanted me to make all the decisions until March, which I believe is the end of the World Cup season. Then I promptly hand the reins back to you and depart to sunnier climes.

Except that now I understand that you've decided to forgo World Cup this year in favor of just the Olympics.''

The word "just" said it all in skiing. To the rest of the world, the Olympics were the pinnacle of an amateur athlete's career. Not so in skiing. The Olympics consisted of a few races every four years, whereas the World Cup was a yearlong contest each and every year that tested the mettle of a real athlete as he traveled from country to country to race against the world's best.

Stephanie's father had netted a downhill World Cup one year. Drake had an impressive two-year hold on the downhill, slalom and grand slalom golds. Rare for anyone, unheard of for an American. The racing world respected him for the four gold medals he'd garnered in the Olympics, but revered him for his two-time overall World Cup title.

Drake's eyebrows rose. "I thought you didn't know anything about skiing."

Stephanie couldn't help but grin. "Even if I'd lived in a cave before coming here, I would have found out everything I wanted to know about you. And from what I've discovered so far, I'd be burned at the stake if I did anything to take you away from your third set of gold medals. The greatest triple threat in Alpine skiing since Jean-Claude Killy, I believe. Your manager, Diane, filled me in with great enthusiasm. You have quite a following."

Drake smiled a bit stiffly. "This is the home field. It's natural."

"Why no World Cup this year?" she asked quietly.

He shrugged. "An injury." Without warning, he launched himself to his feet and began to pace, his eyes resolutely on Stephanie. "Listen, what I told you last night still holds true. The sharks are hungry out there, and you're fresh meat. Why don't you leave the decisions to me?"

Stephanie shook her head. "I can't, and you know it. Jacques was specific. Nothing was to interfere with your racing."

"You don't think worrying about the survival of the Sundance isn't going to interfere with my racing?"

The faster Drake moved, the quieter Stephanie became. She relaxed in her chair, her expression level and passive. "I think if you'll help me for the next couple of weeks or so, I can manage while you're gone. Within the provisions of Jacques's will, it's the best I can offer."

She could tell by the wary glint in his eyes that he still wasn't convinced. Pulling a hand through the unruly hair once more, he sank back into his chair with a sigh. "Just what did you have in mind?"

Stephanie never got the chance to answer. Suddenly the door flew open and a blur in a denim dress and boots tumbled through. It was Diane, the young manager who as far as Drake knew hadn't so much as raised her voice in the entire time she'd worked at the Inn.

"We have to get out!" she gasped, slowing just enough to pivot anxiously toward Drake, a sure sign of who the staff assumed was in command. "There's been a . . . there's been a bomb threat."

Stephanie was so taken by surprise that she could do no more than stare at the young woman's agitation.

Drake was on his feet in one fluid movement. Stephanie saw a mixture of fury and apprehension crowd his face.

"What are you talking about, Diane?"

"The bomb squad's on its way," Diane said to him, still only casting an occasional nervous glance Stephanie's way.

"What bomb squad?" Stephanie asked. "And what bomb?"

That finally made Diane face her. "The desk just got the call. Somebody says it's set to go off in fifteen minutes."

"Are the guests out?" Drake demanded.

Diane nodded, her expression reflecting urgency and fear.

He took her by the arm. "Then go on out with them. We'll be there."

Without so much as taking her eyes from Drake's, Diane backed out the door. Stephanie found herself watching the girl, thinking how great an impression Mr. McDonald seemed to make on the local fans.

"Let's go," Drake said, turning to her.

Stephanie looked up, a little surprised. "Oh, come on," she objected instinctively. "You don't play games like this, do you?"

He scowled, muttering something about thick-headed women, and dragged her to her feet. "I'm the coach. Now, come on."

It wasn't until Stephanie was standing out front and heard the approaching siren that she realized that the staff hadn't, in fact, conspired to pull a fast one on the new boss. Twenty other people stood out there with her, all painfully under dressed for the chilly temperatures, having been roused from their jobs or relaxation around various fireplaces in the Inn to go stand in the snow.

"Do you provide this little welcome for all new towns-people?" she breathed in Drake's direction. "Or is it just me?"

He tried not to notice her eyes. "Maybe nobody pays attention to bomb threats in L.A.," he retorted a touch impatiently, "but we take them seriously in Telluride."

"You actually have a bomb squad?"

"All the conveniences of home. I told you we were becoming big business."

Stephanie shook her head to herself, wrapping her arms around her chest to ward off the creeping chill. It was a pristinely clear day, the blue spruce lush against the snow, the sky that deep cerulean blue peculiar to the Colorado mountains on a December afternoon. The sun rode straight up over the three-story Victorian building Jacques had transformed from a derelict boarding house to a skier's paradise. Painted in dollhouse blues and off-whites, it looked so perfect that, after her years in Hollywood, Stephanie fully expected to walk through the front door and find empty space. A facade constructed of make-believe.

But the Sundance was real. Jacques had invested it with his own brand of humor and hospitality and set it apart from the corporate-inspired condos that sat farther down the hill. Nestled amid twenty undeveloped acres with a view of the valley beyond, it was an oasis where vacation met fantasy. And somebody had evidently planted a bomb to bring it all down.

"Why?" she said more to herself than anyone else as the policemen arrived and made their way inside. The sight of them ignited her fear.

"Because it's the most plum twenty acres left in three counties," Drake all but growled, his own fear filtered through the anger in his eyes. He never looked away from the building, as if he was safeguarding it somehow. "Because in every fight over developing a new area, one side makes enemies of the other. Because," he finished, looking over at Stephanie with as much challenge as empathy, "they might just think they finally have a vulnerable target."

She smiled, her eyes chillier than the air. "I suppose they never heard the adage about bees and honey."

He shook his head. "You'll get that, too. Don't worry."

Stephanie turned her eyes back to the quietly waiting building, her posture slumping just a little. "And to think that a week ago the most pressing problem on my mind was the bad food in Sofia."

*You bequeath your legacies at a high price, Jacques. And because you were such a good friend, you expect the same from everyone else. Well,* she sighed inwardly, her arms tight around her to ward off the fear, *I hope your trust is well placed.*

"Coming out!"

All eyes swiveled to the front door as a policeman in blue padding edged out, carrying a small box. Conversation ceased. All breathing ceased until he had safely reached the truck at the end of the driveway.

Stephanie felt her eyes widen at the sight. She only turned back toward the no longer threatened Inn when the second officer stepped outside.

"Who's in charge?" he asked, notebook in hand.

Drake cocked an eyebrow. "She is."

*For all of four hours,* Stephanie thought dismally.

The officer approached, his attention on the truck until it had crept on down the driveway and away from town.

"What can you tell me?" he asked. He had small eyes and the beginnings of a pot belly.

"Nothing," Stephanie answered, still trying to come to grips with what was happening. "There *was* a bomb?"

"Yes, ma'am. Four sticks of dynamite, looks like."

"Where?" Drake asked.

"In Jacques's old office," the officer said, eyes back on the notebook. "Right under the desk."

# Chapter 2

"Why don't you sit down for a minute?"

Stephanie tried to shake her head as Drake guided her toward her desk. She couldn't quite muster a stern look, though. Her knees were shaking.

He sat her down and walked toward the door. "Be right back."

Stephanie bent over to check beneath the battered oak desk, searching out the shadows where the bomb had been tucked away. She wasn't sure what she was doing it for; the bomb had been driven away in that dark blue van. But it was like cockroaches. You find just one in your bathroom, and you can't overcome the urge to keep checking, sure that all his relatives have followed along.

There was no bomb. Just a little dust and a stray paper clip. Stephanie allowed herself a small sigh of disbelief and willed herself to relax in the padded chair, her trembling hands on its arms.

"Oh, Jacques," she muttered squeezing her eyes shut as a weight settled on her chest. "What did you do to me?"

"Here."

Stephanie opened her eyes with a start to see Drake standing before the desk, a snifter of brandy in his outstretched hand.

"Oh, I don't think so," she demurred with a shake of her head.

His scowl betrayed his impatience. "I don't care if you think so," he said, reaching down for her hand and setting the glass firmly in it. "You look like a warm jelly in an earthquake."

Stephanie had the time to cast a suspicious glance at the pale amber liquid in her glass and cast another up at Drake before he allowed a smile.

Reaching down to where he'd left it on the carpet, he lifted the bottle of Scotch he'd brought along for himself. "Which is just about what I feel like, too."

Sprawling in his chair, Drake took a long drink from the bottle and set it down before him on the desk.

"Kind of traumatic for your first day." He smiled ruefully.

"Kind of traumatic for *any* day," Stephanie corrected him, giving up and taking a sip of her own drink. She raised her eyebrows in surprise. The liquid in her glass was a very fine Armagnac. Her father had kept himself well stocked in the finer necessities of life, and her mother's third husband had taught her to discern the meaning of a finer necessity, so Stephanie had inadvertently become something of a connoisseur.

"Is this regular stock or was it Jacques's?" she asked, rolling the liquid around in her mouth the better to savor the taste.

"Nothing but the best." Drake smiled smugly.

She nodded, smiling softly to herself. "And he said that *my* tastes were exorbitant."

It took Stephanie a moment to return from her memory, a moment Drake spent assessing her. She was cool when it served her like a glass of deliciously chilled wine. Drake had watched her closely when the policeman had broken the news about the bomb. She'd barely blinked an eye, carry-

ing it off as if she were the queen of England discovering an
IRA terrorist crouched beneath the royal throne.

She'd answered the policeman's questions and strolled
back into the building as if returning from an afternoon
outing. And then her knees had almost given out on her.

Now, lost in her private memories, her face took on a lu-
minescence, a soft frailty that belied that smooth control.
An amazing lady, he decided. An enticing composite of fire
and ice. Someone he'd have to get to know better. Especially, Drake thought as he took another pull from the bottle and let the Scotch slip down his throat, if she and the
Sundance were going to survive.

Stephanie shook herself as if coming back to her senses.
"I should get out to see to the guests," she decided, taking
another sip of her brandy before setting it down.

Drake leaned over and put it back in her hand. "Jacques's
staff is handpicked for that kind of thing. Sit here until you
feel a little more settled."

She set the glass down again and shook her head.
"Handpicked or not, Jacques would never have let his
guests face this alone. It isn't appropriate for me to be cowering in a corner someplace."

Drake's eyebrows rose. "Miss Manners has a chapter on
handling bomb threats, huh?"

Stephanie saw the challenge in Drake's crystal eyes and
stopped. "Mr. McDonald, this was absolutely the last place
in the world I wanted to be this winter. Believe me when I
say that. But I am here, and I hope to make the best of it. I
was hoping that everybody else involved would be willing to
do the same."

"You just had a bomb found under your desk," he retorted. "That tells me two things. One, not everyone is
going to let you make the best of it. At least one person in
this town doesn't have your best interests at heart. And two,
unless you're used to this sort of thing, you have a right to
do a little cowering in a corner. You didn't strike me as the
kind of lady who enjoyed doing that in public, so I sat you
down here. You don't like it, fine. But don't get on your
high horse with me and then expect cooperation."

The last reaction Drake expected to see to his tirade was a grin. But that was just what he got, and a sheepish one at that. Stephanie's eyes sparkled with that barely suppressed humor that he found so enticing.

"Jacques and I used to have these little disagreements," she said picking up her glass once more. "I used to tell him that because he grew up in a small town, he trusted everybody, and that that was dangerous. And he told me that since I grew up in Hollywood, I didn't trust anyone. And that was stupid. I'm sorry. It's a bad habit to break."

She finished her Armagnac with deliberate ease. Drake found himself staring. Damn. She was hard to keep up with.

"After I get my breath for a minute," Stephanie said, "would you go out with me to talk to the guests?"

He nodded, unable to take his eyes from her. "Glad to."

She returned his nod, her eyes warming to him. "And then will you begin to explain just what the hell is going on?"

"I thought you flew in." Drake walked around to the passenger seat of the Blazer and opened the door.

Stephanie was already climbing into the driver's seat. "I hate to fly. I rented this and drove in from Denver."

They had spent the better part of the afternoon making amends to the Inn's guests for the inconvenience of being scared half to death and thrown out into the snow. Now, as the sun disappeared behind the western peaks, Stephanie and Drake were heading into town to talk to the sheriff. Stephanie had never thought to ask Drake to drive, and Drake had never offered.

Slipping the big four-by-four into gear, Stephanie turned out the driveway and down the hill. A few horses were still gathered out on the snowy meadow, and the San Miguel River chattered at the bottom of the property. The lights of Telluride lit the gathering dusk like fireflies in late summer, beckoning beyond the solitude of the mountain.

Stephanie couldn't get used to the quiet up here. Oh, there was the string music of wind through firs, a full, throaty sound that you didn't even notice after awhile, and the cowbells one of the wranglers had attached to the horses. There were the birds and the river, even the staccato of small animals if you listened closely enough, but there weren't any human noises. No nightlife, no neon.

After only her second evening, she was desperate to hear a siren, a car horn, even a ghetto blaster as she rode past on the street. A city mouse in a country mouse's world, Stephanie shamelessly missed the smell of smog.

"What do you do around here for excitement?" she asked, scanning the town they were entering. Consisting of a main drag and several side streets, Telluride was made up of lovingly restored buildings from the town's heyday, the mining years of the late eighteen hundreds. The housing that had sprung up around it with the ski boom consisted mostly of the cedar siding and skylight variety Drake had referred to the night before.

"We ski," Drake said laconically.

Stephanie scowled. "Besides that."

"Winter or summer?"

"Right now. While I have to be here."

"Well, let's see—" he was enjoying himself now "—we have sleigh and horse rentals and a skating rink. And there's cable TV and the movies. We are rather woefully short of four-star restaurants or discos at the moment, though."

Stephanie delivered a baleful look. "Who would be most interested in seeing the Sundance shut down?"

"Why don't you know anything about skiing?"

She turned a quizzical eye on him.

"You turn here." He nodded out the window. She turned. "Your father was an Olympian. How come it wasn't passed on?"

Stephanie pulled the Blazer into a parking spot before the sheriff's office and switched off the ignition. Then she gave Drake an answer. "I grew up in a desert climate. There isn't anything I can think of that would convince me that spending a day being cold and wet would be fun."

Her words were delivered lightly, but in the fading light Drake could have sworn he'd caught a flicker of something in those chocolate eyes. Something that belied the ease of her words. An odd chill shot up his spine, as if he'd wandered too close to a shadow he didn't particularly want to investigate. Deliberately shrugging away her answer and his own discomfort, he opened his door to get out.

Stephanie took a moment to scan the town as she, too, stepped out onto the sidewalk. Colorado Avenue was the kind of broad main street classic to small towns everywhere. This one was lined with Victorian facades and old brick and stone buildings that had been around since gold had first been mined here. Structures that had once held assayers' offices and bathhouses now sported T-shirt shops and real estate offices.

On three sides of the town, the mountains were close and sudden, as if the people here had poured themselves into the narrow valley that ended abruptly at Bridal Vail Falls. The mountains seemed to blot out half of the sky, giving Stephanie an unaccustomed feeling of claustrophobia. She wanted to see more of the peacock and crimson of autumn.

Stephanie did like the town, though. It was charming, more authentic than Aspen, more peaceful than Vail, the end of a mountain road where only the hardy still came to vacation. Where a hundred years or so ago Butch Cassidy and the Sundance Kid had pulled off their first real bank job. She had to give the developers credit. Except for the cars that lined the now paved streets, the town still retained its historic flavor.

"It looks like a—"

"Movie set?" Drake finished for her.

Stephanie started at the nearness of his voice. Just the rough sound of it sent shivers snaking through her. Doing her best to ignore them, she smiled. "Occupational hazard. I already had the place scouted for a Western."

Drake took her arm to guide her to the sheriff's office and she jumped. Those shivers again. The climate, she decided disparagingly as she cast a fleeting glance Drake's way to assess his reaction. His eyes were hooded in shadow, revealing nothing.

"So, who would want to see the Sundance fail?" she asked, hoping her voice sounded steady. This was so alien to her. Stephanie couldn't remember the last time she'd stiffened at a man's touch.

Drake held the door open for her. "That's something I'll be happy to take up with you over dinner." She hoped he meant the Inn. "Right after we talk to the gentlemen who dismantled the bomb."

It turned out that the gentlemen hadn't had to dismantle the bomb after all. It was a dud. Someone had gone to the trouble of making it look real enough to scare everyone, but had constructed it so that it could never have gone off. He'd left out the blasting caps.

"Somebody wanted to give you a good scare, Miss Fleming," the deputy said. He was different from the one she'd met that afternoon. Younger, blonder. A definite skier. "Got any ideas who?"

Stephanie shook her head. "I've only been here for about twenty-four hours. I didn't think I had time to make any enemies yet. This kind of thing happen often in Telluride?"

"Not since I've been here," the deputy replied.

An eyebrow lifted as Stephanie remembered her conversation with Sammy the night before. "I seem to have that effect around here."

"Pardon?"

She shook her head. "Nothing."

"Drake," the man said, turning to take him in. "Any ideas?"

Drake shrugged noncommittally. "Not at the moment."

The deputy picked at his papers a little, his eyes lowered to his desk. "You, uh, were kind of vocal about the provisions of the will."

"You're being tactful, Tom," Drake said, grinning dryly. "Miss Fleming knows just how thrilled I was yesterday."

Stephanie couldn't help a small smile. Drake McDonald could be quite disarming when he wanted.

The deputy's gaze rose, his expression still uneasy. It was clear that he respected the man he was accusing. "You also worked the ski patrol for quite a few years. And they—"

"Are well acquainted with dynamite." Drake nodded. "I know. I've blown more than my share of powder. But we're not talking about snow, Tom. We're talking about the Sundance. And I do have a half interest in it."

Tom's eyes lightened. "Yeah, I know. I had to ask."

Drake shared a smile of kinship. "I was expecting it. Anything else you need from us?"

"I don't think so." The young man's smile broadened with relief. "We'll be in touch, okay?"

Drake nodded as he rose to his feet. "See you on the hill."

By the time Drake and Stephanie returned to the street, the light in the sky had died. In its place grew a dusting of stars. The mountains were invisible now, more felt than seen. With the light had gone any warmth.

Even with the protection of her heavy coat, Stephanie found herself shivering, unprepared for the cold. The temperature dropped in L.A. at sundown, but that still didn't match the low twenties she was facing right now. And that wasn't even Colorado's coldest, she reminded herself.

"Dinner?" Drake suggested, a hand on her arm.

Stephanie found her eyes straying to the source of the heat that once again crawled up her arm from his touch. Long-fingered, strong, his hand easily grasped her arm as if it were the most comfortable thing in the world. She wondered if he felt the same surprise at each contact.

"Sounds fine," she answered, her voice unaccountably soft, her gaze slowly traveling back to his, wondering what he was thinking behind those gossamer eyes. They seemed alight in the dusk. "What does Tulleride have in the way of food?"

Drake raised his eyebrows. "Franks and beans."

Stephanie scowled, wishing everything weren't within walking distance. She wanted to snuggle up to the car heater—or, she realized with some surprise, the solid warmth of his chest. She was going to have to stop this. "I hope you come out to L.A. sometime." She grinned dryly, head tilted a little. "I'd like the chance to get even for that chauvinistic little attitude of yours."

"What an interesting thought," he retorted instinctively. The heat radiating from Drake's fingertips increased as Drake unconsciously tightened his hold. He was millimeters away from bending down and tasting those soft lips, closing those luminous eyes with the force of his kiss. His heart thudded in his chest, a sharp ache flaring in him for the feel of this beautiful woman. It didn't occur to Drake that his sudden desire was vividly telegraphed in his eyes.

Stephanie saw the heat flare in that cool gray and felt it envelop her like a sunburst on this dark, chilly street. She shuddered with the impact and saw him straighten.

Drake stiffened. "Why didn't you tell me you were cold?" he demanded, his eyes suddenly brittle. Her chill was as much an excuse for him to pull back as much as it was for her. They'd stepped over mutual boundaries without so much as a word.

"Surprised me, too," she answered a touch breathlessly. "About that food..."

Drake turned and slipped a companionable arm around her shoulders, guiding her on down the street. The strange moment had passed when they'd broken eye contact. Stephanie was grateful.

"Anything you'd like," he offered. "Italian, American, mesquite grill, Chinese, vegetarian, Mexican. We have it all."

Stephanie admitted her surprise. "And here I thought Jacques was living in the sticks."

Drake chuckled, his arm settling more comfortably about her as they mingled with the other pedestrians in search of an evening out. "And, if you'd like local flavor, I can still find you some beans and franks."

"Italian is just fine, thanks."

"Italian it is."

The restaurant they settled on was nestled in an historic late nineteenth-century building. The only difference between it and the neighborhood restaurants in L.A. was that here the waiters were off-hours skiers rather than aspiring actors.

Drake guided Stephanie to a table situated next to a working fireplace and settled her into her seat without the help of the half dozen waiters who suddenly hovered in the still half-empty room. He had barely claimed his own seat before she opened the discussion as if at a business meeting.

"So," she said, draping a napkin over her lap. "What kind of schedule are you going to have to keep for the Olympics?"

Drake looked up with not a little surprise at Stephanie's no-nonsense tone. He saw that her eyes matched it, level and purposeful. It made him wonder what had cost her the spark that had so surprised him out on the sidewalk.

"Would you like a drink?" he answered easily, motioning to the nearest waiter, a young kid from Indiana who'd been out in Colorado for the last two years in search of perfect powder.

"Oh," she said, smiling in the young man's direction, "Yes. Kir, please."

Drake knew by the look on the boy's face that he had no idea what that was, but wasn't about to ask. Stephanie's low voice and elegant carriage were blinding him like everybody else. A hypnotic for the soul. Drake could feel it weave its way through him just as surely, a narcotic that became an addiction before you realized it. After barely twenty-four hours he found himself craving more of it as surely as if it were injectable. The electricity he'd stumbled over when he'd taken her arm had only made it worse.

He was going to have to be very careful. The last thing Drake could allow right now was to let a beautiful lady seep into his life and shatter his concentration. This year he needed that focus more than ever. Maybe more than anything else in his life.

"Drake?" The waiter turned to him.

"Just coffee."

Stephanie smiled at him. "Penance?"

Drake smiled back. "Training. I am, after all, purported to be on the ski team."

"What are your chances of getting three golds?"

He shrugged. "I don't know. I haven't raced since I fell in September. There are two World Cup races I'm entering to get the feel of it again before Calgary. I guess I'll know better after those. Besides, there's another skier who's right on my tail this year. He would have been my top competition in the World Cup if I hadn't had to drop out."

Stephanie nodded. "Chip Markinson."

Drake's eyebrow rose. "Been listening again?"

"Hard not to. According to Diane, this is the biggest fight of your life."

Drake fingered the rim of his water glass. "It will be my last year competing," he admitted. "I'm getting too old for it." He shrugged. "So it becomes more epic somehow."

Stephanie reacted to Drake's words with a wry disbelief. Not for the idea that his contest was an epic one but for the concept that he was getting too old. She knew that it was a fact in sports. The body was a lot more unforgiving than the mind. But she couldn't think of a more vital person than the one sitting across from her. He radiated energy, strength, his movements effortless and fluid. It seemed outrageous that he could somehow be considered over the hill.

"How old are you?" she asked.

He looked up. "Thirty-two. Why?"

"I was just thinking." Stephanie's eyes were colored with an understanding Drake couldn't have anticipated. "If you were a politician, you'd be just beginning. Do you mind that it's your last year?"

The waiter set down Drake's coffee. Drake poured in a little cream, his eyes on what he was doing. "Very much," he admitted, his voice low.

Suddenly he found himself looking up at Stephanie, surprised at himself. He hadn't even told Jacques that. Of course, he hadn't needed to. Jacques had already known.

Stephanie nodded, the empathy in her eyes suddenly intimate. How much wasn't he telling her? she wondered. What did that lost World Cup cost him? She knew all too well what the lost chances had cost her father. Just one more chance, he'd always said. One more bloody chance.

"What will you do afterwards?" she asked.

For a long moment, Drake held Stephanie's gaze, shaken by the suspicion that she was absorbing his loss and unsure why he knew that she well understood what it meant to him. Her eyes seemed to beckon with an unspoken kinship that offered him comfort. Somehow he couldn't formulate the standard line he'd given everyone else.

"Well, well, Drake, your good taste is showing."

Both Drake and Stephanie started noticeably at the intrusion. Drake was the first to recover, turning to take in the newcomer. His expression darkened. A tall, well-groomed yuppie type leaned over the table, all smiles and bonhomie.

Drake nodded without noticeable welcome. "Nathan."

Stephanie looked from one man to the other, and thought that Drake looked remarkably like he had when she'd first come upon him. Their visitor claimed one of the empty chairs and settled in next to her, his bright eyes shrewd beneath the easy camaraderie. He was fair, sun-streaked and good-looking, with only a scar at his left temple to mar the image of bland well-being.

"It's a pleasure to meet you, Miss Fleming," he said, smiling broadly, extending a hand to her. "I'd heard you were coming to town. I'm Nathan Ames."

Stephanie shook hands. "Mr. Ames."

She saw his eyes widen slightly at the sound of her voice and wondered at his surprise. His confusion, really. She could never understand why men were so mesmerized by a damaged set of vocal chords. To her own ears she sounded like sandpaper.

"I was, of course, sorry about Jacques," he went on, now all sincerity, releasing Stephanie's hand as he leaned forward with his message. "He was truly one of a kind. We'll all miss him."

Stephanie could almost see the retort that raced through Drake's mind. Not as much as we'd like to miss you, he wanted to say. She concealed her amusement, wondering what it was about Mr. Ames that set Drake off so fast. He was silently fuming behind his coffee cup.

"Thank you, Mr. Ames," she smiled noncommittally.

"You were related to him?"

The expected question, the unexpected answer. "No. Just friends."

"Oh." He smiled with just a shade too much understanding. "Like McDonald here, huh? Jacques did set a great store by his friends."

How could someone so young sound so much like Willy Loman? Stephanie wondered. She decided to keep her answer to herself.

That didn't bother Mr. Ames in the least. "I stopped over to say that any help you need, just let me know. I've tried to talk some sense into your partner here, but well, you know how we men are. You have a prime piece of property up there, and you're going to have quite a time taking care of it. Have you ever managed property like it before?"

She shook her head as the pieces fell into place.

"Well, like I told Drake here, you have to be careful. And what with Drake so busy with his skiing, you're going to need someone who can advise you."

"You know, Mr. Ames—" Stephanie smiled suddenly with very bright eyes "—I was just telling Drake that very thing. There's just so much to consider...."

Drake almost choked on his coffee. Mr. Ames almost fell off his chair in his rush to provide Stephanie with a solution. "You must call me Nathan," he insisted. "Stephanie?"

Another smile from her was all he needed.

"You're not from around here," Nathan commented.

Stephanie almost laughed in his face. Instead she frowned with the utmost sincerity. "No, Los Angeles. I don't even know that much about skiing, so you can imagine my problem."

He nodded in commiseration, touching her hand in a gesture of support. No shivers from that contact. "A lot of trouble. I understand that you already had some difficulty today."

She nodded, wide-eyed. "A bomb. Right under my desk. I hope this isn't a standard greeting around here."

"Incredible." He shook his head, now patting her hand as if she were threatening to swoon. "That's just the kind of thing I was talking about." A card materialized in his fingers with the dexterity of sleight of hand. "If there's anything I can do to help," he offered, "you call me. I'd be more than happy to advise you on what's a...practical route to take with the property." The quick glance toward Drake that accompanied the word "practical" was telling. Drake, it said, wasn't able to be practical.

"Oh, I see—" Stephanie nodded, reading the card "—you're in real estate." She smiled up at the beaming face. "But then, it seems as if half the town is, doesn't it?"

"Telluride's come a long way since we started," Ames acknowledged. "Well, I just wanted to welcome you. Let me know if there's anything I can do."

Stephanie watched him get to his well-shod feet and delivered her best smile. "Thank you so much. Everyone has been wonderful, Nathan. With all this help, I won't have to be away from home for long at all."

Drake managed to remain quiet just as long as it took Nathan to get out the door. "Just what the hell was that all about?"

Stephanie answered his glower with a satisfied smile. "I'm sorry," she allowed. "I can't keep myself from playing games sometimes."

"What?" His brusque tone of voice reflected the fact that Drake McDonald didn't associate humor with the Inn's future.

Stephanie finally took a sip of her drink. "It's something I used to do in Hollywood. People are happy to underestimate you if they can. So I used to set them up sometimes just to see how far they'd end up falling."

"By people I assume you meant men?"

Her smile grew. "There is a certain...prejudice against women in some circles."

"Is that why you didn't tell me who you were last night?"

Stephanie actually took a moment to think about that as she sipped at the tawny fluid in her glass. "No," she finally decided. "Not entirely. Although you have to admit that you had some pretty archaic preconceptions on the subject.

I just wanted to find out what I was going to be up against. Particularly after hearing your conversation with Sammy."

Drake shrugged without much remorse. "I figured you were some hotshot running around Rodeo Drive in her Jaguar..."

She grinned. "Oh, but I am." Drake's stunned reaction goaded her on. "I do drive a Jaguar. An XJS. On occasion I've shopped Rodeo. And I owe my ill-gotten gains almost exclusively to Jacques."

Her words elicited a completely different reaction than they would have if she'd delivered them the night before. Drake leaned back in his chair, balancing his coffee cup on his crossed leg, his eyes speculative. "Real estate?"

She inclined her head, a look of conspiracy in her eyes. "When my parents divorced, my father didn't trust my mother with the money for my welfare. And rightfully so, I might add. So he asked Jacques to invest it in some of his 'schemes.' By that time Jacques had helped start Aspen. My future was assured in Vail and this lovely little town right here. I assume he did the same for you."

Drake nodded. "He started me off. It's how I've managed to remain an amateur athlete for so long."

Stephanie smiled again. "The gentleman athlete. My investment saw me quite comfortably through film school at USC."

"And the purchase of a Jaguar, it seems."

For a moment Stephanie's eyes clouded over. She turned her attention to her drink to mask the lapse. Drake found himself stiffening.

"No," she finally admitted with a belated smile. "Not that. You don't seem to like Mr. Ames much."

By now Drake was almost expecting her tactful change of subject. He'd seen the pain she'd tried to hide, and wondered about it. Wondered too, why he'd felt himself drawn to it. Her control was a little thin in some areas. Drake found himself wanting to know what areas those were.

"Mr. Ames is one of the sharks," he answered evenly.

Stephanie wasn't in the least surprised.

"That line about 'since *we* started Telluride' is part of the act," Drake continued. "He's been here three years, and he's been after the Sundance every waking minute."

"Do you think he'd plant a bomb?"

"I think he'd try to scare you. He had Jacques in court three times, trying to find a loophole to get the land. And he's suspected to be behind some rather nasty literature that circulated earlier this year to keep people away."

Stephanie scowled. "Nice man. What I just got was the honey, I assume."

"Your hands should be sticking to the table."

"What else should I know?"

Drake offered her a wry grin. "You expect me to tell you that in public?"

"Seems to me you promised."

He shrugged. "I lied. I just wanted to take you to dinner." And he had, he realized with some surprise.

"Me?" She mugged with those elegant eyes. "The bimbo with the Jag?"

Drake mugged back, enjoying himself more than he had since Jacques had died. "Jacques wasn't the only one with expensive tastes."

Stephanie laughed, a throaty music that turned heads. "What about after dinner?"

He shook his head. "It's going to be an early night for me, lady. I'm in training."

"Tomorrow morning."

Another shake of the head. "Workouts, practice runs."

The smile on her face broadened right along with his. "Lunch?"

"Weights."

Stephanie allowed herself a frustrated sigh. "I would like to get this in sometime soon. I have eight or nine commitments in L.A. that I've left hanging until I finish here."

Drake's expression froze at her words. A memory, a tentative trust shaken a little. Stephanie wondered if he'd thought she was going to stay here after all and take on the Inn's responsibilities at the expense of her own. It occurred

to her that she was going to have to end up explaining to this
man why she couldn't change her life like that, even for the
sake of the gift Jacques had given her. It also occurred to her
that it would make a difference how he reacted to it.

"Right after lunch," he compromised. "Your office? I'll
bring the bomb squad."

Stephanie scowled again, playfully this time, preferring
the light banter to the uncharted waters they'd been skirt-
ing. "I'll be there. How much time does this leave us to get
me set up before you leave?"

Drake's eyes narrowed. "I could ask the same of you."

"I'll stay until things are stabilized," she promised.
"Then I'll be in contact for decisions. I have commitments
too, Drake."

He took a minute to answer, time spent considering the
coffee cup he still balanced. Stephanie could see the conflicting impulses reflected in his eyes like swift-moving
clouds in an afternoon sky. Not one to hide his emotions
well, this man. A person who gave full rein to his passions,
and yet took responsibility for them. Stephanie envied that
unspeakably. She had never had that privilege, that luxury,
and found herself mesmerized by the way those emotions
colored him.

"I only have a couple of weeks," he said finally, facing
her with honesty. "I was training with the team at Mount
Hood when I got the call to return here. I should be getting
back. Then I have the two races I entered, and the Olympics in February. I won't be as involved in racing as if I'd
been able...if I'd been participating in the World Cup, like
Jacques thought when he wrote the will. While I'm here I'll
help all I can, and I'll leave my number when I'm not. Good
enough?"

Stephanie smiled with sincere relief. She'd tell him later
about her plan to give him the rest of the Sundance once the
Olympics were over. "Better than I'd hoped, except that I'll
tear up your number when you're away. We'll do fine."
Raising her glass, she met Drake's cup in a toast. "To the
three-time Olympic gold medalist."

She hoped she'd get more enthusiasm from him. He merely smiled and clinked china against crystal. "To the new owners of the Sundance Inn."

Stephanie looked into Drake's cool gray eyes and felt his words incite a sudden tension in her chest. It was going to be a long winter. Correction, it was going to be a particularly long two weeks if she didn't manage to put a little distance between herself and the magnetic attraction she felt for her new partner.

She had to get back to L.A. unscathed and alone. Especially alone. The last thing Stephanie needed was a relationship with a man this dynamic, this compelling, this driven. Her house was built for solitude, and that was the way she wanted it.

But as she sipped at her drink she couldn't help but wonder just how long she could hold out against the heat in his eyes or the fire of his touch.

It was going to be a very long two weeks indeed.

# Chapter 3

Jacques really has been having his problems this year,"
Stephanie admitted, peering at the computer printout in her
hand. Across the desk from her, Diane Taylor studied a
similar sheet. The manager for the last year under Jacques,
Diane was a short, round girl with bright blond hair and a
head filled with figures. Stephanie liked her.

"The census has dropped off." She nodded, peering up
over the rims of her tape-repaired half glasses. "And he had
to spend a lot of time and money to battle the developers
who wanted to persuade the town council to tax him out of
existence or buy out the land."

"He never told Drake any of this?"

Diane shook her head. "Oh, no. Drake had enough on his
mind. We were just getting the census problem under control after those pamphlets that were being circulated to our
mailing list alluding to a buy out and all, when...when
things changed again."

Understanding the girl's reluctance to state the bald truth,
Stephanie merely nodded. "We'll have to get in touch with
everyone on the mailing list again," she said. "Let them
know that it's business as usual. We can make Christmas

something a little special. How are bookings for the holidays?''

"Still full, so far. The count and countess reserved a whole floor. Will you be here?"

"I'm going to try." Looking up, she tapped a pencil against her teeth, an old habit from screenings. "Maybe we could plan some kind of special tribute for Jacques later in the winter."

Immediately Diane's eyes brightened. "I could arrange it if you'd like. Call everyone on his personal list."

Which, Stephanie was sure, was just about everyone who visited the Inn. "We can schedule it for late March, so Drake can attend. And that reminds me—" the peek at her watch closed up business "—I have to meet with him. Oh Lord, it's after one. I wonder where he is."

"Drake?" Diane asked, gathering her own things. "If it's one, he's in the weight room."

Stephanie looked surprised. "Here?"

"Sure. He always trains here." For a moment Diane's assurance faded. "You're not going to make him stop, are you?"

"Not likely," Stephanie assured her. "He's bigger than I am, and he owns half the place. I guess I just assumed . . . I'm not sure what I assumed."

"He's always trained here," Diane added. "At least, when he's not with the team. He has a house in town, but . . . well, he spends most of his time here. I was so glad that Mr. Lavalle left him part of the Sundance. At least he won't have to leave now that . . ."

Diane blushed with fresh discomfort. She wasn't the kind of person to presume.

"I can't imagine that he would," Stephanie assured her. Pushing her chair back, she got to her feet. "It's convenient that he's so close. We need to talk a little business."

"Oh, there's one more thing." Diane scurried through her stack for a list and considered it before facing Stephanie again. "Since you're the new . . . owner, I thought you'd want to check the menus for the rest of the week. We change them nightly. And you may want to okay the shopping for tomorrow."

Stephanie made no move to take the sheets from her. "Jacques always did that?"

Diane gave her a hesitant smile. "He liked to oversee everything."

It didn't take much for Stephanie to perceive the anxiety to please in this well-meaning young woman. "The problem is—" she smiled ruefully "—I don't know the first thing about cooking food, much less ordering it." Not altogether true, but serviceable enough. "Besides, I'd prefer not to get involved in too much since I have to get back to L.A. You've been taking care of it since Jacques died, haven't you?"

Diane nodded, her posture straightening a little.

"If you don't mind," Stephanie suggested. "Maybe you could continue, then."

"Would you like me to handle ordering supplies, too?"

"Anything you've been doing in the interim. Just leave me a list of what responsibilities you've assumed, so I'll know."

Another quick smile and nod, and Diane got to her feet. "Thank you. I'd like that."


Stephanie found the weight room in what once had been a small parlor at the back of the house. A no-nonsense room with a minimum of fuss or decoration, it contained not just weights, but any number of exotic and painful-looking exercise machines intended to stretch and strengthen. When Stephanie opened the door, she found Drake on his back doing leg lifts.

She was just about to greet him when she was drawn up short. Not so much by the sensual look of him, even though there was definitely that. Men had become worldwide movie stars looking half as nasty.

He was clad in gym shorts and shirt, dark with sweat, his muscles straining as he worked. He lay on his back, his legs bent over a bench, slowly lifting them against the resistance of what seemed an enormous weight. His thigh muscles stood out in sharp relief as his body strained to keep the even, methodical rhythm of his workout.

What stopped her was the look on his face. She'd never seen such concentration, such single-minded intensity before. Sweat rolled from Drake's forehead into already soaked hair. His teeth were clenched, the tendons in his neck standing out like heavy cords. Focused on a spot on the ceiling, his eyes mirrored as much pain as will. His expression was fierce. Stephanie was awed by it.

He'd told her he'd had a fall while skiing in September. Stephanie wondered whether this was the price he paid for getting back into shape. She was amazed that anyone could put himself through what was obviously agony to attain a goal and found himself disturbed by the implications. The rasp of his breathing filled the small room.

Backing out as quietly as she could, Stephanie paused a moment, willing the sight of those eyes away from her so that her chest would stop aching. Then she knocked on the door.

There was a pause, then an abrupt, "Yeah?"

"Drake?" She stepped back into the room as if she'd never been there. Nothing in her demeanor betrayed the pain she'd taken out with her. "Mohammed decided to find the mountain."

Drake was sitting up, a towel to his face. "Oh, Stephanie, I'm sorry." Giving his face a last wipe, he draped the towel over his shoulder and offered a wry grin. "Time flies when you're having fun."

Stephanie noticed that he made no move to stand. Then she saw the long scar that traversed his left knee. It wasn't that old. "I bet you haven't even had lunch."

"Yogurt and granola."

She grimaced. "Only yuppies eat that."

Drake managed a smile. "And over-the-hill skiers. Have you eaten?"

"I've had a steady diet of graphite and megabytes all morning. It does nothing to satisfy a need for protein, however."

He nodded, the sweat still glistening along his throat and arms. "Give me a few minutes to shower off and I'll be with you. Deal?"

She smiled, wanting to ask him about what she'd just seen but knowing it was the last thing she should do. The last thing she needed was to get involved with an obsessed athlete. "Fair enough. I'll be waiting by the desk."

As she retraced her steps Stephanie thought of the commitment Drake had made to the Sundance. To Jacques. The two of them were polar opposites, Jacques all gruff good humor and bonhomie, Drake like a stick of hissing dynamite. Where Jacques had enjoyed skiing, Drake seemed to need it. In all the years she'd known Jacques Stephanie had never seen that kind of ferocity in him.

She'd seen it before, though. A long time ago in another athlete, another obsessed athlete who'd wasted the most productive years of his life regretting the loss of that one last chance.

But she couldn't deny that Jacques had chosen well. No matter what faced his little inn in the years to come, Drake would walk through hell to see that it kept the old-world charm and flavor Jacques had bestowed on it. Stephanie could think of no better person to keep the memory of that bearlike Frenchman alive than the dark, passionate Mr. McDonald.

As she approached the foyer area, it occurred to Stephanie that she was rubbing her hands together. Her palms were moist, had been since she'd stumbled over Drake in that weight room. She looked down at them with a certain dry accusal for their betrayal. What was it she'd compared him to the day before, a lightning storm? Well, the lightning was close, and it carried a particular exhilaration. She could almost smell it.

She could still see the sharp ridge of muscle across arm and thigh, the sheen of sweat at his throat. And she could taste the sharp tang of her own arousal.

"Miss Fleming?"

Startled, Stephanie looked up to see a rather disheveled young man considering her. A little shorter than herself, he pushed glasses up his nose and clutched a small notebook that had definitely seen better days.

"Yes?"

He delivered a fleeting grin. "My name's Martin Davis. I'm with the *San Juan Journal*. I was just wondering if you could give me some thoughts on your new position as owner of the Sundance Inn."

"Co-owner," Stephanie corrected.

He shrugged. "Not much left to write about McDonald. You, on the other hand, are a dialogue editor from Los Angeles who doesn't ski."

Stephanie lifted an eyebrow. "Not much left to write about me, either, it seems," she countered easily.

Mr. Davis tried a disarming smile as he motioned to one of the bright blue overstuffed couches that bracketed the flagstone fireplace. "If you have just a couple of minutes . . ."

There were only two or three people scattered over the big rooms this afternoon. Sunlight swept in through the casement windows and warmed the hardwood floors. A fire crackled and popped in the fireplace, scenting the air with the faint tang of wood smoke. It was a nice day. Stephanie thought she could see her way to talking to one reporter.

"You've never managed a resort of any kind before?" he asked as they settled across from each other on the couches.

Stephanie shook her head. "I've spent my better years in Hollywood working on films."

"Jacques was a relative of yours?"

"A friend."

Then came the polite pause, the careful foray for dirt. "He was quite a bit older than you, if you don't mind my saying."

"He'd be the only one who'd mind," she said evenly, her posture carefully relaxed against the thick cushions, her attention divided between the questions and the fresh flowers that needed to be replaced on the table in the foyer. "And I hardly think he can object now."

"How long did you know him?"

"Quite a while. He was a friend of my father's. They skied together in the Olympics."

"Why do you think someone like Jacques would leave you a valuable piece of property like this?"

Stephanie felt irritation begin to build. Crossing her legs, she settled her khaki gabardine shirt over her knees and smiled carefully. "Because we were friends. As I said, he and my father—"

"But one would almost assume that he'd leave the Sundance to a man like McDonald. You don't even ski."

"He *did* leave it to a man like McDonald. He also left it to me. The two of us have decided to run the Sundance just the way Jacques did, as a tribute to him. Now, would you like to hear how I met Jacques?"

It seemed not. Mr. Davis referred to his notes. "Did you see him most frequently in Hollywood, or in his mountain homes?"

"Mr. Davis," Stephanie said with steel in her cultured voice. "There is a very nice story here if you'd care to listen. If not, I think you might as well be on your way, because you'll end up writing whatever you want anyway."

Davis seemed more flustered than penitent, rescuing his glasses once more and squinting at her. "It's just that there are, well, you know, rumors around.... You're a beautiful woman, and Jacques liked beautiful women."

Stephanie thought of the first time Jacques had seen her with braces and bobbed hair and came close to laughing. Instead she got to her feet. "It's been a rare pleasure, Mr. Davis. You must stop by another day when I have more time to talk."

He followed her to her feet. "Then you don't deny that you had a relationship with Jacques Lavalle?"

"Get out."

Both of them turned at the sound of Drake's barely controlled voice. Freshly showered and dressed, he should have looked refreshed. Instead he looked furious. His eyes shot sparks, and his jaw was working in rage.

"I'm talking to Miss Fleming," Davis bluffed, his voice not quite carrying conviction.

"Not anymore you're not," Drake assured him, striding forward. "You've just worn out your welcome."

By the time Drake reached the same floor space as the reporter, it had become too close. Mr. Davis pocketed his ragged little notebook and took to his heels.

"You'll be hearing from me!"

"I was handling that," Stephanie objected evenly, her eyes following the fleeing reporter, amusement tugged at her mouth.

"You were handling it just fine," Drake retorted. "I just thought your sentences needed to be a bit more succinct. He was insulting you."

She did grin then, a wide light that filled her features with wry humor as she turned back to consider Drake. "Seems to me you were laboring under the same misconception just the other night."

"I never labored under that misconception," he retorted. "I just said you drove a Jag." Drake flashed her a grin that was just as unrepentant. "And you do."

Stephanie nodded with a chuckle. "Of course. I didn't appreciate the distinction."

The two of them still hadn't moved from where they stood, considering Mr. Davis's fleeing back. "I probably shouldn't have sent him off quite so quickly," Drake mused, rubbing at a freshly shaved chin.

"Oh?"

"He'll probably end up selling that story to some scandal sheet and trying to smear you."

Stephanie shrugged with a little laugh. "May I remind you that I come from Hollywood?—except for maybe Washington, D.C., the smear capital of the world. He couldn't do anything a dozen other people haven't tried already."

Drake laughed, extending a hand to guide Stephanie toward her office. "In that case, we only have to worry about the dirty tricks Nathan Ames has cooked up for you."

Stephanie was just about to take his hand when Diane reached them at something close to a run, her eyes alight with a furtive excitement. The guests, who had just turned back to their reading, found themselves once again distracted.

"Miss Fleming—" Diane spoke a little breathlessly "—you have a phone call."

Stephanie knew there was more to it than that. She just wondered whether the news was good or bad. It was hard to tell with Diane.

"It's from Los Angeles," the girl went on, then paused for the big news. "Corey Alexander?"

Stephanie sighed. Good old Corey. There weren't many people who brought a hush to a crowd with the mere mention of their name. Corey was one of them. With a package that would have earned her the title of "Blond Bombshell" in the old studio days, Corey was the kind of actress who redefined the word "star." She also thrived on her status the way Houston thrived on petroleum products.

"You do have a full life," Drake muttered at her side.

"It wasn't quite as full until I ended up here," she assured him as they all headed for the front desk and yet another audience.

"Hello, Corey." Eyes widened on a staff that was used to celebrities.

"Stephanie, darling," the voice lilted over the wires. "How are you out in the wastelands?" No one had gotten away with calling people darling like that since Hedda Hopper.

"I'm surviving rather nicely, thanks. Who dialed the phone for you, dear?" Their banter was light and easy, a friendship cemented during weeks of correcting a dismal film in a drab Eastern European country where honesty was born of late hours and no bright lights.

"To think that I only broke one fingernail doing it," Corey chuckled back. "Seriously, love, how are you managing? Aren't there bears and things out there?"

Stephanie thought of the bomb and decided that she'd prefer the bears. "I'll tell you how bad it is," she said with a delighted grin. "There isn't even room service."

"Where?" Corey demanded. "In your little spa?"

"In the whole town."

For a moment Corey couldn't manage an answer. "Why, that's barbaric! I'll send out the jet." She meant it, too. The other end of Corey's umbilical cord was attached to a curling iron. And that was firmly held by her favorite hairdresser.

"I can always come home for a transfusion if it gets too bad," Stephanie assured her dryly.

"Well, tell me, darling," the voice went on in a tone of undimmed curiosity. "What's he like?"

"Who, dear?" Stephanie asked, her eyes on Drake. He was in twill slacks and a V-necked ivory velour pullover, and his hair was still wet. Stephanie noted a delicious increase in her heart rate. He had the most intriguing pattern of creases in his cheeks and at the corners of his eyes when he smiled.

"Who indeed! The gymnast you're playing hotel with. Is he as devastating as he looks on the screen?"

Stephanie caught herself just short of correcting Corey. Drake was watching her, enjoying the humor that escaped from her end of the conversation. Instead, she nodded, her eyes bright with suppressed laughter. "Yes."

"And are you going to immediately if not sooner have an assignation with the muscle man?"

This time Stephanie did laugh. "No." It would have been nice, though. Very nice.

"Well, in that case," Corey sang out in delight, "I can assume it's open season. Reserve the presidential suite for me, darling. I must come check him out."

"Corey..."

"Oh, and another thing. Haven't you been picking up your messages? Franklin is just desperate to get ahold of you. He says you're the only person who can help him."

Franklin was a director Stephanie worked with regularly who was always desperate and forever insisting that she was absolutely the only person who could do what he needed. As difficult as he was to deal with, Stephanie suspected that it was more likely that she was the only person who could put up with him.

"I'll call him," she sighed. "I told him I was going to be out of commission for a while, but you know how well he listens."

"It's what makes him Franklin. Well, do call him. I do so hate it when he uses me as a go-between."

"I'll see you when I get home, Corey."

"Sooner, darling. I must offer solace in your hour of need."

Stephanie was still laughing when she hung up.

"I heard that the last person who laughed at Corey Alexander never worked in Hollywood again," Drake drawled from where he leaned against the desk.

"Ah—" Stephanie nodded with a knowing smile "—but that was a man."

"We do too have room service."

She laughed again and turned for her office door. Drake followed, oblivious to the stares still garnered from the phone call.

"Corey considered nothing less than champagne and pâté for breakfast room service. Peanut butter and jelly sandwiches don't count."

"How did you get hooked up with her?" he asked, closing the door behind them.

"I worked on *Woman of Leisure* with her as the dialogue editor. The conditions at the time invoked comparisons to labor camps." Once again, Stephanie found herself smiling. "As you can imagine, humor saw us through."

"A dialogue editor?"

Stephanie walked over to the coffee maker that was still warm from her conference with Diane and picked up a cup. "My job. I'm the one who makes sure that everything an actor says is heard in the proper order, and that what isn't supposed to be heard isn't."

Picking up his own cup, Drake waited while Stephanie poured. "Like what?"

She grinned, thinking of the last film she'd done. "Jet planes flying over a Civil War battle."

He nodded, interested. "How does one become a dialogue editor?"

Stephanie shrugged, walking over to sit before the fire. Jacques's office was as much a living room as a workroom with a leather couch and recliner complementing the big oak desk. Stephanie chose the couch. "I was trained as a film editor. Putting all the pieces together to make a coherent film. But then I moved on to dialogue editing, because I can pretty much call my own shots. I get to work with the actors in the film, too, which I didn't before. That little room just got a little too claustrophobic for me, I guess."

"Are there many female film editors?" Drake asked, settling in next to her. The steam rose in soft curls from his cup, and he held it in both hands, as if warming himself.

Stephanie nodded. "A fair number."

"How about dialogue editors?"

She saw the sly humor in his eyes with the question and knew he had her. "Me."

The light brightened. "Quite a challenge."

Stephanie couldn't help a grin and a conceding nod of the head. "Just a girl looking for an honest day's work."

Drake chuckled, sipping at his coffee. "You should have told that story to the reporter when he asked how come Jacques gave you the Inn."

"Gave *us* the Inn," she corrected. "And I did try to tell him. That obviously wasn't the story he was sent to get."

She stole a look at Drake as he sipped his drink contemplatively. The light favored him, settling in slashes along the sharp ridges of cheeks and chin. The firelight caught his eyes, their gaze unusually soft and comfortable. His hair still just damp enough for her to want to run her hands through it, tumbled over his high forehead. The lines of his jaw and neck were clean, strong, the hollow at the base of his throat inviting.

Stephanie had known more handsome men. She'd certainly known more famous ones, renowned for their magnetism and charisma. Some she'd dated, one or two she'd taken home. But for some reason she found herself drawn more to the slumbering volcano who sat next to her, the last man she should have ever been comfortable with, much less been enticed by. They'd make good partners, she thought, with Drake's passion and her logic. But how to be partners and not more? How to keep her head when even sitting next to him in the middle of the afternoon incited lightning in her?

"Must be a little dull for you here," he said after a moment. "After working on films and all."

Stephanie raised an eyebrow, the corner of her mouth curving. "Even in L.A. I don't get bomb threats before breakfast. And that's not even mentioning the several referrals to bimbos, buy-out threats, tabloid-style reporters and a possible smear campaign all in the space of forty-eight hours. Even for Hollywood that would be a full two days."

"What about the nightlife here?"

"What nightlife?"

Drake grinned. "My point exactly."

She chuckled, conceding the point. "Yes, Telluride is a little quiet for my taste. But since I won't be here for that long, I think I can survive."

When she said it, Stephanie made the mistake of looking over at Drake. Something about what she'd said, or maybe the offhand way she'd said it, sparked a reaction in his eyes. Anger, frustration. The gray darkened as if the sun had briefly disappeared from the sky.

Stephanie's first instinct was to object, wondering whether he thought she was taking her responsibilities lightly again. Then she realized that the reaction was more personal. For just a moment she had the overwhelming feeling that Drake had wanted to object not to the fact that she was taking the Inn lightly, but that she was taking him lightly.

But then the moment was gone. Stephanie turned deliberately away, her own eyes perilously close to betraying her, her heart once again setting an alien pace. Her reaction had been much too close to treasonous.

"I was wondering," she said, facing the fire, "what you thought of Diane Taylor. She seems to be the best person to leave in charge."

Drake couldn't take his eyes from Stephanie's profile. Outlined in flames, crowned with her own peculiar fire, yet so incredibly calm. He'd seen something in her just now. A

surprise, a sudden confusion as if she'd wandered too close
to something she couldn't handle.

Well, he could sure as hell relate to that. He'd just done
the same thing. Drake couldn't remember the last time he'd
come so close to decking someone over a woman. He
couldn't remember the last time he'd felt so suddenly lost
when a woman said she would be leaving. And damn! He
hadn't even known her more than two days.

"She needs a little confidence," he finally answered
slowly, his gaze still on her. "But she knows what she's
doing."

Stephanie nodded, turning back to him with calm eyes.
She had managed to pull herself together. Drake wasn't at
all sure he liked that. But it wasn't something he could af-
ford to challenge right now. He had too much to do in too
short a time to let Stephanie Fleming drag him down. It
would be his last chance at the Olympics—his last chance at
racing at all. And there was the Inn to consider. He simply
couldn't let himself give in to the magic in those eyes and
become lost.

The sound of a soft rap on the door interrupted them.
Stephanie eased herself out of her chair. "That must be that
room service you're so proud of," she said with a smile.

It was. Peanut butter and jelly sandwiches and potato
chips. Within a few minutes, the two of them had settled
down to their original task.

It was only much later as Drake walked back to his house
that the moment resurrected itself. The evening was crisp,
moonlight skittering off the snow and transforming Telluride into a ghost town. His shadow stretched before him. His
breath rose lazily into the night as he walked down the hill,
hands in the pockets of his leather jacket. He should have
been cross-country skiing on a night like this. It was a perfect time, with all the solitude in the world and the valley
slumberous and mystical.

It was nights like this that made him ache for the future
he was losing. The freedom. All he'd ever wanted to do was
ski, first as a way out of a no-win town, and then because it
taught him to fly. He'd grown to relate to those damn hills,

knowing every turn and mogul as if it were a friend. You knew what to expect on the mountain. You knew where you were going and how to get there, and if the getting there gave you wings, then that was even better.

Drake had had the wings. He'd pushed his limits on the hill so far and so often that just the exercises to keep him in shape were agony. But it was worth it to be able to strap on his skis and take his time alone with the wind.

He had beaten the hill; he had tested himself and come away the best. Now it was all going to be over.

The doctors had given him the news that summer when he'd been in traction and casts. No more racing. Drake had simply abused his body once too often, and it was beginning to refuse to mend. If he continued the way he had, he was going to end up a cripple. The truth of the warning had been borne out by the best orthopedists in California and the pain in his joints. He was mortal.

But he had to go out on his own terms. He had to match himself against the clock one more time. One more season when he was the best, when he could shoot down that hill like a comet. If he could finish with one last win, maybe it would make it better.

The World Cup had been out the minute he'd fallen. He had already spent half the season mending. But there were still the Olympics, and Drake needed those wins to ease the winters when he'd be forced to watch other men take the risks that were so much a part of him. When he would have to sit aside while others picked up the gold.

But he wasn't going to do any winning if he didn't get his mind down to the job at hand. When he should have been working out with the team on Mount Hood, he was giving basics to a greenhorn who couldn't tell a Sno-Cat from a bobcat. A greenhorn with the most unforgettable voice in the western hemisphere.

Drake clomped up the steps to the big porch of the old house. Pulling out his keys, he let himself in and turned on the lights. Spare, almost empty rooms spread out before him.

For not the first time, Drake considered how centered his life had become around the Inn. Around skiing. There was practically nothing of him in this house he'd bought and renovated when he'd first helped Jacques open the Inn. All of Drake McDonald was contained in the pictures on the bar walls up the hill.

Maybe it was time to get out. Maybe this would give him the time to take his life at a walk. He'd been on the run for the last sixteen years. Pulling off his coat, he threw it over the living-room chair where no one would disturb it. He wondered how long it had been since anyone had even been here. And he thought with some surprise that he would like to see Stephanie sitting here. Just the two of them, talking about Jacques and the future.

Scowling, Drake shook his head and walked into the kitchen. Forty-eight lousy hours. How could a person's life change so fast?

# Chapter 4

Telluride was in a skiing frenzy. In the last two days, more than ten new inches of powder had fallen, and even more was predicted. The clouds still hung low over the mountains, wreathing them in soft gray shrouds and sprinkling the valley with flakes. The hills swarmed with bright blurs of skiers coursing endlessly down and then being carried back up by the various lifts and trams. The hills echoed with prosperity and adventure.

At the Sundance, the atmosphere wasn't quite as exhilarating. Tiring of pacing her office, Stephanie decided to go out and walk the grounds. Three more days in Telluride had made things worse instead of better. Unnamed frustrations battled with the named ones to churn in her stomach and sour her sleep.

Wrapping her favorite Irish wool shawl over her heavy sweater and black stretch pants, Stephanie strode out along the driveway to work off some of her frustration, her boots clicking a staccato over the snowy asphalt.

The sense of claustrophobia had begun to consume her. She was trapped in a valley inhabited only by skiers and decorated in the *Gunsmoke* mode. She spent her days going

over books and reports and itineraries, balancing the needs
of the guests, the needs of the staff and those of her partner like bright balls in the air while her own needs festered
within her.

She was not born to rule. Neither was there anything in
her training or inclination that could ever make her a good
innkeeper. Stephanie had grown up an only child of two
other children, then worked her way up in a series of jobs
that called for basic loners. She couldn't think of anything
she enjoyed more than sitting in her little soundstage, a cup
of coffee in one hand and the controls to the Automated
Dialogue Replacement computer in the other, patiently
crafting a sound track until it showed no seams.

She couldn't think of anything she'd rather do less than
listen to endless stories of ski tension and ankle exercises and
powder comparisons. If she heard one more person boast
about vertical feet skied in a day, she thought she'd scream.
Stephanie had done her time on the hill. She wanted nothing more to do with it.

She didn't pay attention to which way she was walking
when she stepped out of the lodge. The afternoon was a soft
one, as they said in Ireland, the air moist against her face,
the world around her gentled by snow clouds. The snow that
drifted down was an easy one, just enough to make the steep
valley look like a Currier and Ives print.

Stephanie slid her hands under the warmth of her shawl
and hunched her shoulders to keep the flakes from sliding
down the back of her neck. Her hair was already dusted with
snow, slightly damping its sunny fire. Deciding that she
preferred to walk away from town, she turned back up the
mountain meadow.

The peacefulness in this damn valley was killing her. She
needed an injection of nightlife. A place where she could
cruise a new neighborhood every day if she wanted, a different restaurant or theater, where she could climb the hills
or walk the beach, or pace herself on Mulholland, the city
spread like a blanket of jewels beyond each turn. Traffic
jams, smog, deal-making over lunch. She had been raised
on that stimulant, and it was always hard when she had to

give it up. It was even harder now, and she couldn't decide why.

Stephanie had just spent six weeks in Sofia and survived better than this. She'd sat on location in deserts and ghost towns, but after five days in Telluride she felt as if she were suffocating.

It could be the skiing, she thought, lifting her face to the wind and the soft touch of snowflakes against her nose. If there was one legacy her father had bequeathed her, it was a healthy distaste for the slopes. Well, no, she amended realistically, not just her father. She'd gone a long way toward creating that situation herself. Her father had simply been the cause and effect. Every time she looked at those bright, red-cheeked faces reflecting the animation of discovery and speed, Stephanie felt her own mortification rise again like bile in her throat. Never again.

It could also, she decided, be the responsibility. Cutting a picture was one thing. You weren't out there on a limb all by yourself. Every time somebody sneezed during the production of a picture there were meetings and screenings and consultations. In the end, it was somebody else's money. This business was going to end up on her shoulders during the worst moment in its history.

Drake had been right. The sharks were hungry in this town, not just for the Inn, but for blood. Rumors were already circulating about Stephanie, innuendos about how she'd acquired her half interest in the Sundance. Curious eyes followed her everywhere until it was all she could do to keep from blurting out that yes, she had bedded down every known skier west of the Continental Divide in the hope of inheriting a choice piece of property.

But that wasn't what hurt business. The rumors of her lack of acumen were beginning to do that. Longtime guests were already starting to cancel on the strength of hearing that friendliness had left the Inn when Stephanie had inherited it. They'd heard that Drake didn't so much avoid helping as want nothing to do with her. The attacks had grown so venomous that Diane had begun to defend her bosses like the castle guard.

Then there was Nathan Ames. Whether he was the source of the rumors couldn't be proven, but he always made himself available to commiserate and offer his own ideas for Stephanie's welfare, which were just beginning to include the word "sale."

Even L.A. wasn't this treacherous. Well, Stephanie amended with a rueful smile. Not always.

But that wasn't all. There was another tension that had begun to eat at her, another problem...

"Hey, watch out!"

Stephanie heard the warning and the whoosh of approaching skis at the same time. Stopping, she looked up to see Drake whip around a last stand of trees and come to a sharp stop right before her.

He was in a sleek red suit, his trademark, and his face was ruddy from the exercise he'd just taken. Stephanie found herself smiling at him, willing the testiness down deep where he wouldn't see it, trying to ignore the sudden new tightness in her chest at the sight of him. He exuded such graceful power in his movements—a sleek energy like a race car at full throttle.

"Jaywalking's a punishable offense in these hills," he told her with a grin, letting go of his pole long enough to push up his goggles. His gray eyes mirrored the color of the clouds that swept the mountains he'd just skimmed. Somehow Stephanie couldn't pull her gaze away from them. They radiated a fierce joy that mesmerized, high spirits she'd never known. She recognized the first tug of envy and just as quickly dismissed it.

"You need better crosswalks," she countered with a tilt of her head. Other skiers appeared from behind the veil of fog and swept by them. She'd wandered right into the middle of a ski run. Thankfully it was an intermediate slope or she would have been impaled on a passing pole. The experts shot their runs like express trains.

"Scouting out the territory?" Drake asked. "Or are you considering a try at it yourself?"

Stephanie glowered at him. "Thank you, my only self-destructive habit is an occasional cigarette. I had cabin fever."

She saw Drake look around in something akin to amazement, and grinned in response. "What—" she mimicked him "—here?"

His almost sheepish reaction gave him away. "People do spend fortunes coming here to cure that very problem," he reminded her.

"Do you know where you end up if you drive an hour away in any direction?" Stephanie demanded with a little too much pique. "Another mountain town. Or maybe just another mountain. I would give Jacques's entire wine cellar for the sight of some concrete and glass."

"But if you drive for an hour in L.A., you're still in L.A."

"Exactly. But you could be in Chinatown, the barrio or Malibu. Or the studios. I find myself positively yearning for all that tinsel and trash."

"Save me from that kind of madness. I'm happy here, thanks."

He was, too. There was a life in Drake's eyes Stephanie had been able to catch in her father's. But she had never been around when her father had been on the slopes. She wondered whether Drake would fare any better when he had to give it up.

"Well, I'll get on with my exercise," she offered abruptly, uncomfortable with the pictures she'd conjured up. "And you can get on with yours. I promise to stay out of the traffic."

Drake wasn't ready to let her go. Leaning on a pole, he kept her from walking by. "I don't think you're giving Telluride a fighting chance. There's more here than just skiing, you know."

"Yes." She nodded. "I know. Cable TV. And the best grapevine east of Hollywood."

He laughed, a soft rumble that the snow kept between them. "I'll tell you what. I'm going to take a break around two. Meet me at the front desk and I'll take you on a real tour. Deal?''

Stephanie frowned, a quick ambivalence sneaking through her. "Oh, I don't want to..."

Drake never gave her a chance to finish. "Two. If you're not there, I'll come find you."

She wasn't there at two. Drake strode in, brushing snow from the shoulders of his jacket to find a couple crowding one end of a couch by the fire and Diane conferring with the concierge at the desk. Stephanie was nowhere to be found.

Brushing off his jacket one final time he leaned across the desk.

"Hi, Drake," Diane immediately beamed, her ordinary features taking on a sweet glow. Other staff members made it a point to assure each other that Drake McDonald could schuss their slopes any day. Diane would never think to put it quite that way. But when Drake smiled at her like that she felt quite special and opened like a hothouse flower.

"I like that sweater on you, Diane," Drake remarked with sincere appreciation. "Brings out the blue in your eyes. Have you seen the boss?"

She took a minute to consider. Drake had a way of flustering her. Diane was not the kind of person to attract attention.

"She was in Jacques's quarters about an hour ago," she finally managed to say, her hand straying to the hem of her baby-blue sweater. "I think she was cleaning up his things."

Drake's face clouded over, his voice suddenly abrupt. "Why?"

Diane shrugged. "She's still looking for the insurance papers on this place. You know how Jacques kept things."

"Yeah," he nodded, his temper easing. "I do. I'll go on up and get her, thanks."

"Why couldn't she be ugly?" the concierge demanded playfully as she watched Drake lope up the stairs at the other end of the room. "Or fat? Give us working girls a chance."

It took Diane a minute to get her attention back to her work. "She's nice," she defended her employer automatically.

"That's the problem," the concierge argued with a dramatic scowl. "She *is* nice."

Drake didn't hear the exchange as he headed upstairs. Jacques's rooms were under the third floor eaves, an old dormer into which the skier had crammed a lifetime of litter. Drake had spent many nights sprawled in a comfortable chair as the two of them had discussed life or planned strategy, a cognac in hand and the mountains spread out before the big window Jacques had installed in the steep roof. When Drake was away, just the smell of drying wool and wood smoke had the power to rekindle for him the warmth of that room.

He stood a moment at the door before knocking. The sea green rug had grown worn, the hardwood floor scuffed with years of traffic. The fact that there was no lock on the door attested to the room's accessibility. Drake suddenly felt as if he were stepping back into the house where he'd grown up, the sweet familiarity at odds with the changes.

He finally gave in and knocked. "Stephanie?"

There was no answer.

He tried again. "Stephanie, are you there?"

This time Drake heard a quick rustle. "Uh, yes. Yes."

Even muffled by the door between them, the sound of Stephanie's voice was disturbing. Tremulous, almost faint. Drake opened the door.

"Are you all right?" he demanded, stepping in. His face was tight.

It wasn't the familiar surroundings that stopped him, the old Oriental carpets thrown over hardwood, the overstuffed couch and wingbacks, the four-poster in the alcove and the trophies that crowded the small mantel. What brought him up short was the stark grief he surprised in Stephanie's eyes.

She was sitting cross-legged on the floor, papers and pictures in piles around her, the door to Jacques's cubbyhole open. In her hand she held a familiar statuette, a sleek gold man most people associated with sealed envelopes and acceptance speeches. Huge tears welled in her soft eyes as they drifted back toward the statuette in her hands.

"Stephanie?"

She didn't answer. Setting the award down before her, Stephanie pulled herself into an almost rigid position and proceeded to pull her control about her like a cloak.

Drake watched her and was amazed. The tears never fell. Her face, as openly bereft as a child's trying to comprehend loss, quickly assumed the more familiar lines of reserve. It took only a second, then the transformation was complete, robbing Drake of the opportunity to reach out to her. Suddenly he found himself standing in awkward silence.

"Oh, it's...uh, two, isn't it?" Stephanie murmured, briefly smiling at him as she again picked up the statuette with hesitant hands. Drake noticed how she kept running one thumb along the sleek lines, as if soothing herself with the feel of it.

"My turn to play Mohammed, I guess," he answered stiffly.

She turned her face up to him, her eyes unnaturally bright and brittle. The well of emotion he'd discovered was more visible than she realized. "I'm sorry. I got lost in this mess. I was looking for the Inn's papers. I haven't been able to find them."

As she spoke Stephanie got to her feet. It should have been an ungainly maneuver, especially since she still held fast to the heavy trophy. Drake saw her glide up with a slow, regal grace that threatened his breathing. How could she be so in control, so contained? The grief he'd seen in her eyes should have had her sobbing, but her shoulders hadn't even lost their proud set. He was at once awed and saddened by it.

"Need any help?" He motioned to the papers, his eyes locking meaningfully with hers.

Stephanie chose to ignore his implication. "No, thanks. I'll finish later. I was just going to put this back on the mantel."

She hefted the statuette easily, obviously familiar with the feel of it. Drake found himself staring anew, trying to ignore the exotic scent of her perfume as she approached, willfully putting aside the sudden impulse to take her into his arms and force that grief to be freed. It made him stand all the more uncomfortably before her.

Instead he motioned to her burden. "Was that here? I never saw it."

She smiled. "In the middle of the mantel. I just saw it when I was sitting here."

A trophy hidden amid the congregation of Jacques's trophies. Drake had never really noticed it before. "Where did he get it?"

Even Stephanie couldn't prevent the wistful melancholy that flooded her soft brown eyes. Standing before Drake, she turned her attention to the statue, now cradled in both hands. "From a snotty film editor he knew."

Drake's eyes widened yet again. "You?"

She met his gaze with wry self-effacement. "They were giving them out in the Blond Bimbo category that year."

He grimaced. "What movie?"

"*The Elopement.* The last time Jacques yelled at me for wasting my life in that 'smog-filled bowl of decadence' I sent it to him." Her eyes drifted again, the loss returning. "He told me he'd put it right where it deserved to be. I'd always figured he meant the trash."

Drake could hear the brusque laughter in Jacques's voice as he teased her, as the old Frenchman and Stephanie taunted each other with the passion they chose not to share.

"Then you're the one he gave his World Cup trophy to."

Her smile lost even more assurance. "On *my* mantel."

Neither could think of anything to say as Stephanie set the statue back in its resting place. The flickering light licked along its gold lines and strayed to Stephanie's fingers as they lingered over it.

Drake hadn't realized that he'd moved closer. But when Stephanie turned back from the mantel he was there. He saw the ache that found its way to her face, the regret and the loss. It was something he knew all too well. He'd spent his share of time alone in this room, sitting before the fireplace trying to resurrect the image of his friend in the light of the flames.

Stephanie stopped before him, suddenly stilled by the protective empathy in his clear gray eyes. For the first time in her life, she found herself staring into a gaze that spoke only to her, and far more eloquently than words ever could. It penetrated her facade and exposed her.

She felt Drake lift a hand to her face, as if the better to communicate his feelings. His fingers were strong and warm against her skin, their scent that smell of wood and soap. But more, they radiated understanding. Sharing. When he bent his head, she knew he was going to kiss her and couldn't seem to object.

Stephanie met Drake's kiss with closed eyes. The world became his touch: his hand, his lips, the soft sigh of his breath against her. She'd never known such sweet communion. The heavy ache that had bloomed in her heart when she'd spotted the Oscar eased a little now with Drake to share it. Loss was given and received within the space of one act.

He wrapped his arm gently around her waist, holding her to him. Lord, Stephanie thought with vague panic, she'd never allowed this before. She wasn't sure she knew how to share with someone, especially pain. She'd never in her life done that.

But, oh, how very gentle that hand was. How very tender were his lips. Drake enfolded her like a fragile flower, afraid to crush her, his mouth searching hers as if hesitant to bruise it.

Stephanie felt his hand leave her face, tracing her throat and crowding the breath in her chest. A new fierce ache ignited deep in her, a need, a hunger such as she'd never known. She'd spent her life protecting herself against loneliness only to recognize it in herself through the power of one man's touch.

Neither of them heard the first hesitant taps on the door. The message was repeated with more force, and Stephanie jerked back, her eyes wide. Drake saw the fleeting ambivalence, the need and the fear that battled in the depths of those earth-brown eyes before she drew that relentless control back around her again.

Stephanie didn't say a word as she drew away from his embrace, nor did Drake protest. He'd met something in her he'd never known in any other woman, an unspoken kinship he couldn't have anticipated, particularly from an outsider. But her kiss had been nectar.

Drake turned to answer the intruder feeling more shaken than he ever had in his life, even when the doctors had told him to give up racing. He'd never really expected to find a soul mate in this world. That intuitive communion, the instinctive understanding and communication that transcended passions and pastimes and plans, had never found its way into any of his relationships.

Drake had always looked for that indefinable something that would create a real bond between him and the woman he would love. He'd discovered it within the space of a kiss.

"I'm sorry to bother you, Miss Fleming." It was Diane, sounding twice as uncomfortable as sorry. "There's a gentleman from the police here. He wants to talk to you and Drake."

A small smile flickered across Stephanie's features as she turned once more to Drake before letting in the rest of the world.

"I'm afraid that guided tour will have to wait."

"Plenty of time for that," he assured her, his own demeanor not nearly as noncommittal. "Let's go see what they've found out."

Stephanie took one last look at him, compelled by the emotion that still fueled his eyes. After that kiss, she felt frayed. She struggled to maintain equilibrium, to gather her calm again so it could protect her. And here Drake was smiling at her with such stark ambivalence that it battered at her even more. How could he possibly allow himself such vulnerable emotions?

Moving deliberately, Stephanie followed Diane down the hall.

Tom was waiting for them, standing stiffly in the lobby as if refusing to get too familiar with people he had to deal with in an official capacity. Stephanie smiled as she descended the last steps. He was so young, so very serious all of a sudden.

"Could we talk in your office?" he asked without preamble, his eyes straying nervously to Drake's, his police cap in a death grip.

Stephanie's own eyes followed briefly to see a wry amusement on Drake's face. "Certainly," she said, nodding in agreement, facing Tom again and leading him toward the room behind the desk. Others were observing the action with interest.

"Something slither out from under a rock?" Drake asked casually.

Tom took a quick glance over his shoulder. His eyes were guilty-looking. "We got a call."

Drake stopped, his eyes narrowing. His gut suddenly told him just what kind of call it was. "And?"

By that time the three of them were settled in the office and Tom had worked his way up to cap-twisting. It was obvious that he hadn't come to work in Telluride for this kind of thing.

"What's the matter, Tom?" Drake asked, perching on the edge of the desk and leaning forward.

The posture seemed too intense for Tom, who stepped back a fraction. "I'm not sure where to begin."

Stephanie, easing into a chair, nodded encouragment. "You got a call."

Tom returned her nod, grateful for the cue. "An anonymous tip."

"My favorite kind," Drake grunted to himself, propelling his frame from the desk. Both Stephanie and Tom watched, she with confusion, he with apprehension.

"Said we'd find the rest of the stolen dynamite on your premises, Drake." Tom looked as if he'd rather be hanging himself than delivering this kind of news. His expression didn't improve any when Drake came to an abrupt halt before him.

"The rest of *what* stolen dynamite?"

Stephanie was back on her feet, too, a new fear crowding her chest.

"Oh." Tom looked from one to the other. "From the construction site. The new condos off Boomerang Road."

Drake took a slow breath. "Mountain Crest Condo."

Tom nodded. "They were reported stolen Sunday morning."

"The morning after the incident."

Another nod, this time not so assured. "We checked the lot number against the sticks used in the bomb threat here. They matched."

Now Drake was nodding, brisk, angry moves of his head that unsettled his hair. His eyes were like storm clouds, heavy and threatening. "A Nathan Ames project."

Stephanie looked up, her eyes widening a little. "He wouldn't."

Drake swung toward her. "Don't bet on it." Then he turned back to Tom. "I don't suppose you found any fingerprints or anything on the bomb."

Tom shook his head regretfully. No one moved.

"So somebody called you and said that it was Drake who stole the dynamite to plant a dummy bomb to scare me out?" Stephanie demanded carefully.

Tom nodded, looking even more miserable.

"But that's ridiculous!" she insisted. "He's half owner."

"It's been known to happen," Tom insisted. "For insurance."

Stephanie laughed then, a jangle of disbelief. "Not likely, if we can't even find the policy."

The young deputy didn't have an answer. "Drake, I'm afraid a search warrant has been obtained for your house. I thought you'd like to be there—"

Drake whipped around. "Are they there now?"

"Do you . . . want to say anything?"

"Yeah," he answered, opening the door and pushing Tom through. "Let's get the hell over there before one of those idiots breaks something."

Without thinking, Stephanie followed them both right out the door.

Stephanie's first reaction to Drake's house was surprise. Not because it was another Victorian dollhouse of turrets and gingerbreading. This was the type of home that would appreciate the fastest in Telluride's climate, a carefully renovated, exquisitely crafted home at the edge of the mountains. Drake would certainly have realized that.

The surprise came when she followed Drake inside to discover the Spartan living conditions he maintained. She'd seen more furniture in unrented apartments.

There was nothing wrong with his pocketbook, of that she was sure. The few pieces inside were as well-crafted as the house. The glossy hardwood floors in the living room bore one heather tweed couch and an overstuffed chair pulled up before the fireplace. There were a couple of ceramic lamps on glass and marble end tables, a stereo system, some andirons, nothing more.

The lack of furniture drew her eyes to the cream walls, and great expanses of space, broken only by well-placed sketches. Mostly pencil and ink, all framed, of skiing and mountains and sunlight. Stark, spare, breathtaking. Drake had enough taste to pick the very essence of his life with which to surround himself. Stephanie was about to ask him where he'd found them when a deputy appeared from the kitchen.

"Drake, I think you'd better see this."

They followed him into the kitchen, another echoing space with little sign of habitation and less of decoration. There were more of Drake's mementos over Jacques's fireplace than in any room in his house.

Stephanie didn't get as much of a chance to study this room. The minute he followed her in, Drake let out a low curse. Another man stood by an open cupboard near the sink, holding up four sticks of dynamite in a plastic bag. Tom looked at Drake with stricken eyes. Slowing to an uncertain halt, Stephanie found herself speechless.

"Dick Benson, Tobacco, Alcohol and Firearms," the gentleman with the bag introduced himself. "I think somebody'd better read this man his rights."

"Don't be ridiculous," Stephanie objected instinctively, stepping forward. Drake held her where she was.

"Did anybody bother to see if one of my doors was jimmied?" he demanded, the weight of sudden rage straining his voice.

Tom had already pulled out his little laminated card, bright with disuse. "You have the right to remain silent..."

"Just do me a favor," Drake snapped as the other deputy pulled his hands around for cuffing, "and check the doors!"

"Anything you say can and will be held against you..."

"Shut up, Tom. If Nathan Ames has anything to do with this, I'll kill him."

Stephanie flinched. "I think you'd better pay attention to Tom, Drake."

Mr. Benson took his first note of Stephanie. "Who's she?"

Stephanie smiled evenly. "His mother. I'm thinking of washing his mouth out with soap."

"Lady, you'd better get out of here."

She had long since lost her fear of police. "You can't really believe any of this."

Mr. Benson wasn't swayed by her protest. "Mr. McDonald was seen cycling past the construction site on Friday and Saturday morning."

"Of course I was!" Drake snorted, his control frayed. "Anybody in this damn town knows that I go out Boomerang every day I'm here. Some days I cycle, some I run, some I ski."

"That's true, sir," Tom spoke up diffidently as if he'd mentioned it before.

Mr. Benson glared. "Don't like your job, do you, boy?"

"It wouldn't make any sense for Drake to plant that bomb," Stephanie insisted.

"Not even to get you out of there and have it all to himself?" Mr. Benson asked.

They were already shuffling Drake out the door, watched by the score of neighbors who had responded to the lure of flashing lights. Drake turned to consider the smug civil servant who seemed so insistent on persecuting him. He shook his head a little, the line of his jaw like steel. If he'd been free, Stephanie had no doubt he would have swung at something.

Stephanie watched the scene and found herself wanting to scream. Another bright little ball in the air, one that would cause catastrophe if it fell. Damn this place. She wasn't sure she was ever going to get home.

"I'll see you in a couple of hours!" she called after Drake as he stepped outside.

"It'll probably be more like a couple of days," Mr. Benson assured her and he then ushered her out the door with everyone else.

"Don't count on that," Stephanie said under her breath and walked out to her car. She was suddenly scared and didn't know why.

# Chapter 5

News in Telluride traveled faster than it did in Hollywood. By the time Stephanie made it back to the Inn, Diane was on the verge of tears, and the rest of the staff was outraged. Stephanie had the vaguely uneasy picture of them lifting shotguns and ski poles and storming the county jail.

"How dare they insinuate that Drake could even consider such a thing?" Diane objected vehemently. "He practically lives here."

"Well they did," Stephanie assured her, dialing for the legal help Drake would need. "Now we just have to figure some way to prove he was set up."

"What are we going to do?"

"First," she said, listening to the ringing on the other end of her line, "we're going to get him out of there.... Hello?"

Diane hadn't quite had her say, though. "I told them he hadn't been anywhere near that office. They didn't even listen to me. They just took away the letter we got."

"Just a moment," Stephanie said into the phone. "He wasn't near the office?" she asked Diane.

Diane shook her head. "Not since Jacques died. Even when I asked him to go in and check for the Inn's important papers for me, he wouldn't do it. He just didn't...well, you know."

Stephanie was tapping the pencil again, the staccato in time with her racing thoughts. "But he could have gone in without your knowing about it."

"Not very easily. I had the key."

"And you told the police this."

Diane nodded emphatically.

Stephanie was just about to go back to the phone when her head shot up. "What letter?"

Diane looked contrite. "We got a threatening letter today. I didn't want to bother you."

"Addressed to me or the Inn?"

"It just said that our tricks would be exposed and we'd be shut down if it was the last thing he—or whoever—did. That we'd pay. It was made of letters cut out from a magazine."

"Sounds like things are escalating," Stephanie mused. "Well, we have something to work with now, anyway." Diane began to make her way toward the door as Stephanie returned her attention to the phone. The manager almost made it out. "And Diane, don't ever keep anything like that from me again. Okay?"

Diane's nod was a quick one. "Okay." She looked rather like a person who had reached the guillotine, only to find it broken.

"Excuse me—" Stephanie apologized to the person at the other end of the phone line as Diane edged out the door "—I'm sorry to keep you waiting..."

She was still on the phone, shuttling back and forth between legal counsel and the police station where Mr. Benson was doing his best to outsmart her, when a commotion blew into the lobby. Stephanie heard the sounds of greeting, then laughter and a sudden silence. She looked up to find a handsome man in her doorway.

"Can I help you?" She hung up the receiver, about to dial again. Her guest was the quintessential ski bum, blond, beautiful, with a matched set of dimples and sparkling blue eyes that seemed incapable of anything but laughter.

"I hear Drake's gotten himself into some trouble. Are *you* the new boss in these parts?"

"I am. You're..."

"Delighted." He marched up and sat himself down on her desk, his smile brightening considerably, his leg swinging in a lazy arc. "Drake didn't tell me you were so, well, younger than Jacques. I'm Chip Markinson." The tone of his voice assumed recognition on Stephanie's part. She reacted instinctively, her eyebrows raised in placid inquiry.

"I'm sorry—"

"I'm on the team with Drake. World Cup? Olympics?" He made a motion like a teacher trying to instill knowledge. "How did you ever get this job if you don't even know who I am?"

"I didn't even know who *Drake* was," Stephanie assured him with a smile, receiver once again in hand.

Her guest waved aside her answer. "Oh, that doesn't matter. He's already past history anyway. I'm the one to watch on the slopes from now on. Take my word for it."

Her smile never altered. "How nice."

Stephanie couldn't fault the pitch. Not with a breezy, carefree attitude like his. Chip Markinson was one of those sunshine boys who barreled through life as if it were all one long birthday party thrown just for them. The fact that they dragged along the rest of the world as they shed their brand of laughter and light was just a bonus. You couldn't help but like the guy.

"So," he went on, leaning a little farther over and concentrating all his boyish appeal on her. "Tell me about yourself."

Stephanie flashed an apologetic smile. "I'd like to, but I have some business to take care of."

"Before you even tell me your name?"

"Stephanie," she obliged, dialing again. "Stephanie Fleming."

His smile grew to wolfish proportions. "Want to go skiing later, Stephanie, maybe when the moon comes up? It's a real kick in the head then."

"I don't ski," she answered evenly, and managed to finish her call while Chip recovered from his open-mouthed astonishment. By the time he found his voice again, she was up and reaching for her shawl.

"That's impossible," he objected. "Even Jacques wouldn't leave a place like this to a nonskier."

"Even Jacques did," Stephanie confirmed, realizing that she instinctively reacted to him like a pesky younger brother. "Now, if you'll excuse me, I have to go."

"Where?" he asked, closing the distance between them. "To get Drake? I'd like to come along."

He wasn't any taller than she, Stephanie realized as she swung the shawl into place and pinned it. "I'm not sure Drake is even going to be in the mood to see *me*," she assured him. "It might not be such a good idea."

"But if I don't see him, I won't be fulfilling my obligation to the ski team," he objected, grabbing her purse and handing it to her. His smile was as bright as a child's, only a hint of malicious glee betraying his intention to enjoy the sight of the two-time World Cup champ in the slammer. "I came all the way from my duties on the World Cup circuit to try and drag him back to training."

Stephanie stopped, a hand on the purse. "I thought he *was* training."

Chip nodded. "When Jacques was alive. Drake split his time between the team and here, since Jacques had always been his personal coach. But it's been a good few weeks now, and the coaches on the team want to see what Drake's accomplished since his injury. He isn't going to get much chance to test out his working parts before the Olympics."

That bothered her. Drake had given her two weeks, but it was obvious that he was cutting his own corners a little close to help her out. He would never think to desert the Inn just when he thought the vultures were about to circle. His last chance at an Olympic gold, and here he was baby-sitting her. Stephanie turned and headed out the door without really noticing that Chip was right on her heels.

"If you're the one bailing him out," he continued unabashedly as he held the door for her, "you must have gotten pretty close to him. How does he seem?"

For a moment Stephanie didn't hear him. Those bright balls were tumbling faster and she was trying to keep track of them.

"Seem?" she finally asked, turning to Chip as they walked out into the sunshine, the eyes of everyone in the lodge on them.

"Yeah." Chip held the door once again and followed her down the steps. "He's got to be up for the competition, ya know? He's got a couple of races coming up, and it's gonna be a real grind. I figured he'd be, well, maybe depressed?"

She nodded. "He misses Jacques, I know. But he's been working hard." A fleeting image of Drake's pain-sharpened eyes crossed her mind and Stephanie shook her head a little. "He's been working very hard."

"Damn."

She looked over to see Chip shrug without much apology.

"I'll never beat him if he doesn't learn to slack off somewhere," he said and climbed into the passenger seat.

"But aren't you the current World Cup leader?" Stephanie asked. "I'd think that would satisfy just about anybody."

Chip shook his head. "Drake ruined all my fun by pulling out. I've never had the chance to beat him. You know, the new gun going for the old pro? Best way to prove I'm the best. Since this'll be his last year, I have to do it in the Olympics instead." For just the briefest of moments his eyes clouded over a little. "Not the same, really, but it'll have to do."

Without even taking a breath, he beamed at her with undisguised anticipation. Stephanie shook her head at his unholy enthusiasm and started the car.

When Stephanie first saw Drake at the station, his face was filled with surprise. "It's only been a couple of hours!"

he protested, gathering his watch and wallet from the desk. "How'd you manage that?"

"Practice," she said with a bland smile. Beyond Drake Stephanie caught a glimpse of Mr. Benson and noted that he wasn't in the least happy. He probably now thought she'd spent her youth springing arsonists from the pen for the Symbianeze Liberation Army. Stephanie decided to let him enjoy his delusions.

"Practice?" Drake countered with the first stirrings of a grin. "One of those notorious friends of yours?"

"More like notorious relatives," she amended beneath her breath, her distaste for police stations not easing any. "Ready to go?"

She missed the question in Drake's eyes.

"Sure. We still have a tour to take."

"Wish I had a camera for the kids back home." Chip had been delayed on the street by an ardent female fan he hadn't seemed interested in dissuading. His entrance couldn't have been better timed.

Drake gaped. "Markinson? What are you doing here? You're supposed to be in Italy."

Stephanie couldn't tell whether it was friendship or pique she heard in his voice.

Chip grinned. "Came into town to scout the competition, son. I went to the hill and they said today McDonald was skiing the great hoosegow run. I had to come see for myself."

He wrung a reluctant grin from Drake as the three of them headed for the street. "Leave it to you to find me with my backside bared," Drake grumbled. "I suppose Hanley is calling for my head."

"Nothing so dramatic. I'm the official emissary begging for the speedy return of the almighty champion so that the company of sycophants may once again worship at his feet."

Even Stephanie rolled her eyes at that. "Never use a spoon when a shovel will do," she intoned as both men guided her through the door before them.

"Congratulations on your win at Alta Badia," Drake said to Chip, then turned to Stephanie. "Can I have the keys?"

Stephanie looked at him with some surprise. She couldn't imagine being able to drive off tension in this town. There wasn't a flat stretch worth cranking an engine over for anywhere in sight.

"If you'd like." She pulled them out and handed them over.

Drake immediately passed her keys to Chip. "Do something productive. Drive us up to the stables and then park this at the Inn."

Now both Stephanie and Chip were staring. "What?" Chip demanded. "Running out on your obligations?"

"Shut up, Chip," was all Drake would say, "and drive."

He did. The three of them spent a very silent ride up to the meadow that spread out behind the Inn.

"You could at least invite me along," Chip whined good-naturedly as Drake helped Stephanie out a moment later.

"Go fascinate your fan club at the Inn," Drake recommended dryly. "Make both of you happy."

Chip shot them a set of raised eyebrows and threw the vehicle into gear.

"Isn't it a little late for this?" Stephanie asked when Chip had turned the car around. The sun was just brushing the western mountains, pouring gold over the far end of the valley. Telluride was already in deep shadow.

"We're not going far," Drake assured her.

The stable hand echoed Stephanie's sentiment. "It's kinda late for long treks, Drake," he objected diffidently.

"Just help me saddle 'em," Drake answered without turning from the roan over whose back he'd just slipped a blanket. "And Bill, can Miss Fleming borrow your jacket? She's going to freeze in that thing she's wearing."

Bill and Stephanie considered each other. "I'll look pretty damn silly in that thing," he objected, motioning to her shawl.

"Nobody will see you but the horses."

It was settled. Stephanie slid Bill's suede coat over her sweater and climbed up onto a sweet-natured dun mare. Bill hung the shawl on a peg, shook his head and muttered as he adjusted her stirrups.

"By the way," Drake said to her as he swung up onto the roan. "You do ride, don't you?"

With a wry smile Stephanie guided her horse through the door. "Thanks for asking."

As hard as she tried, Stephanie couldn't keep herself from being overwhelmed by the panorama Drake served up for her consideration. Walking the horses across the valley, he led them up the far end, away from town, first on a side road, and then up a path only he and the horses seemed to sense beneath the snow. They wound in among the firs and aspen for a good twenty minutes to reach their destination.

Emerging from the trees, Stephanie found herself about halfway up a high meadow that overlooked the valley and surrounding mountains. Sunlight still gilded the snowy crests and swept over the dark firs lower down. A jagged line of peaks stabbed the deepening cobalt sky in sharp relief. The moon, still ghostly translucent in the early evening sky, was just beginning to climb. The valley itself was submerged in shadow, Telluride standing out in a kind of mirrored starlight.

For more than a few moments Stephanie was content just to watch and listen to distant sheep bells and the sound of the wind skittering through the trees. The air was cold on her face, clean and sharp like a tonic. Below her lay the cleanly etched valley, an unnaturally clear sight for someone raised on L.A. smog. She smelled the hidden earth and arching pines and heard the sweet music of bird song. If she weren't careful, she might come to like it.

As Stephanie watched silently next to Drake, their horses patient beneath them, the shadows consumed the valley and climbed the mountains, and night settled over the twinkling town of Telluride.

"Still suffering from cabin fever?" Drake asked softly, the magic of the twilight stealing away his fury.

Stephanie saw Drake's eyes drawn to the mountains, where ski trails could still be seen like white rivers of lava spilling from a silent volcano. She thought she saw the same loss she'd surprised in his eyes that first night they'd met. A longing, as if he watched something he was losing, pacing the time he had left so that none was wasted.

Stephanie felt his loss stab her in a way she'd never allowed before, not since she'd been a child, when there hadn't been any defenses against the sharp ache that could invade your dreams and burden your days.

Because she'd been too good a daughter, Stephanie hadn't had enough energy left to be the same kind of good friend or lover, open to the pain other people brought her. The fact that it now caught her unawares when she was most susceptible, unnerved her. She knew better than to think she had anything to give Drake. Surprising herself with the need to speak, she nonetheless resorted to platitudes.

"You don't have to give it *all* up."

Drake turned startled eyes on her. Whatever he was looking for didn't seem to be visible, because he returned to his contemplation of the serene landscape before them. The bird song had begun to die, and at the edge of the woods a rabbit appeared, shuddering to a halt as it sensed intruders. The wind ruffled Drake's hair and then skipped toward the trees.

"I'm giving up most of it," he allowed quietly, his voice heavy. "Jacques always said it was like putting a racehorse on a track and telling him to walk. The adrenaline is already flowing too fast."

Questions bubbled up in Stephanie like residue from the bottom of a slow-boiling cauldron. Questions that had needed answers for too many years, that had caused too much pain and misunderstanding. In the end she simply didn't have the courage to ask.

Before she could look away, Drake swung toward her. Suddenly Stephanie's breath was stolen. Even in the growing cold, a sudden, swift heat ignited in her with the mere contact of Drake's eyes. She felt a pull, as if some force sought to negate the space between them. A curling kind of apprehension snaked up her limbs and planted its seed in her belly. Stephanie found her eyes on Drake's lips, the memory of their succor feeding the fire.

Her horse shifted beneath her and Stephanie turned to it, too abruptly she knew, her hand on its neck, her eyes briefly closing on her terror.

"I think Chip wants you to go back with him," she said in a controlled tone.

Drake's voice was tight, his breath spilling in sharp little clouds. "Probably be a good idea. I'm only causing you trouble the longer I stay."

She did look over briefly at that. "Didn't the sheriff say something about not leaving town?"

"I'll take care of that." A hard determination had already taken root in his features.

"You're not going to be paying Mr. Ames any surprise visit," Stephanie asked carefully, "are you?"

That got Drake to face her. "I'll be good," he assured her dryly. "I'm just going to clear myself and be on my way."

"Shouldn't be all that hard," she agreed, her own eyes back on the gathering darkness. "Especially since you can prove you didn't have any access to the office to plant the bomb in the first place."

She sensed Drake's quick glance. "Who told you that?"

"Diane. Do you know where she kept the key?"

"No."

"Then you couldn't have gotten in the locked door, could you?"

Drake nodded to himself. Stephanie still patted her mare, rewarding the animal for standing so long in the cold. She was really beginning to feel the chill herself. At least she thought it was just the cold. Those shivers might have another, more unsettling source.

"Were we going anyplace else?" she asked. "It's getting dark—" pause "—and cold."

"No," Drake answered after a minute, his breath taken slowly as if he were hoarding the fresh pine scent to take back with him. "I just had to get away. This—" he motioned around him "—is away."

Stephanie nodded. "You have good taste." Her voice was still hushed, as if she were in church.

She half expected Drake to turn the horses then, but he didn't. He simply sat watching the night for a few minutes more. When he spoke, he uttered the words hesitantly, as if unused to asking favors.

"I really don't want to face everyone just yet. Do you mind?"

Stephanie wasn't sure she understood. "You want to stay here?"

"No. I was thinking of just sitting at . . ."

Stephanie didn't miss the abrupt halt. Drake had been about to say "home" and couldn't. Instinct told her that the home he was thinking of was the overcrowded dormer room they'd left earlier.

She took a deep breath herself, realizing how important his request was, how unprepared she was for it. "Why don't we return the horses and sneak up the back steps to Jacques's room? I don't think I'm quite up to facing Chip just yet, either."

Stephanie didn't miss either the quick inclination of Drake's head in response to her offer, or the appreciation that colored his eyes. "Nothing wrong with Chip," he commented as he turned his horse back into the trees. "Except that he thinks I'm stealing the limelight from his more deserving hands."

"Exactly." Stephanie nodded, her eyes straying to the dark angles of Drake's face, barely visible in the pale moonlight. "He's obsessed. Obsession makes me nervous."

Drake turned to her as she walked her horse alongside his. "Can't have a champion in anything without a little healthy obsession," he said.

"I know."

"I'm just as obsessed as he is."

Stephanie's smile was a little weak. "I didn't say you didn't make me nervous, did I?"

"But your father was a champion skier."

"Yes," she said, nodding slowly, her voice trailing off. "He was."

By the time Stephanie and Drake reached the lodge, most of the clientele were either eating in or down in town. The wide expanse of moonlit meadow was empty, the lights from the Inn spilling long yellow rectangles over the shimmering snow. The drone of traffic drifted up to replace the bird song, and Chip could be heard entertaining an audience in the bar at the side of the building.

Stephanie and Drake stabled the horses and entered the building from the back, taking the outside stairs to the third floor where Jacques's room waited, warm and pleasantly stuffy from the fire that was still smoldering.

Stephanie threw her shawl over a chair and walked around to the small kitchen that nestled in another of the alcoves to assess the supplies. Drake bent to rekindle the fire.

Drake had counted on the comfort of these rooms to further soothe him. It had worked well enough before, the atmosphere and Jacques's brusque camaraderie wrapping themselves around him like a warm cocoon to ward off the tensions outside.

Maybe that was why he'd asked Stephanie to stay with him. These rooms exuded companionship. Some of the warmth went out of them when they were not alone. Right now he needed this place, and he needed someone to share it with. Something compelled him to make that someone Stephanie.

Still on his haunches, Drake turned from the newly thriving fire to see Stephanie considering the liquor cabinet above her head. There was so much peace in those eyes. So much control when he sometimes felt as though he didn't have any. Did he feel drawn to her because he felt she could buffer some of his turbulence, or because he had the irrational feeling that she understood it? Whatever it was, Drake still felt as if of all the people in town, Stephanie was the only one who really understood what he was up against. And she was the only one who hadn't wrapped her life up in skiing.

"I see a full bottle of Scotch up here," she was saying, reaching up for something. "Yours?"

Drake got to his feet. "Mine. Jacques kept it there for celebration and commiseration."

"Want some?"

"No. I'm not in the mood for either."

She looked over, her eyes soft. "What were you in the mood for the other night?"

"Commiseration, definitely. Drowning all my sorrows."

Drake saw the question take form in her eyes, the curiosity, the certainty that there was more that would bear investigating in his answer. He also saw the reticence. She evidently had a far greater respect for barriers than he did.

"You said obsession made you nervous," he said instead, afraid of the questions he wanted her to ask. "Do you mean to tell me you're not obsessed?"

Stephanie paused from pouring herself some brandy and flashed him a scowl. "Do you think we could have one conversation at a time for a change?"

Drake grinned wryly. "Maybe when we get to know each other better."

She nodded and put the bottle down, slipping the snifter into the palm of her hand where she could warm the liquid by swirling it gently in the glass. "I'm not in the least obsessed. What would you like to drink?"

Drake didn't answer. Instead he walked over to a small refrigerator and opened the door. The shelves were filled with various fruit juices. Pulling out a can, he closed the door and faced her.

"How can you have a job like yours and not be obsessed?"

Stephanie was so near him that Drake could smell the clean perfume of her hair. Her eyes lifted to his and he saw the lights in them glitter like diamonds off the sable brown, a warm, life-giving color. Drake saw the pupils widen a little. Saw Stephanie catch her breath. Even so, her answer was a studied one.

"You said it. It's a job."

The quiet character of Stephanie's voice lured him. A fire had sparked in her eyes, one that was totally at odds with her passive stance. Drake felt it radiate from her as surely as if flames danced across her. Stephanie was incongruous, at once seething and deceptively placid. What was it they said about still waters? Hers were the kind that could entice a man to drowning.

"I can't imagine anyone not having something that drove them," he said, neither of them moving, both taut with unspoken tension.

Stephanie's lips curled with wry amusement. "I didn't say that," she objected, her brandy still rocking untasted in her glass. "I said that I feared obsession, and that it wasn't part of my work. A person can be driven without being obsessed."

A fine line at best. "Then what drove you?"

She seemed to stop breathing altogether at the softly asked question. Her lips parted just a little, her hand stopping its unconscious rocking motion, her body stiffening. Drake felt himself drawn closer still, pulled by the soft promise of those full lips and the turmoil that could only be sensed beneath the fragile facade. He suddenly had the fleeting impression of a small animal caught in a trap. Without realizing it, he reached a hand out to her, brushing back an errant lock of hair with gentle fingers.

He actually felt Stephanie sway beneath his touch, her control was so preciously thin, her turmoil so awesome. Drake hadn't realized until now what a lonely woman she was.

His hand returned to her face. Stephanie felt the brush of his cool fingers against her hot skin like a hypnotic balm, their passage marked in ice and fire. His eyes narrowed, their heat building.

Stephanie wondered whether Drake understood the reaction she had to him. She wanted to wrap herself in him, to soak in the passion in his eyes and bathe in his strength. She wanted to feel the rasp of his hands against her like a tool that would burnish her skin to a glowing life. Drake fit his hand against her cheek and she tilted her head to it, closing her eyes. She felt his thumb trace the corner of her mouth and turned her head to kiss the palm of his hand.

When Drake felt the soft caress of Stephanie's lips, he pulled her into his arms. His mind had stopped reasoning why two such disparate people should be drawn together. There was nothing now but the trembling woman beneath his touch, the fluttering heart that beat against his chest. Stephanie's breasts pressed taut against him. Her back remained rigid beneath his hand. Drake turned her face to him and bent to kiss her.

Somewhere deep inside a voice told Stephanie that she should struggle. She should stop this assault to her senses. It was too dangerous. No one had ever breached her defenses so thoroughly or moved her to such living fire. Her body seemed to react all on its own without heeding her racing mind. She arched into the curve of his embrace, lifting her lips to be tasted. Her fingers lost the brandy glass to the counter—somewhere next to the juice can—and rose to delve into the rich silk of his hair. Her legs trembled with the effort to support her beneath the lightning waves of sensation his clever hands unleashed.

Her back against the cool countertop, Stephanie lost herself in the blind desire Drake's touch unleashed. His greedy mouth scorched her, his hands seemed to elicit sparks. She heard a soft, helpless moan and realized it was hers. His hands hungered for her. She knew her own were trembling with the need to touch him. The air swirled with the fierce emotions that had met in their embrace.

The sound of knocking shattered the spell. Stephanie stiffened as if she'd been shot, her eyes unconsciously accusing as she responded to the sound. Her heart still pounded, trying to keep time with her ragged breathing.

"I'm going to have to talk to her about her timing," Drake growled, his arms still tightly around her.

Stephanie pulled gently away, her body shrieking at the loss. "I think her timing is probably perfect," she retorted with a tentative smile.

The knocking resumed.

"What?" Drake yelled a little too brusquely.

"I'm sorry," came the muffled answer. "I was looking for Miss...for Stephanie. Then I found the horses were back, so I thought I'd look—"

Drake swung the door open on the unhappy girl.

"—here." She looked absolutely mortified.

"What's wrong, Diane?" Stephanie asked gently, the surprise in the manager's eyes making her want to smooth her hair. She picked up the brandy glass instead, hoping no one noticed her shaking hands, and walked toward the door.

Drake turned, amazed yet again by Stephanie's monumental control. She smiled as if she'd just been served tea.

Diane didn't notice the exchange. Of course, by this time her search had left her nearly frantic.

"Right after you left to get Drake, you know, this afternoon...?"

"Yes?"

"We got served with a notice that our liquor license has been revoked."

Stephanie found herself staring. "Revoked?"

Diane nodded emphatically. "The notice says that we'd been serving minors. We haven't. We haven't even had any teens as guests in a while. It's crazy! Do you think that that's what the letter was talking about?"

"What letter?" Drake demanded, his eyes suddenly sharp.

"A little poison pen business," Stephanie told him, finally taking a taste of her brandy. "It seems that the opposition has begun to call in the pros. They can't cut off our water supply, so they might as well go after our profits."

Both Drake and Diane stared at her.

Stephanie smiled, setting the snifter back on the counter. "Maybe I've been working in films too long, but this is a plot device right out of a Western. 'Somebody's tryin' ta force us off'n our land,'" she lamented in a perfect imitation of a beleaguered widow woman.

At least she succeeded in provoking grudging grins from Diane and Drake.

"Come on," she offered, heading past Drake. "Let's go see what's going on. Since the offices are all closed down in town, it can't get worse until tomorrow morning."

Stephanie was already at the head of the stairs before Diane worked up the nerve to answer.

"I'm afraid it already is worse."

Stephanie swung around. "Don't be silly, Diane. Is Sammy down in the bar so we can talk to him?"

Diane nodded forlornly. "Yes."

Drake walked past the unhappy manager with an encouraging smile and a pat on the back. It didn't seem to help any.

Stephanie should have known better. After all, she worked in a business that consisted of bad timing and worse luck. It shouldn't have surprised her in the least that she'd walked right into another business just like it.

She didn't get any inkling of what Diane had been talking about until she had almost reached the little bar where she'd first met Drake. Chip was singing again, a little more off-key this time. Certainly with more energy. Stephanie just wasn't sure what it was he was singing. It didn't seem to make any difference to his audience. Every verse was greeted with laughter and applause.

She'd almost made it to the door when a particularly tinkling laugh cut through the rest. Slowing to an apprehensive halt, Stephanie realized just what Diane had meant. Drake almost ran right into her.

"Oh, no."

He reached for her shoulder. "Oh no, what?"

Stephanie looked up at him with very unhappy eyes. "Diane was right. It is worse."

Drake took a look toward the etched glass doors that led into the bar, and then back at Stephanie. "How could it be?"

She just smiled and pulled one of the doors open so that he could see.

There, seated atop the polished mahogany bar like Marlene Dietrich in *Destry Rides Again*, was their problem. Smiling and cooing, their newest guest posed as if studio photographers were in the audience. Chip stood alongside, winging into another verse, a full magnum of Dom Perignon in hand as he attempted to pour another serving into the new guest's sequined pump. The rest of the patrons were wide-eyed and mesmerized.

It only took the new guest a moment to realize that her audience had grown. Turning her glossy head toward the open door, she let out another delighted giggle and brandished the shoe, careful lest the champagne drip on her bright red silk dress.

"Stephanie, darling, there you are! And here we thought you'd been eaten by a bear. You almost missed all the fun. *We* almost missed all the fun. Your scrooge of a bartender wouldn't break out the bubbly, darling. You simply must have him beheaded or something."

Doing her best to suppress a heartfelt groan, Stephanie smiled wanly. "Corey. Nice to see you're surviving the wilderness."

# Chapter 6

"Corey, dear, get off the bar," Stephanie said with a smile as she walked in. "Sammy, throw that bottle away before the authorities catch us."

"Oh, c'mon!" Chip slurred his words a little, a possessive hand on Corey's shoulder. "We were just beginning to have fun."

"You just finished," Drake amended as he relieved his teammate of the bottle in question. Behind them Diane came to a hesitant stop in the doorway, her face set for a new disaster.

"You can't possibly mean that, my dear," Corey purred to Stephanie, her eyes only on Drake. Without blinking, she drained her shoe and slipped it back on her foot. It was all Stephanie could do to keep from laughing. No one else seemed to be considering how very sticky Corey's foot would become any moment.

"We'd love to serve you coffee or juice," Stephanie announced pleasantly to the assembled guests. "Or soda. It's all on the house. For the moment, though, I'm afraid we're restrained from selling liquor."

She had the feeling that as long as Corey was in the same room, she could serve the patrons shoe polish and they wouldn't complain. They were there for the show and nothing else.

And they got it.

"W-e-e-l-l, what have we here?" Corey was smiling as she slid her sleek curves from the hand-carved mahogany, her eyes nailed to Drake. Her smile brightened considerably as she flipped her thick blond tresses over her shoulder with a well-practiced move. "You must be the wrestler."

Drake stared at her. "What?"

"Oh, you know—" She giggled, waving a hand in the air. "The other athlete in this primitive little hamlet. Stephanie's told me all about you."

Stephanie turned from her guests to see Corey damn near glue herself to Drake's chest. It was something Stephanie was very familiar with, one of Corey's quaint little ways of making introductions. The more handsome the man, the less airspace between them when she said hello. Stephanie was sure that in this instance, they were going to need a micrometer to measure the distance.

Tonight for some reason, it irritated her. She felt rare color flare in her cheeks and an abrupt urge rise to snap off a bitchy comment. Absurd, she thought immediately with an unconscious shake of her head. This was Corey. It was just the way she was. But she was doing it to Drake McDonald, and all of a sudden Stephanie wanted him to know better.

"I've seen you ski, of course," Corey went on, leveling her emerald-green eyes on him like a snake handler. "You're magnificent."

And that had nothing to do with his ability on the hill, Stephanie could almost hear her add. She noticed, too, that Chip wasn't a lot happier than she with the little display. His eyes narrowed a fraction as he saw Corey completely forget him in her attempt at a new conquest. Evidently he felt Drake's competition more than just on the slopes.

Before Stephanie could get a good handle on Chip, he turned to find her considering him. Within an instant, he was flashing her that disarming, little-boy grin that had won him such a following the world over. It at once negated the effect of his reaction and called to mind her own. He reacted to her blush almost as he had to Drake's incarceration. Just another amusing slice of life to become grist for his storytelling mill. Stephanie smiled back, wishing he weren't so perceptive.

"Let the man breathe, darling," Stephanie suggested dryly to Corey as she walked by to talk to Sammy.

"He can do that any time," Corey cooed. "How often is he struck by kismet?"

Then Stephanie did laugh. "Corey, at least don't use lines from your movies. By now every man in America knows them by heart."

Corey laughed back in delight. Stephanie was the only person who could get away with calling her hand. She was the only person Corey knew in Hollywood who had never had an ulterior motive in dealing with her. Stephanie had always been painfully honest, a friend who'd kept Corey's best interests separate from her own.

"Where did the champagne come from, Sammy?" Stephanie asked quietly, merely curious.

Sammy looked uncomfortable.

"You have to ask?" Corey piped up, still doing her best to paralyze Drake on the spot. She'd already made a point of asking *all* about his career, his hopes and his exercise techniques. Stephanie had heard all that before, too. "It's from my CARE package, darling. I knew you were desperate, so I dropped everything and flew to your aid."

"And I appreciate it," Stephanie assured her. She couldn't stay mad at Corey for long. If only she'd just be a bit more discreet. A number of the customers were in danger of falling from their chairs.

"I tried," Sammy said. "I didn't want you to get into any trouble."

"I know," Stephanie assured him with a nod. "Corey's what you call an irresistible force. You haven't noticed the alleged minors around, have you?"

"Absolutely not." His vehemence matched Diane's. The Sundance was a source of personal pride to all her employees. "The whole thing's a crock of—"

Stephanie jumped in, prudently cutting him off. "I know. I just had to ask."

"Shall we go somewhere more private and talk?" Corey was asking Drake, running a gleaming red nail up his shirtfront.

"What about dinner?" Chip asked from behind the bar. "I was going to take you to town."

Corey didn't hear him. She was still basking in the soft gray of Drake's eyes.

"Sounds great," he accepted with a quick smile, hooking her arm with his.

Suddenly Chip wasn't the only one staring.

Corey turned around, her eyes flashing in delight. "You don't mind, darling, do you?" she asked Stephanie.

"Of course not," Stephanie was unsure exactly how to react. "Have a lovely time. And have another shoe of champagne for me."

"How 'bout you?" Chip asked Stephanie after the other couple had closed the door behind them. "Want to one-up your friend and go out with a real champion?" Diane was still standing in the doorway, her mouth slightly agape.

Stephanie almost accepted. That bright, little-boy smile was a real charmer, and she really didn't feel like ferreting through the latest Inn problem tonight. But she shook her head with regret.

"I'd love to, Chip—" she demurred "—but I have an awful lot of work to finish before I can go back to L.A. More than ever if you and Drake are going to desert me."

Chip slid over to her, closely mimicking Corey's position, his breath a touch too potent. "All you have to do is ask, and I'll make sure he forfeits the whole season for you."

Stephanie chuckled. "I'm sure you would."

"All right, then." He chuckled back. "*I'll* do it. We'll go upstairs right now and I'll call the team, tell them to take their skis and go stuff them."

"Okay," she agreed, linking her own arm through his. "Let's go."

First Chip hesitated. Then he laughed. "Asking the king to abdicate," he admonished her, keeping Stephanie standing where she was. "Not a very noble thing to do."

Stephanie smiled. "Just a girl with no class." With a pat, she let him go.

Chip's response was not half so light. "You've got that all wrong, lady."

That was when Corey came storming back in the door. Fifteen heads swung around for the next scene.

The actress was truly flummoxed, her eyes glittering, her hands restless with disbelief.

"Back so soon?" Stephanie asked calmly.

"Back?" she retorted, her voice musical in its outrage. "Do you know where that barbarian wanted to take me? Into the snow!" With an extra glance around for sympathy, she delivered the final insult. "On a *horse*! Who does he think I am, Annie Oakley!"

With the reflexes of a champion, Chip slipped right in to console her. "Unspeakable," he murmured, taking her by the arm. "You can't depend on McDonald to be civilized. An intimate dinner for two. Some flowers..."

Letting herself be escorted by the young man, Corey flashed Stephanie one more look of arch disbelief. "You could at least have warned me, darling."

Stephanie smiled passively, wishing she could have seen it in person. "Some things are simply not to be believed, Corey."

Corey snorted with self-righteous indignation as she left with Chip. "Well, at least now I know where he gets his animal magnetism."

Then Stephanie laughed outright, more wholeheartedly than she had in a long time. Her new employees and guests watched with interest.

The next morning Stephanie fended off the licensing board, only to discover another setback. The board informed her that they had received a complaint from a man who claimed that his seventeen-year-old son had been served in the bar. The son had said that the spot was a favorite for underage drinkers, especially since Jacques had died.

When Stephanie had asked where the complainant was, she found out that his vacation had ended and he'd returned to his home in Denver. He'd offered to return for the hearing, though. Stephanie went away wondering who had bought off whom.

She spent another hour unsuccessfully trying to find the missing policies, and the early afternoon at the insurance agent's trying to figure out why the records had also disappeared not only from his office, but his computer.

As she walked back up Colorado toward her car, Stephanie found herself battling a new sense of unease. She felt like Custer when he'd spotted that first smoke signal.

"Well, Stephanie, how ya doin'?"

Preoccupied, she didn't even see Nathan Ames until she was almost upon him. Her first reaction was that on one really wore too much after-shave. Her second was that his offices were in the same building as the insurance company. She'd seen his name carved over the old wooden door frame.

"Mr. Ames," she said, returning the greeting and trying to walk on. He deftly blocked her path.

"Heard about your license," he commiserated with a concerned shake of the head. "It's hard to keep track of those kids today. Particularly the ones who want to go out and party."

Stephanie's smile grew fixed. "I know. The problem is that they've been partying somewhere else. The Sundance is clean."

Ames nodded emphatically, a hand out to her arm in a show of support. "Of course it is. But that's just another worry for a motel manager, isn't it?"

Stephanie wanted very much to tell him that not only was the Sundance very definitely not a motel, but that she wasn't a manager. Instead, she decided to play the hand through.

"So much to worry about," she agreed, a slightly breathy edge to her voice. "And now the police have some ridiculous idea that Drake might have had something to do with that bomb...."

Ames's eyebrows shot up. It occurred to Stephanie that he obviously didn't realize he was dealing with a woman who worked with better actors than he on a day-to-day basis.

"Have you had lunch yet?" he asked. "Perhaps you'd let me treat you. We could talk."

"Over your dead body, Ames."

Both of them turned to see Drake on final approach, a rather confused-looking middle-aged woman in tow. Drake's eyes were thunderous, his posture like a tree battling a windstorm.

"McDonald," Ames greeted him with something akin to a growl. "You do have a way of showing up at odd times. I'm surprised you're out on bail."

Drake's face broke into a piratical smile. "I'm out for good, you bastard. And don't ever try setting me up again, or you're going to find yourself reduced to fine hamburger."

Stephanie found herself staring. Ames was closer to blanching. "I don't know what you mean," he objected. "I just found out myself."

Drake's smile grew broader. "Sure you did. Now get going."

"I was just about to take Stephanie to lunch."

Both men turned to Stephanie for an answer, but she was still trying to figure out who the lady in the ski suit was.

"Mr. Ames was just going to help me with some matters, Drake," she managed to say. "And since you're leaving, you know..."

Stephanie wasn't sure whether Drake understood or not. He certainly didn't look appreciably happier. Without another word, he turned to the lady he still held and guided her past.

By the end of lunch, Stephanie felt she had the true measure of Nathan Ames. He was everything Drake claimed him to be. Stephanie had met some of the other realtors in town, hardworking, up-front people who spent their time building Telluride into a viable and far-reaching community. She liked them, men and women, mostly her age, who'd settled here for the skiing and stayed to build, not unlike the old gold rushers who'd first founded the town.

But Ames was another story. No one understood him, no one respected him, no one appreciated what he'd done for the town. At least that was the story he served over lunch. In between that and the umpteenth play for the Sundance, Stephanie saw somebody who would have sold his mother for an acre of property near a ski run, and who wasn't above a bit of collusion to achieve his ends. He went as far as to promise she'd be more than adequately compensated for her time there, above and beyond the asking price of the Inn itself. For the first time since she'd had a bout of mono, Stephanie left a nice restaurant with a raging case of indigestion.

Then she went to look for Drake.

Stephanie drove by his house, but he wasn't there. Neither were all the crime scene warnings that had been there the day before. She drove on up to the Inn. Again, no luck. Diane suggested the ski runs. This time of day, she said, Drake would be making his last runs down the north face, site of the expert runs that swept right down to the edge of town. Stephanie hopped back into the four-wheel-drive and turned it back down the hill into town.

She'd only been standing at the bottom of the hill for a few minutes when she spotted his red-suited figure. It wasn't just the color; there were other people in red on the slope. It was the style. Drake swept down the face of the mountain like a bird gliding on air currents, never quite touching the earth, his body crouched into a tight Z, his arms tucked close to his sides, as he swept over the snow. Stephanie stood rooted to the spot like the other spectators, watching him weave and bob, flying from the bumps and sweeping over the curves without hesitation.

Just the sight of Drake on that hill took Stephanie's breath away. She watched the bright blur plummet down the shadowy slope and found herself sailing with him. He was every bit as good as Jacques had said. Better. He was the finest, most graceful skier she'd ever seen. And today he wasn't even paying attention to what he was doing.

Drake wasn't even breathing hard when he pulled to a stop in front of her. Some of the others around Stephanie were still staring. She was smiling.

"Had a little too much weight on that inside ski on those last two turns," she said nonchalantly.

Pulling his goggles up, Drake looked at her with some surprise. "You're right. I also came off some of the bumps much too high, but my knee's a little tender."

A little tender? There was pain in his eyes, a tightness to his forehead that spoke volumes of what that run had cost him. Stephanie felt his admission catch in her chest like a hard knot and lost some of her smile.

"Thought you didn't ski," he was saying, guiding her away from the crowd so that he could unfasten his skis.

Stephanie refused to face him. "I don't."

"But you did. You raced."

"My father raced."

Drake's eyes betrayed his disbelief as he bent to his skis.

"Do you really think you should be shooting those expert runs like that if you're not paying attention?" Stephanie asked, her own eyes back on the hill. "That slope is mighty steep."

"So's the downhill course at Val d'Isère," he said. "And I have to be on that in another couple of weeks."

Point well taken. Stephanie looked down at the shadows that were collecting at her feet, still not wanting to be witness to the pain that creased Drake's forehead and robbed his movements of grace. "I imagine you're still pretty distracted by the business with the bomb."

"Nope." Drake straightened, carrying his skis with him. "That's all taken care of. How was lunch?"

Stephanie raised surprised eyes to him, but he'd already turned to the car. He was limping ever so slightly, and she noticed that he held his head very carefully, as if he had a headache. "What do you mean it's taken care of?" she asked, following.

Drake flashed her a smug grin. "If you'd forgone your little tryst, you might have found out. You headed back to the Sundance?"

"Eventually. I came to talk to you. About lunch."

His smile grew wicked. "Want to do it while I work out in the weight room?"

No, Stephanie thought. I don't think I can stand to see that agony on your face again.

"How about after you work out in the weight room?" she countered. "I'm not really into sweat."

It was a silly thing to say. She'd been ready to eat him alive when she'd seen him sweaty that first day. How many days ago? It seemed like forever, as if Drake McDonald had always been a part of her life. Maybe in a way, Stephanie thought, he had.

Drake's grin grew a little, deepening the gullies that creased his cheeks. His eyes were pale against his tan. Stephanie found herself drawn to them.

"Where's your friend?" he asked, setting his skis alongside her car.

"Who, Corey?" Stephanie checked her watch. "Probably just getting up. She has a rule that if she's not on a set, daylight is worthless."

Drake chuckled to himself. "She's a real piece of work."

Stephanie couldn't help but chuckle back, her arms brushing Drake's as they opened the back window of the vehicle and slid the skis in. The brief contact left her tingling.

"She called you a barbarian."

"I am." He turned in time to catch a glimpse of the yellowing sunlight gild Stephanie's hair. Suddenly the pain he'd carried off the mountain was forgotten. Drake was mesmerized by the warmth of Stephanie's eyes, by the color the wind had brushed onto her delicate cheeks, by the small crease that appeared above her eyes when she was worried. Absurdly, he wished she were worried about him. "I can be tamed, though."

He couldn't believe he'd said it. Or that Stephanie's eyes grew wider and her lips parted ever so slightly with the words. For a momment Drake fell as still as Stephanie, the chill of the afternoon wind as forgotten as the dissonance of the skiers who thronged the area like noisy children. The two of them were suddenly the entire universe, an eternity trapped between them as they expressed more than words could say.

"I doubt it," Stephanie finally ventured with a breathless little smile. "But be careful. Corey may just try."

Drake wanted to say that Corey wasn't the person he'd want to try. He didn't. He'd already overstepped his boundaries. Snapping the window shut, he turned back to Stephanie.

"You know who she reminds me of?"

"Corey?"

He nodded. "That femme fatale from the sixties. Want me to drive? You remember her. She did all those musicals. A thinner Monroe."

Stephanie motioned Drake around to the passenger seat without mentioning the sore knee he'd have to use to shift gears. "You mean Belinda Carson?"

He nodded, his eyes lighting with the memory. "Yeah, that's her. I spent the better part of my adolescence fantasizing about her. Corey seems to cultivate that same larger-than-life aura."

"She's also a lot smarter."

Once both were settled inside, Stephanie started the engine. She didn't move off though. A patient expectancy had stolen across her features, as if she were waiting for the inevitable.

"Smarter how?" Drake asked.

Stephanie's smile was enigmatic. "Corey knows exactly what she's doing."

"And Carson doesn't?"

"Belinda runs on instincts alone. And those aren't always functioning a hundred percent."

Drake shot her a bemused look. "You sound like you know her pretty well. Have you worked with her before?"

Now the smile grew, colored by tolerant amusement. "After a fashion, I suppose. She's my mother."

Drake swung around so fast that he winced at the sudden pain. He'd almost forgotten the soreness in his shoulder and neck that had grown tighter over the afternoon.

Belinda Carson. Good God! He remembered sitting for hours in a dark theater watching those famous brown eyes and listening to that slightly breathy voice promise paradise—and believing every half-whispered word. Belinda Carson had been every woman and every child, a bewitching blend of beauty and innocence. The quintessential dumb blonde. The idea that she could have given birth to this eminently self-contained, serene young woman completely astounded him.

Even as Drake watched her, Stephanie downshifted the vehicle to take the hill toward the Inn, her eyes reflecting her private amusement. She was patiently waiting for him to get over the shock. Drake had the feeling that his reaction was undoubtedly painfully familiar.

"I bet it makes for some interesting conversations when people find out," he ventured.

Stephanie shrugged, her eyes still on the road. "Not really. People generally want to know three things. Is she really that beautiful? Yes. Does she really talk like that? Again, yes. And what kind of mother was a woman who was a worldwide sex goddess? As good a mother as she could be, considering who she was."

"It must have been pretty difficult on you," Drake said.

At that Stephanie looked over with fleeting surprise. Evidently that had not been one of the more familiar reactions.

"Not really," she answered, returning to her task. "My father saw that I was always financially well-off, and I got to live in at least seven cities and five countries when I grew up. Quite an education. And fortunately, I liked most of my mother's husbands."

"How many was it?"

"She's presently on number nine—if you don't count Baron von Trager, whom she married twice."

"But what about stability? What about security?"

"Oh, Belinda always married wealthy men. And she managed to divorce them even more profitably. She didn't have much of a head for money, but she usually had enough around to keep her in swimming pool services."

"I don't mean her," Drake retorted, his concern sincere. "I meant you."

The car bumped over the bridge that spanned the small river, Stephanie glanced at Drake briefly, his words giving birth to a renewed expression of surprise in her eyes. When she turned back to the road, she was smiling in that quiet way that made people assume that she was always content. Her eyes, however, held a rare spark. "I made my own stability," she allowed without rancor.

As ever, Diane appeared the minute Stephanie and Drake opened the front door. There was a couple checking in at the battered old mahogany desk and another making arrangements to go snowmobiling. The big front room with the fireplace echoed with conversation.

Stephanie was glad to see all the activity. She knew it didn't hurt that they had Corey Alexander as a guest, but it was still good to see the Inn with a full complement of guests who were enjoying themselves.

"Oh, Drake, congratulations!" Diane beamed as she emerged from the office. "I heard about the police."

"What about the police?" Stephanie immediately asked, her attention on Drake.

He grinned. "That's what I was going to tell you. We came to an amicable agreement. They've agreed to drop the charges and I've agreed not to make any more threatening comments about Ames."

"Dropped the charges? Why?"

Slipping out of his jacket, Drake lifted an eyebrow in her direction. "I thought that was what we were going to talk about after my stint in the weight room."

Stephanie knew it had something to do with that woman Drake had in tow when he'd come across her and Nathan. She could see it in his eyes. And now he wanted to taunt her, especially in the face of her decision to lunch with the enemy. She smiled back at him and unpinned her shawl, the little game giving rise to an odd sense exhilaration.

"All right," she agreed amicably. "Say an hour? I'll be in Jacques's rooms since I still haven't found those papers."

"And you'll tell me," he countered, grinning crookedly "about lunch?"

Out of nowhere the most delicious shiver shot up Stephanie's spine, as if Drake had just put his hands on her bare flesh. "Every word," she promised.

Stephanie didn't observe the attentiveness of the guests in the great room. Nor did she notice that they all greeted her with unusual animation when she strolled over to chat with them before heading for her room to change. But then she couldn't see the fetching rose that tinted her cheeks when she walked away from her verbal duel with Drake.

She did notice her smile in the antique mirror that topped her bedroom dresser. It was a heartfelt smile, not the kind she displayed for actors when they needed calming or producers when they needed to be placated. This was a hundred-watter straight from the soul, where so few of her smiles resided.

It had dawned on Stephanie as she topped the stairs that beneath all that sexual chemistry and smoldering intensity, her partner was a really nice man. That didn't lessen his other qualities any. Rather it made them more exceptional that they were simply part of a character that didn't have to be completely selfish to support them.

Drake's reaction to Stephanie's revelation about her mother had been telling. His first questions had been for her rather than for the legend who had borne her. An almost protective anger had appeared in his eyes for the little girl who had so long ago grown up in eight separate households. Drake hadn't wanted to know just what Belinda Carson was like, or what Stephanie could do to get him to meet her. He'd wondered how she'd survived in a family that had Belinda at its core. Stephanie could think of no more than a handful of people who had reacted similarly. It had, maybe selfishly on her part, become something of a touchstone by which she judged people. After all, Jacques had been the first.

Stephanie sat on the old brass bed, suddenly feeling tremulous and a little foolish. What a silly reason to feel excited. After the emotional upheavals she had survived while growing up, she had carefully cultivated her life to exclude any more. Yet here she was, with her hands clasped in her lap, suddenly wanting to believe in a man. She was so scared she could hardly breathe. Even though she was doing everything she could to protect herself from Drake McDonald, she wanted nothing more than just one more look from those eyes.

There was only one thing for it, she thought, abruptly standing, the sudden ambivalence unnerving her. Get back to work. Get in touch with the world she was comfortable in so that she could balance this out. She'd do better once she got home. Her house in the hills was what she needed to get her head together, and work would have to do the rest. She had no business falling in love with a man who reminded her so much of what her father had once been. A disaster was a disaster, no matter how empathetic his eyes or enticing his smile. Unconsciously wiping her palms against the sides of her slacks, Stephanie walked over to pick up the phone and put her plan into action.

In the weight room, Drake worked steadily, the sweat rolling from him in rivulets, the expression on his face fierce. It looked as though he was trying his best to purge himself of something. Or someone.

# Chapter 7

Stephanie lit a cigarette and took a slow drag. "No, Franklin," she said evenly, "I cannot just put down what I'm doing and fly home. I've already told you."

The only time Stephanie smoked anymore was when she was having phone conversations with Franklin. He was one of those people who felt that the entire world existed to answer his beck and call. It didn't help that he was one of the most talented people in the business. He was also one of the most neurotic. Stephanie had worked for him in a variety of capacities over the years, and had seen herself evolve as the sane eye of Franklin's hurricane.

"But you don't understand, Stephanie honey," he all but whined. "It's time to do the dialogue editing, and you're playing snow bunny. I need you here!"

"Not if you haven't locked that film, you don't," she assured him, the cigarette already stubbed out. They'd become a waste of money, a reflex that turned sour without any enjoyment. "I'm not moving until you have a final print, Franklin. I'm not going to hold your hand while you trim out your megalomania."

"It's almost ready," he hedged, which meant that it wasn't ready at all. If Stephanie tried to go in and work on a film that was still being edited, it would mean six times the headaches and time spent while the director changed his mind and reshaped the film just one more time. Until the pictures were in the right order, the sound was superfluous.

Stephanie had such a position in the community by now that it was a demand she could easily make, unless the actors wouldn't be available to work. Franklin's would.

"Call me when you have a locked print," she suggested. "I'll be in my chair the very next morning."

Someone knocked on Stephanie's door just as Franklin started another round of objections. Putting her hand over the mouthpiece, she called a welcome. A quick glance at her watch proved that she'd spent more time in her room than she'd anticipated. It must be Drake coming to look for her. Franklin went on without taking breath.

"Stephanie, darling, we simply have to—" Corey came to an abrupt halt, her hand still on the doorknob, a bath towel held in a manicured hand rather like an unhappily discovered rat. "I see you got ahold of Franklin," she said grimacing at the look on Stephanie's face.

Stephanie's expression was answer enough. The voice at the other end of the line went on unabated. "Something wrong?" she asked Corey, hand still over the receiver.

"Oh, just the towels," Corey said with less assurance. "I only got two in my room.... Come to think of it, I only got a room. What happened to the suite I requested?"

"The closest one is on the other side of town," Stephanie advised her evenly before turning back to her phone conversation. "Of course, it's going to be the best thing you've ever done, Franklin. I'm sorry I can't get there any sooner for screenings, but you really don't need my opinion. You need my ADR. Call me when you're ready for it. Bye."

"You know you're the only one who can get away with that," Corey accused brightly, coming to roost on the bed.

Stephanie slipped into her gold flats in preparation for meeting Drake. She'd changed out of her sweater and slacks into a cotton denim dress with a drop waist. It was a bit too sweet for her taste, still more so with the lace collar, but at least it was comfortable.

"Everyone needs a bit of logic in his life," Stephanie shrugged offhandedly. "I'm Franklin's."

"You're Hollywood's," Corey disagreed.

Stephanie couldn't help but chuckle. "Heaven forbid. Now, then, Corey, if you insist on demanding that I play the hosteler, just what is it you want in your room? More towels?"

"Company," she retorted. "It's positively hallucinatory facing all those middle-earthers alone. Darling, I need your eminently practical support."

"Middle Earth hasn't existed since Tolkien," Stephanie informed her friend dryly. "And you're a little too far west to consider yourself in the Midwest. What's wrong? All this reality too much for you?"

Corey wrinkled her nose. "It's positively bleak. I mean, most of these people would rather discuss powder—whatever that is—than the worth of my movies. And of course you were already asleep when we came back to fetch you."

Stephanie shrugged, quickly running a brush through the mass of hair that framed her face. Always maintain appearances, Belinda had preached until it became instinctive.

"I never have been a late-night person."

Behind her Corey made a moue in the mirror, checking her own reflection. "You've never been any kind of partyier, darling. The most boringly normal person in all of California. No wonder you get along so well with the masses."

Stephanie hadn't realized that Corey had left the door open until she caught a shadow in the mirror.

"Be careful, Corey," Drake warned, stepping in. "You're ruining her reputation."

Stephanie didn't have to look to see that the tight edge to his features hadn't eased any. He was still hurting, yet he smiled for Corey as if he'd waited all day to see her. Then he turned to Stephanie and his smile transformed. It was nothing dramatic, no definite change that could be easily labeled. But its crooked cant settled into Stephanie's chest to ignite a sweet fire.

"Her reputation could use some ruining," Corey retorted with a flick of her head. "She can't even have the decency to be neurotic or self-destructive like the rest of us. She sits in that dreary little house of hers and practices Zen gardening or something. Talk her into a bit of debauchery, Drake, won't you?"

One of Drake's eyebrows shot up. Stephanie had just turned, and he caught her discomfort at Corey's accusations.

"I'm afraid debauchery wouldn't fit into my training schedule," he apologized, his eyes still locked with Stephanie's. Neither of them saw Corey's attention sharpen. "Zen gardening?"

Stephanie didn't answer, so Corey did. "Rocks and things." She shrugged.

"Minimalism," Stephanie said smiling dryly. "After seeing your house, I imagine you'd appreciate it."

Drake shook his head. "Yours was done out of patience," he disagreed. "Mine out of laziness. Am I in time to discuss our respective lunches?"

His question brought a faint trace of relief to Stephanie's eyes. She nodded, her hair stirring in silken waves against her shoulders. Its fiery color softened against the washed-out blue of that denim, the lace that swept the base of her throat in quaintly feminine counterpoint. Drake found his eyes drawn to it the way a prospector's eyes are drawn to the glitter of gold, and knew that he'd had no luck sweating Stephanie out of his system down in that torture room. She was settling in even more deeply.

"Are you sure you don't want to learn how to ski?" he asked abruptly, as surprised as Stephanie at the question.

"Learn?" Corey immediately demanded incredulously. "Are you—"

Stephanie silenced her with an abrupt turn of the head. Corey allowed herself a raised eyebrow and a pretty pout, then gave in. She also dispatched a smug smile to her friend that warned of retaliation.

"I'm sure," Stephanie told Drake, turning back to him. "Let's go on down to the office. That way we won't be keeping Corey from her adoring fans."

With the practiced air of a teacher herding schoolchildren, Stephanie cleared her room and shepherded Corey and Drake down the steps. She couldn't get that knot of tension to slide back out of her throat after Corey's unintentional slip. Stephanie knew that she was going to end up telling Drake the truth, but she wanted to do it in her own time. No matter how she ended up telling Drake, there was no way she could think of to dispel the mortification that still stained the memories or the sick realization that she'd tried so very hard—only to be rebuffed.

"Well, darlings," Corey sighed grandly as they reached the bottom of the stairs. "I suppose I'll go find Chip. I'm sure he'll have an idea or two on what might be fun in this sleepy little hamlet."

Stephanie and Drake watched her sweep into the main room before Stephanie sighed, too. "Do you have any other idea where Jacques might have hidden those papers?" she asked as they headed toward the office. "I think I've torn up everything in the place. I can't even find a safe deposit key."

Drake shook his head. "He didn't believe in them. Did you try his wall safe?"

They had reached the front desk, where Drake out of habit always ran a hand over the scarred, polished wood. He'd helped install this one, too, a front desk from a ghost town up by Cripple Creek. On the bottom left of it there were still bullet holes from a particularly rowdy night in the old mining town. As his fingers ran over it this time, Drake wasn't thinking about miners, but about film editors.

"Jacques didn't have a wall safe," Stephanie countered instinctively.

Drake walked ahead to open the door for her, a smug smile taking shape in his eyes. "You just didn't know where to look."

Guiding Stephanie past him with a hand to her shoulder, Drake noticed that she was tense, her sleek muscles taut beneath his fingers. Anticipating? Afraid? She'd tightened up the minute Corey had tried to argue about teaching Stephanie to ski, shutting them both out as if she could indeed disappear into a shell.

It was the skiing, he knew. Something about skiing had touched a live nerve, one that she didn't yet want exposed. What, my beautiful lady? he wondered. What kind of memory would need such a solid barrier to protect it from the light?

Once inside the office, Drake walked right over to the bookcase on the left of the fireplace. "Behind the *Collected Plays* of Molière," he instructed.

"I looked there," Stephanie said, her voice more interested than outraged.

Pulling a book out, Drake ran his hand along the shelf's back edge. Without so much as a click, a small panel swung open.

"He loved his little secrets." Drake grinned offhandedly as he reached in to discover a healthy wad of papers and thick manila envelopes.

Stephanie did no more than raise an eyebrow, her lips curved in mute appreciation. "Some coffee," she suggested. "I think we're going to be here a few minutes." Her next thought was communicated with dry dispatch. "It would have saved me a lot of trouble if you'd remembered this before."

His hand inside the deep recess, Drake didn't appear unduly repentant. "I was a little preoccupied. Besides, Jacques kept everything important in his desk so he could find it, Right where they found the will."

Stephanie was already running coffee through by the time Drake opened the first envelope. Inside were pictures, a compilation of the skiers Jacques had trained and raced against. Drake couldn't figure why Jacques had wanted to lock them away, unless he just wanted to make sure he didn't lose them among the haphazard disarray of his possessions.

The stack went all the way back to the beginning, with shots of a young Jacques racing in the school competitions in Quebec, the shots of the '48 Canadian team, some duplicates of photos on the walls, others he'd never seen before. Drake skimmed them quickly, deciding he'd rather go through them later at his leisure. Then one particular photo caught his eye.

He looked up at Stephanie, then back to the garish color print in his hand. He found others, always the same variation. A smiling Jacques, a lithe young girl in racing numbers and a trophy. Aspen, Sun Valley, Vail. They graphically explained the what of Stephanie's reaction, but not the why. The smile in these pictures was heartbreaking—a child seeking praise.

Looking at the beaming pride in Jacques's eyes, the enthusiasm of his embrace, Drake knew that the smile hadn't been for him. For someone else? Someone not so easily pleased, perhaps?

Drake remembered winning his own first big race. The first people he'd turned to on that cold, raw day had been his parents. After they had shared his joy, it had been the property of the world. But not until then. At that age, maybe twelve, it was still the most important approval in the world.

Who had Stephanie turned to? And had he been pleased for her?

"Have you found them yet?" Stephanie asked from where she stood behind the desk.

Drake's head popped up, the pictures still in his hands. He looked at her quiet features, then down at the younger version. "Uh, no," he answered, slipping the photos back in the envelope. "Not yet. So far all I've found are his old Olympic pictures."

She grinned. "The way Jacques hoarded things, you'll probably find the title to his first car in there next. Bring them on over to the desk and we'll go through them all."

Not knowing why, Drake included the packet of pictures. "Corey was trying to tell me you ski," he said quietly, carrying the load over to divide it up on the massive desk Stephanie was clearing. Drake didn't really expect an answer yet, merely a crack in that perfect veneer. Maybe he could slowly work his way into that soft, sad center. "You do, don't you?"

Stephanie actually found herself bracing for what was to come. Needlessly, she thought. But then, childhood hurts were the hardest to overcome.

"Did," she amended without looking up. "Could I find out about the police first?"

To Stephanie's relief, Drake seemed agreeable. The paperwork was ready to be gone through, and the two of them took chairs, Stephanie's facing a window scene bathed in low clouds and sudden shafts of sunlight. A tranquil scene, meant to soothe. For Stephanie it unaccountably stirred up unwanted images.

"The police, huh?" Drake countered, easing onto his chair as if his joints had seized up. Stephanie didn't miss the quick wince, the setting of his shoulders against the ache. He wrapped strong fingers around the hot coffee mug and nodded. "The long and short of it is that I was right. Somebody broke into my place to plant the dynamite. My neighbor saw him yesterday morning. Since she's only been here a couple of weeks, she didn't think anything of a blond man in my kitchen when I wasn't there."

Stephanie's head came up. "A blond man?"

Anticipating her, Drake shook his head. "Not Ames. I asked her after we met him in the street. Anyway, the police checked, and sure enough, the door had been jimmied. They also checked with the construction site. Since there hasn't been any blasting in a couple of months, the dynamite could have been taken anytime during that period. An anonymous phone call sent them checking Sunday morning. And a couple of other bikers I rode with told the police that I didn't go anywhere near there when I was riding. I'm off the hook for now, Benson says." His smile was wryly amused.

Stephanie nodded, that deceptive calm enveloping her features. "A blond man...."

Drake shrugged, returning to the papers before him. "Just about every other person in Colorado right now. It wouldn't be any mean trick for Ames to get somebody to plant that." He held up a fat envelope. "Loan on the Inn."

Stephanie nodded, going to her own pile. "Did you know that Ames is in the same building as the Inn's insurance broker?"

Her question wasn't what surprised him. "No protestations of innocence for our builder friend?"

"Let's just say that I wasn't bowled over by his sincerity and warmth."

Drake chuckled, one hand rubbing absently at his knee. "Well, let's see what Jacques rabbited away here before we go blaming Ames for a missing insurance policy, too."

They found everything but the insurance policy. Bills of lading for repairs made, drawings for renovations and additions, even the original correspondence when Jacques had set out to search the ghost towns of Colorado for his furnishings. Stephanie discovered that the bar had once supported the famous elbow of Charles Dickens during his American tour.

There was, though, no sign of the insurance policy that both Diane and the agent, a Mr. Hammersmith, vowed Jacques had kept on the place.

"I don't think this bodes well," Stephanie said, her pencil tapping away as she considered the dwindled pile of documents. All that was left was the large manila envelope of photos that Drake had first picked up.

"Doesn't the home office have the records of the insurance policy and payments?" Drake asked, his eyes straying to the same envelope.

"Mr. Hammersmith's checking."

Drake nodded and stood to refill their coffee cups. "When he does, we can get some interim documents drawn up until we find the real ones. The question is, where they'd be. I'm more surprised that the other documents were in that cubbyhole than I am that the policy isn't." Then he shrugged, his attention on his task, his back to Stephanie.

"Maybe Jacques was just getting things in order. He never had a will till August either."

Raising his eyes to the scene that spread out from the window, Drake allowed his thoughts to return to his friend, to that last day when Jacques had lost his fight to live, his once powerful bulk wasted by a sudden and ravaging disease, his eyes still bright with that wonderful Gallic obstinacy. Jacques knew he would die, but he wasn't going to give the reaper any easy task seeking him out. Lost in memory, Drake didn't hear the rustling of the envelope behind him.

"You saw these, didn't you?"

The sound of Stephanie's voice dragged Drake back. He turned to see her attention on the photos he'd stuffed back in the manila envelope, her own face smiling out at her from fifteen years earlier. The eyes Stephanie lifted to him were bleak, their soft brown brimming with the weight of the memories those pictures resurrected. For the first time since Drake had known her, she didn't hide her feelings.

Taking the time to return with the refilled coffee mugs, he perched himself across from her on the edge of the desk, his leg brushing hers. "I did," he admitted quietly, his own expression carefully passive. What Drake wanted was Stephanie's confidence. He didn't want to scare her off by offering sympathy or judgment when she wasn't ready.

"It's funny." She smiled tentatively, her gaze fixed on the jumble of photos on her lap. "I was afraid Jacques had thrown them all away. He'd always said he would after I gave up racing, since I didn't want to see them. But I didn't really want him to..."

"How long did you compete?"

"Oh, three years or so. Until I was fifteen."

No explanations or apologies. Stephanie simply sat staring at her lap as if willing back the elation of that moment. She looked curiously vulnerable in the lace and denim dress. Drake knew that most people mistook Stephanie for a woman beyond her years. It was only at times like this that her true age peeked through, in the softness she would not allow otherwise. It didn't occur to him how privileged he was to see it.

"This was my first NASTAR race," she was saying, reaching blindly out to pick up her coffee. Stephanie didn't notice that her hand trembled as she drew the mug to her mouth for a sip. "I finished second. Quite a feat, considering the competition."

"Jacques was your coach?"

She nodded, her eyes brightening. "He told me I was doing it for all the wrong reasons, but that I was a natural just the same. If I wanted to chase gold, he'd help me do it."

"You didn't want to race?"

"No." Stephanie looked up, the surprise of her admission in her eyes. Drake didn't seem quite so surprised. His eyes were calm and level, bathing her in a wealth of understanding. He seemed to have anticipated her, knowing her answer before asking his question. Stephanie had the feeling that he knew her reasons, too. She'd never shared that verbally with anyone, not even Corey, who still on occasion wondered why Stephanie had given up one brilliant career for another, even though she could never understand anyone's fascination with the snow. Jacques had known without asking, but he'd known her father. He'd seen the obsession burn bright in those troubled eyes over the years, the fever of it eating at her father's soul just as surely as the cancer had eaten at Jacques's body.

Jacques had spent Christmases with the Flemings, watching the child Stephanie trying to please her troubled, mercurial father. Today, people often wondered why Stephanie preferred holidays alone, but they had never been the target of Edward Fleming's drunken rages across the Christmas table.

"I...well, I thought I'd please him by following the sport he'd loved so much."

"It was after your father had given up racing," Drake said, a statement rather than a question.

Stephanie nodded, her eyes briefly straying to the pictures. "Yes. He'd had to quit before I was born."

"An injury?"

"His leg. He walked with a cane after that. His left leg ended up being about three inches shorter. No real handicap for a cinematographer, which he became. He has four Oscars of his own." She shrugged now, almost a wince. "But it did effectively end his career on the slopes."

Drake's attention remained concentrated on Stephanie, his eyes responding with empathy to the story of her troubled past. Because he understood the obsession of the father, he appreciated the misgivings of the daughter.

"No small wonder you can't stand to ski," he acknowledged. "I imagine he was a tyrant when you won."

Unable to sit still any longer, Stephanie rose to her feet and set the pictures down. Drake had moved too close, physically and emotionally. Closer than anyone else had in her life. Jacques had known her in an unstated way, trying his best to protect her from herself and her father until she'd finally gotten up the nerve to quit the racing that she'd hoped would unite her with her father—but had ended in only driving them further apart. Jacques had bluffed and laughed and sung, swinging her around whenever he saw her like the small girl she had always been to him. He had never thought to intrude into her soul.

What confused Stephanie was that after all the years she had so assiduously protected herself from others, it was now so easy to open up to Drake. Why now? she wondered. Why with him? Because he understood? Because he saw seeds of her father in himself? Did he appreciate what she told him, or did he pity her because of it?

Stephanie walked to the window, soaking up the stillness in the scene before her, wishing she had the chance to escape to her own house where nothing and no one intruded. She was beginning to hope, and that was the most devastating of all emotions.

"He began to hate me, I think," she finally admitted, her eyes as dry as the day she'd won her last race and her father had walked away from her. "I had what he never would again, and he couldn't live with it."

As much as he wanted to, Drake didn't approach her. Stephanie couldn't tolerate his intrusion right now, he realized, her armor as bright and brittle than ever. The fact that she'd even told him was enough of a milestone. Drake

watched the proud set of her head and marveled at the
weight she had carried alone all these years. Wondered at the
woman she had become. He didn't really understand it but
felt almost possessively proud of her.

"Compared to that," he said at last because he couldn't
think of anything else that wouldn't intrude, "being Belinda Carson's daughter must have been small potatoes."

Stephanie didn't answer for a moment. When she did, it
was facing him, a grateful smile wreathing her features.
"Medium potatoes." She shrugged with self-effacement.
"Shock training for the real world was what Jacques always called my childhood."

"If you ran away from skiing," he asked, "why didn't
you run away from the movies, too?"

She shrugged once again, the angle of her shoulders now
a little softer. A hurdle passed, a fear resolved. Drake had
respected her privacy enough not to try to coddle her, yet his
eyes held all the support she could ever want. Maybe,
Stephanie thought, maybe in a little while she would ask him
to swing her around as Jacques had done.

"It was something I knew and liked. And I spent more
time on the set with Belinda than with my father, so the experience wasn't quite as traumatic." Her smile when it came
was self-deprecating. "I find I enjoy those neurotics that
Corey talks about."

"You're just used to caring for them."

Stephanie looked up, a little startled at Drake's percep-
tion. She hadn't really looked closely enough herself to an-
alyze it. Belinda had relished her therapists, waving them
about like flags of achievement. Stephanie preferred to sit
in the silence of her garden and arrange rocks.

"Someday," Drake said a companionable smile, "I'd like
to see you work."

"Someday—" she nodded as she battled that unfamiliar
taste of hope "—I'd like you to."


After twelve more hours of mountain solitude, Corey decided that this was about all she could tolerate. Awakening
at what for her qualified as the crack of dawn, she called for

a jet to pick her up and then proceeded to pack. Still waiting for word from Mr. Hammersmith on the insurance, Stephanie helped.

"So, darling, what news do I take back to the rumor mill?" Corey demanded as she unceremoniously stuffed brightly colored silk dresses into a suitcase. It was all Stephanie could do to keep from pulling them all back out and folding them properly, just as she'd done for so many years.

"Tell every one of them to come out for the holidays," Stephanie answered agreeably as she gathered her own armload of silk. "It would do them good."

Corey made a face. "Oh, don't be so boring. I'm talking about the devastating Mr. McDonald. Did you fail to tell him about your illustrious career because you want him to teach you all about skiing?"

"You only know by accident, my dear," Stephanie retorted, the threat implicit in her voice. "So, as I've said, I'd rather that past remained in my past."

"Oh, a mystery woman," Corey crowed with delight. "It's a new twist for you, darling. Do you think he'll bite?"

"Bite what?"

Another face. "Don't be so provincial. The bait, of course. Men love nothing more than a woman with an untold past. Of course, yours would have been much better with another man in it, but there you are."

Stephanie couldn't help a rueful shake of her head as she grinned at her friend. "You know, I really appreciate your coming all this way for me, Corey. After all, you've been forced to spend more than forty-eight hours without spreading one rumor or buying out a single shop on Rodeo."

"Oh, Rodeo," Corey dismissed. "Passé, darling. I've found the most wonderful shop in Newport Beach. For the woman who can't bear to break a thousand. Don't you love it?"

"To die for."

"Tell me the truth." Her eyes lit with unholy interest as she leaned over the opened Vuitton luggage. "Just what are your plans for this skier?"

Stephanie arched an eyebrow. "Drake?"

Corey giggled. "I'm certainly not talking about that child he travels with."

Instincts kicked in to prevent Stephanie from admitting the tight pleasure just the mention of Drake's name set up in her, the fear she couldn't escape. "Until the season is over," she said instead, "he is going to be my business partner. Then I sell him the rest of the Inn and never darken its doors again. Are you satisfied?"

"That man is no business partner, my darling," Corey objected with outrage. "He's a gift from God."

"Be that as it may..."

"Then you really wouldn't mind if on my way out of this place I set my considerable cap for him."

Stephanie saw the challenge in Corey's eyes and knew exactly what she was up to. For all her egocentrism, Corey did have a rare streak of protective friendship in her. One simply had to wait long enough to see it.

"Feel free, dear," she answered with just as determined a smile. This was not the time to be pushed, even though she was a lot less assured than she sounded. "I'm sure you'll positively adore those long horseback rides in the moonlight."

Corey's eyebrows did a long slide northward. "I'll make it a point to."

True to her word, as she made her way out the door, Corey waylaid Drake as he came in from skiing to plant several highly suggestive proposals and an even more suggestive kiss in the vicinity of his ear. The audience in the main room was impressed. Stephanie, seeing the look in Drake's eyes, was hard-pressed not to laugh.

For the first time in her career, Corey had struck out. Drake looked as if he were entertaining his favorite little sister. It was something Corey couldn't comprehend or tolerate.

"I'll be seeing you again," she promised, her eyes just a touch steely as she regarded him.

"It will be my pleasure." He smiled, and with a kiss of the hand sent her on her way.

From where she stood against the desk, Stephanie couldn't keep the wry smile from her features. When Drake turned to her, though, her smile faltered. His eyes had taken on a new warmth, an intimate greeting that needed no words. The spark from that look crackled along Stephanie's skin and shot through her chest leaving a breathlessness that she didn't understand.

She tried to smile back, to give greeting for greeting. In the end, though, her instincts won out. With a stiff nod of the head, Stephanie turned and walked away, so afraid of the promise Drake had begun to offer that she couldn't even face it.

Drake watched until Stephanie had closed the door, then walked past with a shake of his head. In the office the afternoon before, he'd decided that the benefits outweighed the risks in getting to know Stephanie Fleming. He'd been captivated by the glimpse of her secret self. Maybe if he just played it safe until the winter was past, they could build something worthwhile. Maybe he could convince her that he wasn't the same man her father was, and thus free her of the ghosts the older man had left her.

Drake had awakened this morning with a rare pleasure, anticipating the sight of Stephanie, the throaty music of her voice. He wanted to be able to get a foothold in a relationship before he had to go, and as he'd turned to tell her that, she'd run.

Patience, he told himself, realizing how little patience he had. You have enough to worry about with the Olympics. Put your mind on that and let your relationship with Stephanie grow at its own pace.

But as he opened the door to the weight room, Drake knew that he was going to spend another hour trying to purge the feel of her from his system—without success.

## *Chapter 8*

Two days later, Stephanie was waving Drake and Chip goodbye. With the downhill competition at Val d'Isère in France bearing down on them in another week, and Chip due immediately back in Switzerland for the competition at Laax, there was no more time to waste with the Inn's problems.

Stephanie drove with both of them to the airport, putting up with Chip's terminally bright humor and Drake's silence the best she could. It would amuse her at another time, she thought, that she could find just the act of putting Drake on a plane depressing.

She was just nervous, Stephanie kept telling herself. She was going to be left alone with the shaky future of the Inn, the questionable attentions of Mr. Ames and a still unresolved insurance policy. Drake's knowledge of the Inn had been lifesaving in the time she'd been there so far, and now he would be unavailable for consultation. That was the reason that every time she looked over at the dramatic angles of his face, the contrasting soft gray of his eyes, that she was plagued by the most curious sense of loss.

That was why she wanted to feel the gentle caress of his lips against hers just one more time before he left.

"You've got the number if you need to reach me?" Drake asked suddenly, his eyes straying briefly from the mountain road they were traveling. Squeezed between Drake and Chip in the front seat, Stephanie nodded, her attention more on the delicious pressure of Drake's leg against hers and the heat that radiated from it. Another thing she would miss, that wonderful rare chemistry. But that was all, she kept telling herself, even as she met his eyes and felt their impact more intensely even than the physical contact of his leg.

"Pay attention to your skiing," she advised with a dry smile, her voice just a little throatier. "We'll handle the Inn."

"I'll probably be back after Val d'Isère," Drake assured her. "There are a couple of weeks after that until the grand slalom at Ebnat-Kappel, so I'll have time to spend Christmas at the Inn."

"What about me?" Chip immediately demanded from Stephanie's other side. "Don't I get to come out for Christmas, too?"

"Only if you don't talk about skiing," Stephanie informed him.

His reaction was less than enthusiastic. "Might as well sew my mouth shut."

Chip was to skiing what Corey was to the movies. The world revolved around their craft, and their craft revolved around them. Take any of that away, and the world stalled to boredom.

"We just don't appreciate you," Stephanie said with a grin and a pat to his hand before he had the chance to say it.

Chip's corresponding smile was knowing. "You're right there. Just try and find somebody else to fix your A drive while I'm languishing in the cold."

Stephanie's eyebrows rose. "My A drive?"

"The computer," Drake offered. "It went down while you and I were in Mr. Hammersmith's office yesterday."

And an unprofitable afternoon that had been, too. Once a computer threw you out of its system, it was loath to put you back in again. The insurance company would do its best, but it would take a while to straighten out that particular mess. "It wouldn't have mattered if I'd been sitting on top of the computer when it went down," Stephanie assured him in all sincerity. "If it doesn't match a film and a sound track, I don't know what to do with it."

Chip shrugged. "All you have to do is be logical with it," he suggested. "And hit it with a blunt instrument if it acts up."

The airport was a tiny affair stretched across a high meadow just outside the town. As they pulled up to it, the small Lear that transported vacationers to the isolated little community was just coming to a stop. The three of them tumbled out of the Blazer and began pulling ski equipment and luggage from the back.

"Remember," Drake told Stephanie, his hands on her arms. "Call me if you need me."

"She remembers," Chip groused, swinging a heavy ski bag over his arm. His features brightened into a friendly leer for Stephanie. "Call *me* if you need some fun."

Stephanie laughed, accepting a less than chaste kiss from him.

"I really am more fun than he is," Chip assured her before turning for the little prefab terminal.

Drake was left shaking his head, a rueful grin tugging at the corners of his mouth. "Losing him as a roommate almost makes forfeiting the World Cup worthwhile."

"But you'll have him for the Olympics," Stephanie retorted. "Won't you?"

"Unfortunately." Without noticeable hesitation, his eyes grew serious. "Don't let Ames get away with anything, Stephanie. The Inn is solvent, and unless something major happens, it should stay that way."

"I'll call you if there's a problem," she assured him.

Drake tightened his hold on her. The wind set Stephanie's hair dancing and raised color in her cheeks. With those PreRaphaelite eyes, she looked like a goddess. God, how he wanted to stay. Instead, he bent to kiss her goodbye.

Stephanie met the kiss with her eyes closed. Drake's mouth was so warm on hers, so compelling. Before she realized what she was doing, she found herself fitting into his embrace, her arms around his shoulders, her head pushed back with the force of his kiss. Standing together with him on that high plain, Stephanie lost all sense of the wind. Her soul sang with the heady elixir of Drake's touch, the sweet comfort of his embrace. In the space of moments, Drake McDonald did what no person had ever done before. He made Stephanie forget her obligations and deny her common sense. She wanted nothing more from that moment than to remain where she was, with the mountain sun warming her and Drake's strength suffusing her.

The music of his own blood surging in him, Drake straightened as to see exhilaration in Stephanie's eyes. There was uncertainty there, too, a sudden restraint that betrayed her insecurity, but Drake didn't care. He would be more than happy to teach her how to let herself go. In time.

Still holding Stephanie to him, Drake drew a thumb along the line of her cheek, her softness intoxicating him. "Will you spend Christmas with me?"

Stephanie couldn't help the surprise that surfaced on her face. Her first instinct was to say no. Anything but Christmas. If she were anyone else, it would be an easier time to share, to anticipate. She still regarded it with the same revulsion she felt for skiing.

"Nothing much," he assured her, instinctively interpreting her reaction correctly. "Just a day by ourselves and maybe a turkey for dinner."

"You're inviting Chip?" She grinned slyly.

Drake chuckled. "I have to go, Stephanie. But I'm not getting on the plane until you say you'll at least spend that day with me."

The breath Stephanie took was not an even one. The confusion Drake's touch incited still bubbled in her. Stephanie wanted to be able to get a safe distance from him before answering. She needed to go far enough from the electricity of his nearness that she could think of something besides being held in his arms. Caressed by him, undressed by him. . . .

"All right," she agreed abruptly. "Now get on your plane."

Drake boarded his plane and Stephanie turned back for the Inn, her arms wrapped around her to ward off the sudden chill. She wanted to go home to Los Angeles. Everything made more sense there. At least it wasn't as threatening, she thought as she climbed into the Blazer and switched on the ignition.

"Where did you find him?"

Stephanie stood in the office, her back to the window, her posture rigid. She held the phone in one hand, a pencil suspended motionless in the other. The knuckles that surrounded it were white.

"He was in Dallas, Ms. Fleming. Would you like the full report?"

Instinctively Stephanie shook her head, her eyes bleak. "No, thank you. You may send it to my home address. It's enough that you found him. I've been looking for three years."

"He doesn't want to return."

Her eyes closed, the pain sharp at the words she'd so long anticipated. "Not to me, he wouldn't. If you don't mind, I'd like someone there to try and unobtrusively guide him to some help."

"It would cost extra."

"I know. Can you send me a recommendation and I'll call you on it?"

The tiny voice sounded as resigned as Stephanie's. "Of course. We'll be in touch."

The click on the line signified the end of the conversation, but Stephanie couldn't hang up. So many months, so many leads. So much guilt. It hurt worse to realize that the resolution wasn't one at all. She didn't notice her hand tighten around the pencil, the tendons sharp slashes along the length of her wrist. The office had grown dark, the sun lost behind the mountains and the air still.

Stephanie's voice unsettled the silence with its weight. "Oh, Daddy...."

With a sharp snap, the pencil broke in two and fell to the carpet.

In the end, it was the phone call that saved Stephanie's life, and possibly the Inn. She took the call to bed with her, the pain it had churned up eating at her, setting her gaze blindly on the shadowy ceiling in the little room. It had been almost two days since Drake had left, and suddenly she wanted to see him, to talk to him.

Drake would understand. He'd hold her and run his strong, callused hands over her hair and accept her tears. Maybe he'd even really understand what that phone call had meant.

Stephanie had tried so very hard all her life to make her father proud of her. To make him love her. Wasn't it ironic that she was in fact the one person he couldn't love? Even now the tears refused to come. As the night crept along the earth and lit the sky with starlight Stephanie lay dry-eyed and hurting.

It was some time in the early hours of the morning when she first smelled it—an acrid tang in the air like the first flash of a match. Stephanie didn't pay it any mind for a few minutes, her attention resolutely on the pattern the window's frail light threw across the ceiling. The night was crisp and cold, a sharp contrast to the companionable warmth of the comforter that sheltered her. She didn't want to move. She didn't want to think, just feel, as she'd done when arranging her garden with such exacting precision.

The tang sharpened, strengthened. Stephanie sniffed with more curiosity than alarm. She was too preoccupied to really consider what that particular aroma meant. Since her room was located in the rear of the Inn right over the restaurant, she was used to waking to the smell of freshly baking bread that changed to the fragrance of mesquite as dinners were being served. It was an old building, and the aromas drifted easily through the ventilation system.

But at two in the morning?

She was suddenly on her feet and running for the phone.
"Desk," a sleepy voice answered on the first ring.

"This is Stephanie," she said, her voice controlled even
as her hands shook. It was smoke she smelled, the faint
warning of a new fire. The smoke alarms hadn't even
sounded yet. "The Inn is on fire. Call the authorities. I'll
start waking guests."

Her words brought the young desk clerk to abrupt life.
"Yes, ma'am."

Stephanie didn't think to rescue her purse or clothes.
Swinging into her robe, she ran out the door and down the
hall. There were three floors of guests spread over the wings,
fifteen rooms in all. Stephanie pounded on the first door she
came to until it opened, then followed suit down the hall.
With an old wooden building like this, she wasn't going to
have much time. A deathly dark fog had already begun to
creep along the hallway after her as the first alarm finally
sounded.

"Wake up!" she called as she went, raising a babble of
excited voices around her. "There's a fire! Hurry!"

After that the night dragged with the frustrating fight
against time and the fire. Sirens cut through the cold air and
red lights shuddered against the snow. Within minutes the
entire Inn was emptied, some twenty-six guests huddled
alongside the still-shaking night clerk, a high school stu-
dent named Billy Martin. He'd been the one who'd stayed
behind calmly calling rooms to make sure everyone was out
as firemen swept past him with axes and breathing equipment.

Stephanie patrolled her guests like a collie her sheep,
making sure no one went after their belongings. Finally she
settled the majority of them in the comparative warmth of
the barn under the supervision of the soon-to-be-promoted
Billy, while the fight went on. The flames had already
claimed a portion of the back wing, her room included. If
the call had come in ten minutes later, the chief said with a
shake of his head, the entire Inn would have been a pile of
cinders. Water soared in a leaden arc against the thick, oily
smoke, and shouts and clattering echoed from within.

Stephanie stood out in the frigid winter night in only her nightgown and robe, her feet clad in slippers sodden from the snow, not even feeling the discomfort. Her eyes were trained on the solid front of the building, willing it to safety, much as Drake had done that first day with the bomb.

Diane materialized after only an hour, taking over from Billy and marshaling the town's Red Cross resources to keep the guests warm and hydrated while the Inn was saved. She and Stephanie worked nonstop until all the guests were temporarily placed and the last of the firemen were sitting around the pumpers sipping at the Red Cross lemonade and coffee.

The sun had come up, the first shafts of it glinting against the traces of smoke that still drifted from the back of the building. Water dripped from exposed beams and froze into huge icicles. Hoses were being recoiled and a pile of charred furniture lay scattered over the pristine white of the meadow. Original antiques, collected with individual care like favorite children, had been ravaged. The kitchen was gutted and the back wing of four rooms a total loss. The rest had been saved, but, as the fire chief pointed out, that sometimes meant it had been ruined by his water rather than destroyed by the fire.

Stephanie spent the rest of the day walking the ruined, half-ruined and miraculously whole rooms of the Inn with Diane making out a damage report for the insurance company and outlining plans for repairs. No one had yet thought to tell Stephanie to change from her gown; after all, she had nothing left to change into.

As the last of the firemen who'd stayed to watch for new outbreaks finally departed, Nathan Ames swept up the driveway in his Mercedes, a large box from a clothier under his arm.

"I heard it was your room that went first," he said without preamble as he came upon Stephanie trying to arrange for someone to temporarily close off the back wall and restore the heating system to life. She was sooty and exhausted, her hair pulled back in a knot. Instead of looking unattractive, the hairstyle had the odd effect of making her look like a tragic heroine, her great eyes serene in the face of disaster.

"Hello, Nathan." She nodded a greeting, jotting notes on the pad in front of her before placing another call. The outside phones were intact, so she talked from the front desk, a space heater whirring mightily against the chill wind that swept in from the back.

From where she stood, it was hard to accurately assess the damage. Confined to the area beyond the great room, it was largely out of sight. A fire danced merrily in the fireplace and the dying sun slanted in the long windows, just as it did every day. But one of the maids was trying to clean mud from the beautiful hardwood floors, the furniture was all pushed to the side, and the carpeted hallway that stretched toward the back wing was water-soaked.

"You should be half-frozen," Nathan protested, lifting the box he held onto the desk. Stephanie barely looked up. "And unless I miss my guess, you're a perfect ten."

She smiled distractedly, picking up the receiver again. "I'm a little busy right now."

"Clothes." He nudged her gently, motioning to the box. "Sweaters and some slacks. Not what you're used to, I'm sure, but serviceable until you can get home to your own. I heard all your clothes were lost."

And now probably out on that smoldering pile in the snow. "Thank you." Stephanie smiled with as much sincere gratitude as she could muster. "I appreciate the gesture."

"Why don't you let me make those calls while you change? Maybe you could slip on down into town and take a nice, long bath. There are a couple places I manage that are available, if you'd like. I'll put you up gratis." Out of habit, his voice had taken on a patronizing tone.

"No, thank you," Stephanie answered with a small shake of her head. "I'm fine here. I moved into another room, and the hot water tank is intact. I just haven't had time yet. Thank you for putting up what guests you could, Nathan."

Stephanie didn't notice the bemusement in Nathan's eyes at her matter-of-fact attitude. After the past two days, the last thing on her mind was the little game she'd played to lead him along. Nathan had hurried up here fully expecting her to be prostrate from the fire, unable to cope with the loss of a few sweaters, much less the running and rehabilitation of the Inn. Yet here she was, still in a sooty robe and nightgown, her bare feet inches from the warmth of the space heater, carrying on conversations with contractors as if she were sitting in a Los Angeles office.

"Mr. Bellvue," she was saying, her eyes on her notes. "How long do you think it would take for you to come by and inspect the roof?...No, as far as I know it's intact, but I want to be sure before I make any other repairs."

Nathan Ames stood at the desk like a boy unsure whether he should ask a girl out on a date, a frown deepening on his features. He'd apparently figured all he had to do was come up here and take over, now that McDonald was out of the picture. Not so easy, it seemed. Even a half-ruined Sundance Inn seemed no closer to having his name on its title than a whole one, now that Miss She-Can-Do-It-All Fleming had moved in.

"Keep the clothes," he finally said as she hung up. "I'll be back in the morning when you've had some sleep. By then we can figure out what to do with this place."

The way he said it, the Inn should have been that pile of smoldering cinders the fire chief had worked so hard to prevent. With a slightly preoccupied look around her, Stephanie turned her attention to the concerned look on Nathan's face. Then she smiled.

"What we're going to do to this place is fix it back up," she informed him. "We only have a few weeks left until Christmas."

Nathan barely blinked an eye. "Of course," he said, nodding with encouragement, as if his grandmother had just said she was going to climb the north face of the Eiger. "But if it doesn't work out, we have to have contingency plans." Nathan took his own look around. "It's going to cost a lot to fix this place up in time."

Absentminded from stress and exhaustion, Stephanie came within a hair's breath of committing an indiscretion.

She almost said something about the insurance. But then, maybe Mr. Ames already knew the exact state of their insurance. Maybe he'd been the one to somehow sabotage it. "That's all right," she said instead. "It's worth it, don't you think?"

Stephanie had barely gotten the ubiquitous Mr. Ames out the door before Corey called.

"Stephanie, darling, you'll be so pleased to know that you've made the columns."

Stephanie continued to scribble on her list, the numbers she still had to call stretching far down the page. "I'm thrilled."

"Wouldn't you like to hear? It might just be a nice ornament for your wall for when all those people come streaming back to the Inn."

"Of course I'd like to hear." What she heard first of all was the concern that edged Corey's voice, and knew that her friend was trying to break the news to her the only way she knew how. Oh well, Stephanie thought, what was another problem? It didn't occur to her to burden Corey with the new crisis she faced. Stephanie had never felt comfortable farming out her worries; she'd seen how effectively her parents had done it for too many years.

"Ahem!" Corey started with a grand clearing of the famed throat. "'It seems that Stephanie Fleming has inherited the same killer instincts as her legendary mother Belinda Carson. Need we remind you how many rich, older husbands La Belinda has snared in her career? Evidently the daughter doesn't even wait for marriage. Consider the case of Jacques Lavalle, beloved innkeeper and superstar skier who died recently. Stephanie ended up with a split of the profits, without ever tying the knot. At least not *that* one. She purports to be running the same inn in the Rockies, to our chagrin. It galls to think of supporting such classic deceit with patronization, don't you think?'"

There was a pause, and then Corey's voice came back, now tinged with scorn. "Everyone else in Hollywood is lily-white. I'd be angry if I *were* guilty, darling. You must be livid. Give me the word and I'll have Marvin at your little hamlet before sunrise.''

Stephanie found herself wishing for a chair. Suddenly she felt very tired. Rubbing at the strain she felt like a band across her forehead, she smiled at her friend's outrage. Marvin was Corey's personal lawyer who had seen her through early skin-flick scandal and divorce. Corey invoked his name like a child would her father.

"It's not necessary," Stephanie assured her, thinking that thanks to the fire they wouldn't have to worry about filling the Inn for a few weeks, anyway. "We'll take care of it from here with a subtle goodwill campaign."

"You know I can't deal with you when you're reasonable, darling," Corey protested.

"Thanks for calling, Corey. I'll see you when I get back."

"Oh, Franklin says that you only have a few more days. He's being perfectly surgical with his whims."

"I'm glad."

She wasn't, though. Hanging up the phone after lengthy goodbyes, Stephanie finally went in search of that chair. Diane had gone down into town to finish delivering personal belongings to guests, so the Inn was quiet. The wind still whistled through the tarp they'd thrown up, but the heater chugged away. Stephanie had got as far as the office door when the phone rang again.

"Ms. Fleming?" a worried voice said. "It's Frank Hammersmith. I've been on the phone all day with American Mutual, and I'm afraid I have some bad news."

Drake's first sight of the Inn was a relief. From the frantic call he'd gotten from Diane, he'd figured the whole place had gone up. It rose dark and whole before him, the front facade as meticulously painted and groomed as ever. Only the muddy jumble of tire tracks and footprints betrayed the fact that anything had happened here at all. Pulling his Jeep to a sharp stop before the door, he swung out and climbed the steps.

The front door was unlocked, the hallway dark and quiet, the only light coming from the lamp at the desk. Drake stepped in to find that the big fireplace in the great room stood for once dark and cold. A space heater took the bite off the winter night. The pervasive reek of sodden ashes and scorched wood filled the air, hinting at the wreckage that lay at the back of the building.

"Stephanie? Diane? Anybody here?"

There was a rustling sound from the office, no more. Drake walked over and pushed open the door.

At first he couldn't see anything. The room was illuminated only by the light that spilled over from the desk area, the window open to the cold, starry night. Then Drake heard the sound of breathing and looked toward the desk.

Stephanie sat there. Not on one of the chairs, but on the floor, her knees drawn up to her chest, her arms around them. Her hair was slipping from the knot she'd worn it in, and her face was smudged and streaked. Stephanie looked utterly forlorn and lost, her eyes cavernous in the dim light, her body trembling with the cold.

"You still have your robe on," he said tightly when she finally noticed him. He didn't get much of a reaction. A hard ache for her settled in his chest, a fear and a possessiveness he'd never known. That someone usually so controlled and self-contained should look so very helpless tore at him like a knife.

"I don't have anything else to wear," she managed to say with a weak smile, lifting a listless hand up to brush a stray strand of hair from her forehead.

Drake's eyes widened and his attention briefly wandered toward the door.

"It's the entire back wing," Stephanie said. "We were lucky."

Wasting no more time, Drake walked over and crouched down before her, a hand out to her now dry cheek. "So you decided to sit on the floor and think about things."

Stephanie shrugged, her eyes melting at his tenderness. "I guess I just wanted to curl up for a few minutes. Things have been pretty busy."

Her voice wavered on that last word, betraying its inadequacy to describe what she'd had to face. The sound brought Drake to her. With hands that wouldn't be refused, he drew her into his arms and held her, her head close to his own.

She was cold and limp, and her face pressed instinctively against his shirt. She'd needed to curl up, all right, Drake thought savagely. What she'd needed was someone she could turn to for support, warmth and tenderness. But there was no one she'd allow close enough to do it. Well, she was damn well going to allow him.

For a minute Stephanie didn't move, didn't breathe. Drake was afraid she'd pull away from him, but she didn't. She simply curled into his embrace like a child seeking a haven. He could actually feel the warmth stealing back into her skin as he massaged it.

"How did you . . . know?"

He held her tighter, feeling the first shudder of new tears. "Diane called. She figured you wouldn't want to bother me."

"She shouldn't have."

The shudders grew in the silence, as if Stephanie couldn't even admit to them or to the tears that had begun to dampen Drake's shirt. Drake lifted a hand to her hair, running his fingers along its tangled strands, thinking how even now they felt like silk.

That act seemed to somehow purge her. Suddenly her hands came up to him, clinging, and Stephanie buried her face in the solid strength of his chest. Her tears fell freely, the sound of her small sobs muffled against him.

"Ssh," Drake murmured, his own eyes stinging with her pain. "It's okay, Stephanie. I'm here . . . I'm here now."

"I'm just . . . tired," she protested.

"I know."

"And . . . cold. . . ."

"Mmm-hmm."

Stephanie's hold on him tightened, almost as if she were afraid she'd fall. Drake brushed his lips against her forehead, tasting the grime and weariness, and gathered her more closely in his arms.

"And glad . . . you're here."

Drake held her until her sobs eased away to the soft emptiness that follows tears. He stroked her hair and cheeks and rocked her a little. And when she'd settled into silence, he straightened to consider her puffy, tear-stained face.

"Come on," he commanded, not yet moving. "You're coming home with me."

Stephanie immediately stiffened in protest. "But the Inn—"

"Will wait till morning. You need some food, some sleep and some clothes. In that order."

That actually got a smile out of her. "Nathan already brought some clothes by."

Drake scowled. "Like I said. . . ."

There was little to close up before they left. Drake took care of it, his eyes always on Stephanie's forlorn figure. As the two of them walked out to Drake's waiting Jeep, he knew that tonight would be the night he would begin teaching Stephanie how to love again.

# Chapter 9

Stephanie stepped out of the shower to the smell of frying bacon and perking coffee. There was something about those two aromas that resurrected such pleasant memories of breakfast on the patio, the yard heavy with dew, the air full of bird song and Cook singing in the kitchen. It had always struck her as something straight out of Tennessee Williams to call their housekeeper Cook, but her mother had done it as long as Stephanie could remember. So the affable Mexican woman named Maria Louisa Santiago y Perez had always been known as Cook. Stephanie inevitably connected Cook with her better memories.

Stephanie bent forward to towel her hair dry. Her body felt refreshed after the vigorous shower even though her brain still harbored cobwebs from lack of sleep. After running on sheer adrenaline all day, Stephanie hadn't realized how tired or hungry she was. That explained why she'd so uncharacteristically fallen apart on Drake, she thought. She'd have to apologize. Drake had enough on his mind without hysterical females. She'd eat the dinner he was fixing, then reassure him that everything was under control so he could get back to his skiing. Right after she explained that episode in the office.

If only she hadn't felt so at home while he held her, so comforted. His arms had been stronger than Jacques's, gentler and more giving. Stephanie fingered her hair, remembering how Drake had stroked it as she'd cried, and a reluctant smile bloomed.

"How do you like your eggs?" Drake called through the door, startling her.

"Oh, it doesn't matter," she stammered, raising a hand unconsciously to her throat where her pulse had suddenly begun to skitter. Stephanie had been with men before. But she'd never felt that she belonged to one. Not until now, anyway, and the thought frightened her.

"Well, dinner's ready when you are," Drake announced, his voice fading back toward the kitchen.

Stephanie slipped into the short terry cloth robe Drake had provided and belted it. Any other day of her life, she would have refused to step from the bathroom without at least blowing her hair into order. Somehow tonight she felt more comfortable with it left damp and loose around her shoulders.

At home. How could she possibly feel at home in a place she'd never been before? She did, though, the comfort an intangible thing that transcended the Spartan decorating and delicate beauty of the building. Shaking her head at her fancies, she stepped out to join Drake for her meal.

"I wanted to apologize...."

At the sound of Stephanie's voice Drake came to a shuddering halt. She stood in the kitchen doorway, barefoot and tousled, the white robe snug against her curves and parting gently at the knees to hint at shapely legs. The top lay open just enough to show the soft rise of her breasts, the pearly skin below her throat still damp and glistening. Without makeup and with her hair tangled to her shoulders Stephanie looked like a sea nymph who had happened suddenly on land, her skin glowing and her eyes luminous and dark.

Drake's breath caught in his throat. He clenched his hands against the sharp desire that slammed through him.

Damn. Damn. Damn. There was going to be no patience, not after this evening. He was skidding faster than a downhill on ice. It was all he could do to keep from pulling her into her arms and savaging that delectable mouth until she moaned with need.

Stephanie saw Drake's eyes widen. She felt the heat rise in her body until it glowed against her skin. After everything she'd been through, her defenses against him were sorely weakened, just as his arousal left her breathless.

"Do you want some coffee?" Drake asked, his voice a rasp, his stance easing a bit as he fought to regain control.

Stephanie nodded and smiled. "Anything I can do to help?"

Drake grinned wryly. "Stay out of arm's reach."

She remained in the doorway as he filled their plates and poured her a cup of coffee.

"Isn't the team a little upset that you ran back out on them?" she asked.

"Most of the team is on its way to Laax," he replied shrugging. "With Markinson, thank God."

That got a grin out of her.

"Cream, no sugar?" he asked, the creamer in hand.

She nodded. "Thank you. I can fill you in on what we're going to need to do, if you'd like, so you can get back."

Drake's eyebrows arched in disbelief. "Are you saying that you don't want me around?"

Yes, Stephanie wanted to say. You distract me. You make me want too much.

"Of course not. But the purpose of Jacques's codicil was for you to be free of the Inn's worries while you finished out the season."

"There is no season," Drake reminded her. "He wrote that before he knew I was going to forfeit the World Cup."

"You still have the Olympics to consider," she reminded him as she edged toward the table. Even running on empty, her body still sang in response to his the closer she got. It exhilarated and disquieted her.

Drake wore a black turtleneck tonight, creating a dramatic contrast to his features and accentuating the lean toughness of his physique. Stephanie's hands itched to roam him, studying muscle and sinew, savoring the savage grace of his beauty and the untamed fire of his passions.

Reaching her chair, Stephanie sat down abruptly. Drake cast a quizzical glance her way, but couldn't seem to interpret her erratic moves.

"I think this is just a little more involvement than Jacques even considered for you," he observed as he set plates of steaming food on the table. "He really didn't know how carnivorous Ames would get."

"Even so," Stephanie retorted, more at ease now, "you're supposed to be skiing, not holding my hand."

"And you're supposed to be running the Inn," he countered, "not rebuilding it."

"I'll tell you what," she suggested, motioning to their meal. "I'm really hungry. Could we call a truce until after we eat?"

Drake relented, easing into his chair and picking up a fork. "I think I can manage that. What did Ames want in return for the clothes?"

Stephanie had to laugh. "You're wasted on skiing, Drake. You should be writing gossip columns."

"I don't trust the guy, all right?"

"We'll talk about it later. How do things look for the downhill at Val d'Isère?"

In the end Drake gave in, filling Stephanie in on the team's chances for the cup and the Olympics, and giving a rough outline of his plans for the games. Stephanie heard disappointment crowd his voice for the record-breaking World Cup win he'd wanted so badly, and the delight at competing in the Olympics again.

He wasn't like her father, she realized. Her father had been propelled by rage, needing something to focus on. As long as he'd had the physical release of competition, brutalizing himself and his competitors, he'd been tolerable. After he'd lost that, he'd needed to find something else.

Drake needed his skiing like a musician needed a melody. It made him whole and free, set just a little above the rest of the world. Stephanie had the feeling that he thrived on the speed, the challenge, the risk. Drake liked living on the edge, and skiing down a hill at ninety miles an hour was as close to the edge as one could hope to get. The question was, what would happen to him when he had to give it up?

By the end of the meal the two of them were chatting like old friends, comfortable in the warm familiarity of a kitchen and a shared meal. It seemed natural afterward to follow Drake into the living room to sit before the fireplace.

"That's one thing I could get used to in this place," Stephanie admitted, crouched before the crackling fire, her hands stretched out to the warmth.

From where he was setting a disc in the player, Drake could see the flames reflect and dance across Stephanie's drying hair. She straightened with that elegant grace and turned to him. He wanted to pull her into his arms.

Drake had never had anyone but Jacques here in the quiet of the evening. And yet the first time Stephanie stepped into his house, she fitted into it as if she'd always walked its floors, the soft spring scent of her hair trembling on the air, her laughter filling the empty places with sunshine. He'd been right to want her here.

Pushing the comfort of those thoughts aside, Drake turned his attention to the sound system.

"What's that?" he asked.

"Fireplaces. They're a bit superfluous in L.A. You don't spend much time here, do you?"

"Not till recently." The soft moaning notes of the blues rose from the speakers, melting into the background where they best belonged. Giving the system one final adjustment, Drake got to his feet and joined Stephanie on the couch.

Feet curled up beneath her, she watched the fire, her eyes quiet and sleepy. When Drake joined her, she smiled at him, a surprisingly shy smile for so mature a woman.

"Thanks for the TLC," she said, a hand on his arm. "I'm beginning to feel human again."

Stephanie had new smudges below her eyes from lack of sleep and rubbed a tired hand over her forehead from time

to time, but after what she'd been through, Drake was
amazed at how controlled she could be.

"My pleasure," he assured her with a gentle smile,
brushing a hand along her cheek. Her skin was so soft
against Drake's fingers; he almost let them stray to the
tempting line of her lips. Instead he slipped an arm around
Stephanie's shoulders and drew her against him. "After you
get some sleep tonight, we'll start work on putting you and
the Inn back in business."

Drake reveled in the way Stephanie's body fitted against
his. She laid her head against his shoulder and the scent of
her hair filled his nostrils. Stephanie was a fragile flower
coated in armor, a temptress who never meant to tempt. The
room seemed more friendly with her in it, the music richer.
For the first time, Drake had an idea of what it would take
to transform this house into a home.

Drake realized that more than anything right now, he
wanted to make love to her. He wanted to play her body
with his hands, to watch her eyes grow wide and languid,
feel the heat spark across her skin. He wanted to grant her
the solace of his embrace and waken the life in her eyes.

He didn't realize that he was letting his hand drift along
Stephanie's arm, tracing its slim line beneath the nubby
material that covered it. He was aware that her breath
fanned his throat, that the robe she wore stretched taut
across her breasts, the open neckline hinting at their fullness. Nuzzling his cheek against her hair, Drake soaked in
its texture and scent, his eyes briefly closing against the
sudden pain of longing.

Stephanie had thought that resting her head against
Drake's shoulder would be soothing. She'd been so tired, so
strung out by her father, and Ames and Mr. Hammersmith, not to mention Corey's long-distance dramatic reading. The feel of Drake's embrace seemed to ward away the
world that worried at her. The hollow of his shoulder cush-
ioned her against the morning. Stephanie didn't rest,
though. She didn't relax into sleep as she'd hoped.

Just the intimation of Drake's body against hers roused
her. His hand was making slow forays along her arm,

spreading shudders in its path. When she turned her face closer to the protection of his chest, Stephanie felt his cheek against her hair and knew the pleasure of being cherished. Drake's actions were fraught with restraint, his hand trembling, his breathing harsh. He wanted her, Stephanie knew that, but he wouldn't force her.

She wanted him, too. On this tranquil night when the threnody of a sax climbed into the air and the world was held outside the door, Stephanie wanted nothing more than to satiate herself with Drake McDonald. She had seen the infinite tenderness in his eyes. She wanted to savor the fierce life of his hands, wanted to share with him something she had never really shared with anyone before—herself.

When she lifted her face Stephanie found that she didn't need to say a word. Her message was carried in her eyes, the need, the yearning, the loneliness that only Drake could assuage. His eyes softened. Raising a hand to her cheek, he brought her to him.

Stephanie's eyes closed as her mouth met his. She welcomed him, meeting his greedy lips with her own. He tasted, tested, explored the fullness of her mouth, pulling her lower lip in between his teeth to ignite sharp thrills in her belly. Stephanie's hands came up, steadying her against his chest as the new headiness threatened her balance. Her skin ached for him, anticipating his touch with agonizing hesitation. Drake wound a hand through her hair and eased her mouth open to plunder it deeper, and Stephanie lost her strength to resist.

Stephanie felt Drake pull her onto his lap, where he cradled her against him. His fingers at first danced against the nape of her neck, then the length of her thigh, edging the robe further apart. Drake's heart thudded against her hand, and his breathing grew erratic. She knew that her heartbeat matched, even outdistanced his. And it wasn't just his touch, the clever madness his tongue was inciting. It was fear of this man. Of Drake, who had held her when she'd cried and kept his distance when she hadn't. She should stay away from him, from all men who were passionate. But Stephanie wanted him more than ever.

Drake's hand slipped up along the outside of the robe, teasing Stephanie through the thick material, nearing her breasts but stopping just shy and driving her to take his hand in her own.

Drake misinterpreted her gesture. Pulling away abruptly, he tried to rein in his desire. "I'm sorry, Stephanie…I can't seem to stop around you."

Stephanie faced him, her own eyes bright. "I don't want you to stop," she whispered, wondering at the almost pleading note in her voice. Drake's expression was fierce, the cost of control measured in the light lost from those magnificent gray eyes.

He shook his head. "You're tired. I'm taking advantage of you."

Stephanie brought his hand to her lips and kissed it. "You're not doing anything of the sort," she assured him softly. "If I didn't want to be in your arms, I wouldn't."

"You need sleep," he persisted, as if that alone made him guilty.

Letting go of his hand, Stephanie smiled, her fingers at the belt of her robe. With a single movement, she opened it and let the terry cloth fall from her shoulders. "I need *you*," she said simply.

For a moment Drake couldn't move. Stephanie sat nestled in his embrace, completely naked except for the robe that still hung from her arms. Her skin was milky white in the soft light, her nipples the fragile pink of roses. Her breasts were full and round, her waist narrow and her hips sleek. Her eyes, now dark pools of tranquility, brimmed with anticipation, the anticipation of sharing, of affirming, of determination. Slipping the robe the rest of the way off, Drake picked her up and carried her to his bed.

Stephanie helped him undress, letting her hands travel his skin and revel in his vitality. She could never remember knowing such a possessive delight in a man's body. His was all muscle and sinew, strength and softness. Stephanie traced it as if claiming him for herself.

When Drake was undressed, he laid Stephanie back and took his time with her. A hall light spilled into the room at an angle casting shadows across them, pouring molten gold over their skin. Drake followed the light across Stephanie's belly with his hands. She was so soft, her curves full and filling his hands to perfection. He celebrated the feel of her as if it were the first time he had discovered a woman; for in fact it suddenly seemed like it.

His hands still splayed across Stephanie's skin, Drake turned so that he could see her eyes. It was there he would find what mattered the most. He wanted to see satisfaction, joy, communion, wanted to know that he could give her what she gave him.

He found his answer. Brightly, tentatively, Stephanie smiled at him, her eyes now seething with desire. Her skin shuddered beneath his touch as her eyes welcomed him. Drake bent to her, reclaiming her mouth with a hunger that surprised even him. And then he feasted on her.

Stephanie arched beneath his hands, her body on fire, her mind a swirling light where needing and giving danced too close to distinguish. Drake's touch was sure, as if he had anticipated each place he claimed. He maddened and delighted her with his attentions, his tongue dancing along her breast and drawing sparks from her throat. His hand ravaged her; his hard desire committed her. Stephanie had never known such ecstasy. She had never allowed it. But when Drake poised himself to enter, only to draw away, she pulled at him, her nails clawing at his back with the need to have him in her.

Drake dipped his mouth to hers, taunting, tempting, his tongue seeking hers and then leaving. He rested his weight on hands that bracketed her shoulders and insinuated his knee between hers. Stephanie welcomed him, instinctively rising to meet him, groaning with the urgent fire he'd built in her. Then, when she thought she would only be denied release, he returned to her.

Drake knew that the moment he entered Stephanie he would be lost. He heard her breathless moans, felt the sharp sting of her nails and even then held back. He wanted her, wanted to possess her completely, feel her shudder to release within his arms. Her hair was fanned out over the pillow, sunset gold at the edge of night. Her eyes were wide and smoldering, her lips open as the excitement seized her. Drake felt the tremors begin to build beneath his quick fingers, the slick, sweet feel of her stabbing him like sweet fire. She was waiting for him, balanced on the precipice, and he wanted her to surround him when she soared.

Stephanie felt the hard length of Drake against her and brought her legs around him, her hips urging him on, his name a plea on her lips. His touch was torture, driving her so close and then denying her, stoking the fire in her belly until it all but consumed her. Then, pulling her to him, Drake drove into her and the light broke.

There was no longer any thought or intention, only the maelstrom that overtook them. Drake wrapped his arms around Stephanie, his hands to the firm mounds of her buttocks to bring her even closer, their bodies dancing in perfect rhythm, their hearts hammering and their eyes wide for each other. The once empty house echoed with the music of their whispers, the joy in their eyes. Beyond them a lone saxophone soared into the shadows, its keening painfully sweet. Stephanie heard it far away and thought its pure sound bittersweet counterpoint to the sweet joy that washed over her as Drake shuddered to stillness within her arms.

Drake woke with the first shaft of sunlight that crept through the window. He hadn't even remembered falling asleep, only the delicious feel of Stephanie as she slumbered in his arms. She'd fallen asleep quickly, the exhaustion of the day overtaking her even as she smiled her satisfaction.

Now she lay on her side, facing away, her body nestled against his in a close harmony that seemed the most natural thing in the world. Back to chest, leg along leg, her hair spilling over his arms as they wrapped around her in easy companionship. Drake lay very still for a while, savoring the elusive spring of her hair in his nostrils, the gentle brush of her breasts against his hands.

The feel of her in his arms stirred embers Drake had long since thought dead. Yearnings for just such a communion, waking to the same woman every morning, knowing her special scent and texture even in his sleep. He wanted to fit this naturally, knowing that if he turned, she would ease against him, always there, always a part of him so that she even lived in the depths of his subconscious.

Just as suddenly, he knew that he wanted Stephanie to be that woman. Not only for last night, tonight or a month. Always meant always. Drake wanted to wake to her and slip off to sleep alongside her, having her there to share the good and the bad.

He'd put off a commitment of any kind until he'd attained his goals in skiing, since those goals took so much out of him. It would all be over soon, though, and suddenly his life yawned empty and open, a page waiting for some kind words to fill it. Jacques had given him the Inn to have a future beyond his medals. What Jacques had never been able to give him was the reason to anticipate a future away from racing. If that savage thrill was gone, what could replace it? Cradling Stephanie's soft body to him like a precious gift, Drake suddenly knew.

By the time Stephanie woke, it was to an empty bed. The room was bright with daylight, the world outside bustling. She pushed back her hair, stretching against the delicious sensation of sheets against bare skin. She should have felt spent, the long hours and traumas of the day before dragging at her and sapping her energy even now. Instead she felt refreshed. Her body still remembered the symphony of delights she and Drake had generated. Her mind remembered the protective warmth of his embrace. She smiled with it, wishing with all her heart that she were the kind of person who could learn to count on something so wonderful. But she hadn't survived her childhood to forget its lessons. Trust was a hard-won commodity. When it came to commitment, she couldn't even consider the price. The most she might take with her from last night was the treasure of that one moment. She'd learned that to expect more would be foolish.

Well, she thought with a less than self-assured expression as she swung out of bed and padded across to the bathroom. You've certainly let your better judgment ruin a beautiful morning with those depressing thoughts. Might as well ruin the rest of the day and get back to business.

Stephanie came out of the shower in the same bathrobe as she had worn the night before, wondering if she weren't tempting fate a little. Just the rough sensation of it against her skin ignited shivers of anticipation. She could still feel the heat of Drake's eyes as they'd strayed toward the line of her breasts. She remembered the moist pleasure of his tongue as it taunted her nipples to attention.

"Do you have anything else in the wardrobe I can wear?" she asked him when she came upon him in the kitchen.

Looking up, Drake discovered traces of an almost belligerent defensiveness in Stephanie's eyes. He also saw the outline of her nipples where they strained against the robe. His body reacted predictably, but he smiled all the same.

"Sweat suits in the second drawer," he managed to reply, deliberately turning his eyes from the tempting familiarity of her.

Stephanie slipped into a hunter-green sweat suit and returned to the kitchen, more comfortable with the shapeless garment than with the robe. There was coffee on the table for her across from where Drake sat poring over a pile of paperwork.

"What are you doing?" she asked, taking her seat.

He looked up. "You could wear a sackcloth and you'd still be sexy," he warned with a friendly grin. "You're just lucky I'm busy with these estimates. What's this note about Hammersmith? It just says 'report' and then 'damn.' I can assume it wasn't what you wanted to hear?"

Stephanie found herself staring. "You went to the Inn already and pulled all that out?"

"Already?" Drake countered. "I've had nothing else to do all day with you snoring away in there."

Stephanie looked around her, feeling a little disoriented. When she couldn't find a clock in the room's decorating scheme, she turned back to Drake.

"Three in the afternoon," he obliged.

"I do not snore."

"Of course you do. It's kind of cute, a little rumble like a cat purring. Are you hungry?"

Stephanie shook her head, finally going for the coffee. "What do you think?"

"I think I like women who snore. Proves they're human."

"About the estimates." She scowled. "We can get most of the workmen to start day after...uh, tomorrow, I guess, now."

"I think you're right," Drake said, reaching for his own coffee and taking a sip. "You don't need me here to make decisions. The only thing I've been doing today is listening to people tell me what a hell of a job you did yesterday...and how cute you looked in your robe and slippers, ordering the firemen and maintenance gangs around."

Stephanie lifted an eyebrow. "You're in quite a jovial mood this morning."

Drake found a smile for her. "Like a ticket to the Olympics?"

"No."

Her reaction had been instinctive. Not because of Drake, because of her father. She hadn't meant to be so curt, but Drake had surprised her.

"I'm sorry...."

"Don't be," he retorted, the light in his eyes a little dimmer. "I forgot for a minute how much you love the sport."

For just a moment Stephanie faced Drake honestly, her eyes recalling what they had shared the evening before and asking him to be content with it. He faced her without flinching, understanding in his way and accepting. At least to a point. With an almost sheepish smile, he turned back to the paperwork in his hands.

"About Hammersmith...."

Retreating behind her raised cup, Stephanie nodded. The coffee she sipped was bitter. Right now she didn't seem to mind. "We have the worst timing in the world, according to our agent. If we could have waited another week or two until the computers were all happy with the policy they were trying to put back in, he would have had a man out yesterday with an estimate and a check in our hands today."

"But now?"

Stephanie shrugged. "Now, he can't give us any kind of time frame. The company smells a rat, so they want to investigate, which means that all repairs will be out of pocket for the time being. And you know that the only thing Jacques had in the world was that building."

Drake nodded thoughtfully. "Not one for material gains, our Jacques. He always said they corrupted him."

"Especially after he went through three separate fortunes," Stephanie commented with a grin.

"Tell you what," Drake suggested. "I have a tidy sum available. We'll go to the bank tomorrow and put your name on my account. Use it."

"I'm not exactly destitute," she objected. "I can use my money."

"Do you think Jacques would want you to use your money?"

"Do you think he would have wanted you to use yours?"

At a stalemate, the two grinned at each other. "We'll split it," Drake decided. "If worse comes to worst, I'll put Diane in charge of fair play. Just so you don't spend too much of yours."

"When will you be going back to training?" Stephanie asked, the hesitant note in her voice a barely suppressed plea. Go soon, it said, because she so much wanted him to say never.

Drake's expression betrayed the pain her question brought. The trust he still had to nurture in Stephanie was like the first buds of a wildflower. They had been lovers the night before and now she couldn't even bear to depend on him. The sooner he left, Drake saw, the sooner her life would return to equilibrium.

"Probably a couple of days," he answered. "But don't forget Christmas."

"I won't." Maybe by then I'll be more ready for it, Stephanie thought. Maybe I'll look forward to the disruption you bring to my life, the heady exhilaration that can so easily descend to pain. "How about if we have it here?"

Drake couldn't answer. Stephanie had made another tentative step, one so sweet it took his breath. The rooms he had avoided as holding no special fulfillment for him were beginning to change. With Christmas there would be more of him in the house, enough maybe to balance out his past on the Sundance wall.

Two days later, to the sound of ringing hammers and whining saws, Stephanie said goodbye to Drake once again. The two stood before the unspoiled front of the building, the sun bright on the snow and gleaming in the gold of Stephanie's hair. She wore black and green, a turtleneck and heavy sweater that cast her features in a dramatic contrast. The smile she bestowed on her business partner lit those features with a fire more special than the one dancing along her hair.

"Do me a favor and beat Chip," she said with a smile.

"I'll do myself a favor and beat him." Drake grinned back, slipping his arms around her, the leather of his jacket creaking comfortably. "If anything else happens, would you mind being the one to call? It took ten minutes to bring Diane to the point of coherence."

"I promise. I'll have champagne ready."

His eyes softened, their gray luminous against his weathered face. "I'll be happy to share it with you."

With a final kiss, he turned to go, and Stephanie was left alone with the task of rebuilding the Inn. She didn't mind. What she minded was the fact that that feeling of loss grew every time she said goodbye to Drake McDonald. One way or another, she was going to have to do something about that soon.

She watched until his Jeep crossed the San Miguel. Then she turned, hands in pockets, to continue her work.

# Chapter 10

Pushing her glasses to the top of her head, Stephanie took a moment to rub at tired eyes. On the screen before her a couple still argued. The men and women scattered over plush seats on either side of her continued to comment in hushed tones.

It had only been two days since she'd returned to Los Angeles. The Inn was in the midst of renovation and Diane was all too capable and eager to handle the job for Stephanie to stay and look over the younger woman's shoulder. Franklin had called again, vowing that the movie was ready and begging her attention. So Stephanie had come home to edit. In her lap she held a clipboard full of her scribbled notes, and next to her her mixer sat with a similar one. Franklin perched on her other side, biting his nails and puffing on Gauloise cigarettes.

"Stephanie," he snapped, whirling on her. "I asked about that last line. Do you think it needs redoing?"

Stephanie turned to him, surprised that she'd missed it. Usually she could gauge the quality of a movie's sound and catch up with her notes even if she were half asleep. According to the numbers that continued to advance along the bottom of the screen, she'd just completely missed five minutes.

"It *is* your job, sweetie," he nagged, changing positions in the chair yet again as if he'd been sitting there for days instead of just shy of seventy minutes. Franklin positively delighted in agonizing over his films, berating them just to hear everyone else tell him how wonderful they were.

"I'm sorry, Franklin," she apologized evenly, turning to her assistant rather than face the director's snit. "Jack?"

Jack nodded, eyes a little wide at the boss's gaffe.

"We'll do it," she said. "Next time, Franklin, try and search out an actress who can speak above a whisper on a freeway."

"She breathes the part!" Franklin protested, the register of his voice climbing.

Stephanie smiled, pushing her glasses back in place and returning to the clipboard. "Exactly."

"I hope Fawn likes small places," Jack whispered into Stephanie's other ear. "She's going to be in our closet for weeks."

"And the line at 256," Stephanie added with a private nod for Jack. "We might as well just loop all her lines and be done with it."

The film had no sooner ended, the various gofers and execs applauding Franklin yet again for his newest masterpiece, than a voice called out from the projection room.

"Miss Fleming."

"Yes, Martin?"

"Call. Corey Alexander."

"Invite me this time," Jack pleaded, unfolding his long frame from the chair next to hers. "I want a crack at that nut."

"Jack," she protested with a grin and a pat on his shoulder. "You've cracked just about every nut in town. If you don't slow down, you're going to be dead by the time you're thirty."

"But what a legacy I'll leave!" he retorted, dropping a kiss on her forehead. "Everyone in Hollywood slept here but Stephanie Fleming."

"And Corey Alexander."

"Time, my sweet. Give me time."

"Have all the notes put together and we'll start making up the schedule after lunch," she suggested, turning finally to an undoubtedly impatient Corey.

It was the seventh call Stephanie had received from her friend since she'd been back, three of them promising dire consequences on the answering machine. Corey was having a party this weekend, and she wanted Stephanie there. It was going to be fun (of course), with a not-to-be-missed guest list (undoubtedly), and absolutely bleak if Stephanie refused to show.

A month ago Stephanie would have gone without thinking. Corey's parties reminded her a lot of the kind Belinda used to throw—all good times and fun and pretty harmless, as parties went these days. Stephanie would sit by the pool and watch the various famous and semi-famous faces she'd worked with and grown up around swim and talk and sometimes make fools of themselves. Best of all, she'd station herself to catch Corey's running commentary on the scene, which made it all worthwhile.

This time was disturbingly different. It wasn't that she didn't want to see Corey. Between Stephanie's cool outlook and Corey's claws they always had a wonderful time. But to a preoccupied mind, the foolishness somehow seemed unpalatable. It grated when Stephanie needed rest. Except for work, she hadn't set foot out of the house and didn't feel the urge now.

It all boiled down to Drake and the approach of Christmas. Stephanie hadn't seen him since she'd waved goodbye that day in front of the Inn, but she'd talked to him in Oregon and yesterday when he'd arrived in France to compete. They had never let their easy conversation drift past anything but surface topics, but the undercurrent couldn't be denied. He would return to her at Christmas and try to build more than they'd left. And she, sitting alone in her house or in the viewing room at the studio, was terrified to try.

If she had the nerve and didn't think he'd come right out to find her, she might even consider disappearing during the holidays. But that would only put off the confrontation, not deal with it.

Drake filled her waking and sleeping hours; his voice, his scent, his compassion. Stephanie even found herself turning to look for him when she smelled that particular dark honey of his after-shave. She relived the hours she'd spent in his arms and reviewed the tentative commitments he'd tried to make. But when she'd returned to L.A., the reality of that kind of commitment awaited her.

Belinda was getting another divorce. It seemed that the Mexican businessman had been too possessive, so she'd returned to the "palace" she maintained out in Bel Air. Not that she asked Stephanie to wait on her. Belinda had always been slightly dismayed at having a grown daughter to betray her own age. But there was going to be a tribute in a few nights. Of course, Stephanie would be expected to attend and answer the questions she so hated.

Maybe this year they would stop asking after her father, the discomfort of his slide to ruin all to evident in their eyes. "There but for the grace of God go I" had been the theme of too many conversations.

For Stephanie had also returned to the detectives' report on Edward Fleming. Living on the streets, with no outward intention to change. As requested, the attempt would be made without her name being brought into it. It seemed nothing ever changed. It only got worse.

Love brought burdens, and Stephanie already had enough. Surrounded by the consequences of what love meant, steeped in the self-indulgent attitude this city and business had toward it all, she couldn't seem to see her way past.

"You're coming tomorrow," Corey sang without introduction when Stephanie answered the phone. "I've put this little shindig together with just you in mind, so you can't say no."

"Corey..."

"My darling," her aggrieved voice said, "it's the least you can do after I risked life and limb to join you in the arid desert."

"Brutal mountains," Stephanie corrected instinctively.

"*Cultural* desert," Corey amended patiently. "Now that you're back in our bosom, we must celebrate. And bring that delectable mixer of yours. I hear you've nabbed him for another film."

Why not? Stephanie thought. It would serve both of them right.

"What time?" she capitulated.

"I'm doing something radically different. Breakfast. Be there at ten for the time of your life."

Stephanie was back at her desk organizing cues and footage numbers when she got the call from Diane.

"Just tell me the Inn isn't on fire again," she said when she recognized Diane's breathless voice.

It stopped the girl for a moment. "Uh...no. No, it's not. But the fire was arson. The police finally proved it. The insurance company thinks we did it."

Stephanie rubbed at her forehead. "Of course they do. Why wouldn't we set fire to a building while the insurance was in question? How was it done?"

"Some kind of timed acid system. Very intricate and calculated, they said, so that Drake could have set it before he left. Oh, and Stephanie? We got our liquor license back. The man from Denver disappeared."

Stephanie didn't tell her that a liquor license wasn't top on their list of problems at the moment. "Has Nathan Ames been by?"

"Like clockwork. I think he misses you."

"If he gets to be a pest, set the stable hands on him."

That produced a giggle from Diane as she proceeded to update Stephanie on progress. Stephanie hung up thinking of the mountains and that high meadow Drake had taken her to.

Jack escorted Stephanie to the party, dressed in his best Armani jacket and jeans. Stephanie, more used to Corey's extravagant tastes, dressed in a simple blue jumpsuit with a gold paisley scarf thrown over her shoulders. It would be a long day, she knew, already feeling unaccountably tired.

The day became longer then she'd thought. At exactly eleven, Corey had her caterers wheel out a six-foot TV and set it up for the guests' pleasure.

"We're going to watch the races, darlings," she crowed, her eyes on Stephanie.

Stephanie had no idea what she was talking about until the screen came to life and she found herself on the hills of France. Val d'Isère, to be precise, where Drake was skiing. Her eyes wide with apprehension, she turned on her friend. Corey looked like the cat with the proverbial canary.

"It does pay to have a certain status, doesn't it?" Corey sang. "I was able to convince a little man down at that sports network that he'd love to give me their tape of the event that took place just this morning...since I didn't want to get up at five to watch it. We're going to get the chance to watch a simply divine man I met ski down a mountain for...what do they ski for, dear?"

"First place." Stephanie grated at the words. Her stomach churned and her breath caught in her throat as the announcer familiarized the audience with the course, the contestants, and the wonderful story of Drake McDonald, last year's World Cup champ who was on the comeback road from severe injuries that fall.

"Having to forfeit the World Cup in favor of the Olympics," the suavely good-looking ex-skier said against the background of bright spectators and a slash of mountain, "McDonald will appear on the circuit only a few times to test his readiness for the Games. If he is truly recovered from his injuries, his greatest competition will be Chip Markinson. And a fierce competition that's been already."

Stephanie didn't notice Jack supply her with a drink, nor did she realize that she was downing it with measured determination. She didn't want to see this. She didn't want to see Drake compete at all. By immersing herself in her work and her patient gardening, she'd successfully put this weekend's competition out of her mind. Behind her, Corey was providing her own color commentary, but Stephanie didn't hear her, either.

She should leave before he ever set foot on the hill. Close her eyes and walk away. She didn't want to know this much about him. But she couldn't move. Trapped on the couch between Jack and Corey, Stephanie watched with growing fatalism as the first and second skiers sailed down that dangerous, demanding mountain.

Stephanie saw the red suit and stopped breathing. Drake waited up in the gate, crouched, rocking on his haunches in rhythm with the timing beeps, his arms stretched up to his poles. Alongside, a man mouthed the fleeting, swift seconds toward the start. Stephanie saw the fierce concentration behind the dark goggles, the taut hard line of Drake's windburned cheeks. She remembered the times she'd been in the gate, the clutch of fear, of anticipation, the breathtaking view down the savage slopes of the course that was obliterated by the concentration on the finish line.

"He's off!" Corey cried.

"That's a horse," somebody retorted dryly.

Stephanie sat forward, her hands tight around the glass, her eyes on the set.

"Look at him take those turns!" the announcer cried. "He's just this side of losing control, windmilling to regain his balance coming off those bumps. Nobody competes like Drake McDonald. Every one of his runs reminds you of the famous Franz Klammer downhill of the '78 Olympics. I can't watch him without my heart in my mouth."

"Oh, my God!" Jack breathed in true awe. "Look at him!"

Drake was a different skier on a racecourse. Instead of that smooth grace Stephanie had seen in Telluride, he radiated a savage will to win, a breathless ferocity that took him right to the edge. His body fought against space and gravity as he hurtled down the treacherous turns and hills. His speed met and surpassed the ninety-mile-an-hour mark. In trying to keep up with him, the announcer became as breathless as the audience.

The finish line was in sight. Two more turns. One was in the shadows where ice formed, a turn that had already claimed one skier. Stephanie watched with her heart in her throat as Drake sped nearer, his need to win greater than his need for caution. Maybe she'd been wrong. Maybe he was more like her father than she'd thought. He was ferocious on the mountain, a person she didn't know.

It happened in that same corner. Drake never made the turn. At those speeds they could only guess what went wrong, but suddenly he was tumbling, skis arcing free in the air, his body a tangled projectile that slid down the mountain without stopping.

Stephanie didn't realize she'd cried out. She was on her feet, hand to her mouth. She had never heard her glass fall to the floor. Sudden tears stinging her eyes, she watched the screen in horrible fascination. The announcer had nothing to say.

Drake came to a halt within a group of bystanders, the medical crew already on the run. Stephanie watched, but he didn't move. He lay in a jumble in the snow, his suit as red as blood.

"Honey, I'm sorry."

Corey was at Stephanie's side, an arm around her shoulders while Jack made sure the caterers brought in the next delicacy to distract the others. Stephanie would never forgive Corey for exposing her terror to others, and Corey knew it. What she couldn't have known was how very hard Stephanie had fallen for her skier. Corey couldn't remember ever seeing her friend's eyes so stark. And to think she'd arranged this little silliness to amuse her.

On screen they brought out a stretcher and took Drake away as everyone waited. The next racer took his turn and the next. Chip came in third in the final tally behind a Swiss and a French skier. Drake's time would have put him well ahead of them all.

Finally the word came that he was all right. He'd suffered a concussion and a dislocated shoulder. He was lucky, considering the frightening speeds he'd been doing when he took that tumble. The guests in Corey's white and peach room sighed with relief and went back to entertaining themselves. The screen grew dark, and Stephanie, the shock of that moment still lodged implacably in her heart, asked to go home.

Four days later she sat in a darkened sound stage, coaching the capricious Fawn Deering on volume control and emoting.

"I thought that was just fine," the young woman bubbled, flouncing her long ebony hair behind her.

Well, Stephanie decided, asking for the next track, at least she didn't perpetuate the myth about dumb blondes. But the brunettes of the world were certainly going to be in trouble.

"One more time," she suggested softly, tapping her pencil lazily against her notes, pressing the earphone against her ear. "Just so I have something to choose from." She cast a quick look at what she'd written, as if she didn't know it by heart. "I think Franklin wanted to try just a little more force at this point. After all, your lover has just shown up with another woman."

Franklin had said no such thing. Just make the bloody thing audible was all he'd told her. He knew enough to leave the rest to her.

"You mean . . . shout?" the girl asked.

Stephanie smiled encouragement. "Try it. Let's see how it sounds. And don't forget to take a breath after that third beep. Jack?"

Seated in the safety of the soundproof mixing room, Jack finished punching up the cue. "Ready on channel three, take forty-seven." From his spot behind the board, he could just make out Stephanie's weary smile in the soft light from her desk. Dead center, Fawn held up her own earphone and turned to study the film that was beginning to replay, the same clip for the forty-seventh, and he was sure not the last time.

"Jack?"

The clip had barely ended. "The last couple of words were a little hot, Stephanie. I'm sorry."

"That wasn't my fault!" Fawn protested.

"No, Fawn, it wasn't," Stephanie assured her. "It was Jack's. I'll beat him later. Let's go again."

"Is that a print on 36?" Jack's disembodied voice floated over the darkened sound stage sometime later. Only the small light at Stephanie's desk and the music stand that held Fawn's script illuminated the room beyond Jack's window. For the first time in her career Stephanie considered just drifting off to sleep. After four more hours, she'd only made it another page down her schedule.

"It's a print. Channel 3, take 42. We'll review the film first thing in the morning." Gratefully getting to her feet, she signaled the end of the day.

"Praise the Lord," Jack sighed where they couldn't hear him.

The lights came up, revealing the scattered furniture, the microphone that hung before a now frazzled Fawn, the screen that covered a wall, the digital display for cues and the lights that blinked from blue to red to green for the different functions of rehearsing, taping and replaying.

"Thank you, Fawn," Stephanie said smiling. "You've been really patient. See you tomorrow?"

Walking over to Stephanie with arms outstretched, the young woman bestowed a rare smile of genuine warmth. "Sure."

Then it was Jack's turn to leave.

"You're not going to stay again, are you?" he demanded, massaging Stephanie's shoulders.

"I'm just going to clear up a few things." She was going to keep busy as she had for the last four days. In that time she hadn't slept a full night or managed a full meal. She hadn't worked up the nerve to call Drake, either.

"Listen, I've been by the garden, and I can tell you're neglecting it," he protested. "Your rocks are dying."

"Water them for me, will you?"

"You know I have a black thumb."

He finally left, closing Stephanie into the room with the screen, the computer and the silence. She carried the tape onto which they'd collected all the cues they'd printed back in her cutting room where she would see that it matched against the film. Then she'd go home and try to sleep.

Stephanie was just about to slip on her earphones when she heard the door to the cutting room open behind her.

"No, Jack," she said without looking up. "I am not going to change my mind."

"I wouldn't want you to."

Stephanie whipped around at the sound of that voice—at the sudden hint of soft night in the air. It wasn't Jack in the doorway. It was Drake. Clad in an open-necked shirt and jeans, he stood before her, his right arm bound to his side and in a sling, and a white bandage covered one-fourth of his forehead.

Stephanie stood, unable to feel anything. "How did you get here?"

"Right behind Corey." He grinned sheepishly. "She doesn't take no for an answer."

Drake could hardly bear the sight of her. He'd thought so much about her while they'd been apart, resurrecting the precious gilt of her hair, her classic beauty, her grace, the throaty music of her voice. But the memories couldn't compare with reality.

Where just about every other technician he'd met was clad in jeans, Stephanie wore a simple jersey dress, the skirt swirling gently against her elegant legs. She looked comfortable and dignified at the same time, the apple-green material swelling deliciously over her breasts and baring her throat. She stood, poised like a dancer and watching him with a turbulent expression in her eyes.

"Corey said that you wouldn't be home for a while. That you'd been working pretty hard on this movie." Drake took a moment to look around at the room that was packed with reels of film and sound tape, the desk, and the corkboard with schedule notes. "So, this is where you work."

Stephanie couldn't take her eyes from him. He was so nonchalant when the last time she'd seen him they'd been carrying him unconscious from the snow. God, how could he do this to her? The pain rekindled, the terror, the certainty. Stephanie had known she was in love with him when she'd seen him tumble off that mountain, because she couldn't possibly hurt that much for someone she didn't love. And now here he was, as if he'd just returned from across the street.

"Are you...all right?" Never in her life had she stammered.

Drake took a step toward her. Stephanie backed away in an odd dance. "I'm fine," he assured her. "I've dislocated my shoulder before. I'm probably going to get it fixed for good after the Olympics is all over, but it would lay me up too long right now."

"After the Olympics?" Even Stephanie couldn't keep the outrage from her voice.

"Sure. I have plenty of time." Drake followed her eyes to the arm that lay imprisoned against him. "Oh, this. I usually take it off after a week. It's more a reminder than anything, really. The shoulder doesn't hurt at all once they pop it back in."

Now Stephanie took a step forward. "But Drake, you can't possibly—"

"Compete?" he asked. "Yes, I can, Stephanie. Nothing is going to keep me from those games." She hardly recognized his voice, it was suddenly so harsh. "Nothing."

The memories stirred, sharpened. Stephanie's features clouded over and she turned her face away, afraid Drake would see the tears that threatened.

"Are you going to show me your job?" Drake asked, trying to make amends.

She shook her head. "Not tonight, I think. I'm a little...tired. I think I'm going to close up."

He nodded.

"Can I drop you by your hotel?"

His wry grin was followed by a shrug. "You could if I had one. I came straight from the airport."

Stephanie stopped, her eyes widening. "Well...why don't we call from the house? I'm sure I can find you something."

She didn't see the small glint of triumph that crept into Drake's eyes. "That would be fine."

Stephanie led them out past a guard she said had bounced her on his knee when she was a baby, and to the parking lot where her hunter-green XJS sat between a Porsche and a Volkswagen.

Drake saw the license plate and laughed. "XSF? The lady has a sense of humor."

"Keeps me humble," she assured him as she unlocked doors and slid into her leather seat. "How do you like MGM?"

"But it isn't...."

Stephanie shook her head. "I don't care who owns it now. Even if he decided to call it Burger King, to me it will always been MGM. I grew up here."

Drake waited to answer until Stephanie had started the engine. The powerful purr under the hood made him itch for the stick.

"I had to see this car with my arm in a sling," he groused.

Stephanie grinned, her aviator sunglasses hiding her eyes. The sun was setting across Washington, tinting a shell-pink the whitewashed walls that kept the studios separate from the street.

Drake took one more look around as they reached the gate and waited for the traffic. "It's smaller than I thought."

"It's smaller than it used to be. Kind of a facade of its own now," Stephanie answered, her eyes on the rush hour traffic that whizzed by. "When I was a kid, it was immense. There were whole towns in here I could get lost in. It used to drive Belinda and the nanny crazy. They'd be screaming after me, and I'd show up on horseback with one of the stuntmen. But now..." She shrugged; the changes in the movie industry were sometimes painful to her. She harbored a lot of sweet memories among that make-believe. "They sold off the back lot and most of this one. It's nothing but subdivision anymore. More of the technical work's being done in the valley, anyway."

"Where do you live?" Drake asked, savoring the rich comfort of the car and the richer seduction of Stephanie's proximity. God was in his heaven and all was right with the world.

"Up in the hills," she said. "Hollywood proper."

Caught in all the street traffic, the Jaguar never got a chance to shine. It was still the most painless way to face rush hour, though. Weaving her way in and out with the dexterity of long practice, Stephanie shot up to Sunset and over to Highland, climbing toward the hills that were home.

By the time they turned the last corner on the tight little streets, Drake could make out the buildings of Hollywood spread out below them in the dying light. The sun had disappeared behind a band of clouds somewhere over the ocean to the west. The street was quiet, steep and well cared-for. Flowers tumbled over retaining walls, their scents cloying in the early evening air, and trees shaded with their own blossoms. Faced with all the foliage, Drake had to remind himself that it was December. No wonder people couldn't deal with reality here. Neither, it seemed, could nature.

Stephanie led him to a white Spanish-style stucco house with red tile roof that perched on the side of the hill. The other houses on the street, stately and well-groomed, were built in the same style. Drake had always thought of Hollywood as a seedy remnant of bygone glory. Evidently no one had told the people who lived in this neighborhood. There were three stretch limos tucked alongside the curb.

Unlocking the grille to the yard, Stephanie walked on through. Drake cast an appraising eye on what was obviously the front door and followed away from it.

Stephanie led him down a set of steps down to a lower level where an awesome view of the city appeared below them. The house seemed to go on forever, various levels were layered down the hill like a terraced garden. Drake noticed that all the houses in the hills clung to the earth in the same precarious manner as Stephanie's. For all the size of the city that lay below them, it was curiously quiet up here.

"This is minimalism," he demanded, coming upon a plot of ground that was riotous with wildflowers, some tall, some peeping out beneath other foliage. The scent was indeed like Stephanie's.

She smiled. "No. That's around the corner. This is my English garden. I like contrasts."

"Obviously."

Drake was in for another surprise when he entered the house. This level was one long sun-room, the apparently endless windows supported by sturdy columns and folding into cubist geometrics as they followed the floor plan of the building above.

The rooms went on and on, stepping gradually down the hill, all filled with spring flowers and light wood furniture, the colors white, apple green and pale pink. The rooms were in quaint disarray, plants sharing space with books and stuffed pillows that were perched on couch and table alike. The effect was charming and bright—another side of Stephanie that Drake hadn't anticipated.

"Sit down," she offered, heading for the kitchen area. "I'll get something to drink."

Drake walked to the window to see the clouds scurry up from the coast as Stephanie tapped her answering machine.

His attention was immediately drawn to the breathy voice that filled the room.

"I do so detest this thing, Stephanie dear." Belinda Carson. No question. Her voice still provoked pleasant shivers. "I'm just calling you to remind you about tonight. I know you won't let me down. It's the biggest night of my life. See you at nine."

Stephanie groaned. All the effort she'd gone through to forget had evidently worked. She'd completely forgotten her mother's benefit.

"Stephanie."

She turned at the quizzical note in Drake's voice.

"I thought you'd like to know. There's a man out here watering rocks."

Stephanie couldn't help but laugh. Drake didn't sound terribly surprised. It was probably no more than he expected from L.A. Joining him at the window, she found Jack bent over the stark simplicity of her back lawn. The few plants and rocks it held were carefully placed and the little gravel walks raked into designs—a passion she'd acquired from one of Belinda's gardeners, a Mr. Yamamoto.

Tapping on the window, she succeeded in getting Jack's attention. He waved the can at her with a smile and she waved him inside.

"Do you know him?" Drake asked.

Stephanie handed Drake a Scotch, straight up. "His name's Jack Randolph. He works with me."

"Oh."

"He also lives upstairs."

Drake took a long drink. "You live in his house?"

She smiled. "He lives in mine. I rent the top floor to him."

"Of course."

Jack walked in without knocking to see Drake dispatching the rest of his drink in a gulp.

"Hey, Corey's racer!" He grinned brightly, causing Drake to almost choke.

"Not really," Stephanie obliged, enjoying herself immensely.

"Nice to meet you," Jack went on unheeding. "I watched you ski…well, till you danced down that mountain on your face, anyway."

Drake took the man's proffered hand with admirable restraint. "You work with Stephanie?"

If there was an answer to that, Jack wasn't immediately forthcoming with it. Bending to give Stephanie a resounding kiss, he motioned to her yard.

"You ask; I do. One problem. Tonight's out, I'm afraid. Will you survive?"

Sensitive to the new thunder that was brewing in Drake's eyes, Stephanie gave Jack a pat on the arm. "I imagine. What came up?"

Jack's smile was piratical. "Corey."

She gave him a dry grin. "Congratulations. Where do I get a date so that Belinda won't start badgering me again?"

It took Jack a minute to consider. "What about him?" he asked, raising an eyebrow toward Drake. "He'd probably at least fit into my tux, which I'm sure I won't need."

Stephanie turned innocent eyes in Drake's direction. "What had you planned for tonight?"

Drake shrugged, beset by the odd feeling that he'd just stumbled into a hurricane of some kind. "Finding a hotel room."

"Stay with us," Jack offered with an offhand wave. "That way you two kids don't have to be home early."

The humor of the situation glinting brightly in Stephanie's eyes as she faced Drake. "Well?"

He shrugged again, suddenly wishing he had more Scotch. "How can I turn down an offer like that?"

## Chapter 11

Belinda's tribute was held at the Beverly Wilshire Hotel. Promptly at eight-thirty, Drake and Stephanie were picked up in a stretch limo and transported into town. Drake had managed to fit into Jack's tux after all, the sling and bandage forming a dramatic counterpoint. Stephanie wore a stunning strapless black taffeta and velvet dress with a full skirt that whispered as she walked. Diamonds glistened at her throat and ears, and she wore her hair full and long, framing her face with drama. Drake couldn't keep his eyes off her.

He'd been to quite a few ritzy parties in his time, between knowing Jacques and fund-raising for the team. The crowd that turned out for this affair, though, redefined the word legendary. The room swam in champagne and drew light from the jewels that crowded a hundred throats. It was a long way from Mount Hood.

Although he was sure he should have known better, Drake was still amazed that these people greeted Stephanie like one of the family, with a hug, a kiss on the cheek and a "Doesn't Belinda look wonderful, dear?" from each of them. Stephanie glided through the crowd like a politician's wife, perfectly at ease in the rarefied atmosphere. Come to think of it, he thought, she outshone any female in the room.

When Drake was introduced, most of the guests recognized him, the Hollywood crowd being big on skiing. He answered questions about the racing season, his own prospects and the accident that many of them had by now seen. He followed Stephanie through the crowd, he watched, listened and smiled appropriately when called for. They'd made it almost to the far side when, for the third time, someone greeted Stephanie with the word, "Anything?" and a frown. She just shook her head, at which point the other would shake theirs. The attitude bore a striking resemblance to someone discussing a friend with a terminal illness or a tragedy. The frown, the downcast eyes, the uncomfortable pause. Drake waited for Stephanie to explain, but she never did.

"Ah." Stephanie smiled, a champagne glass in hand as they broke through the press of bodies. "The holy of holies."

Drake turned at her tongue-in-cheek observation to discover a receiving line by the windows, where several huge sprays of exotic flowers served as backdrop for the guest of honor.

Standing before them like a rare peacock, Belinda Carson greeted her friends and fans like a queen accepting homage. Her pink satin gown flattered her blond features, and her jewels sparkled with just enough ostentation. Even with a few wrinkles that had escaped plastic surgery, she still stunned. Drake took a moment to live out a childhood dream and then took Stephanie's arm to approach her mother.

To Drake's surprise, instead of joining Belinda, Stephanie stepped to the end of the line just like all the others. He didn't know quite how to react. The aging TV queen who stood before them was sharing Belinda stories with Stephanie while her husband commiserated with Drake on his injury. Around them the crowd murmured and waiters circulated, and Stephanie waited like a fan to say hello to her own mother.

"Oh, there you are, dear." Belinda smiled, the expression on her face no different than for the last three people she'd greeted. "I was so afraid you'd forgotten me."

Stephanie bent forward to kiss the proffered cheek. "You're surviving the divorce nicely, I see."

Belinda rolled her eyes. "It's such a wasteland down there. I don't know what I ever saw in Mexico in the first place."

Stephanie smiled with genuine warmth. "Solitude, if I remember correctly."

Belinda returned the smile, one girl to another as she leaned close for a confidence. "It's nothing to settle for, darling. Believe me. Are you going to introduce me to your dashing friend?"

"Belinda, this is Drake McDonald," Stephanie announced, surprised at the bemused expression in Drake's eyes. He nevertheless took Belinda's hand in his left and bent to kiss it, earning the star's pleasure.

Drake walked away from that line feeling he'd gotten a true measure of Stephanie's childhood. She'd never had either family or a mother to scold and cosset and worry after her. Her mother had been a child, unable to focus her attention on anything beyond herself. Her child must have been just another adoring subject to dress up and take out and hand over to a nanny. Who had, after all, been devoted to Stephanie?

Drake's mother had been older, and not often completely well. But he could remember the security of coming home each day to her soft hug, and the fierce scolding she'd give him when he'd followed his friend Jimmy over to the construction site to play. Had anyone worried about Stephanie?

"You're awfully quiet," Stephanie said a moment later as the two of them stood alone at the side of the room. They would be sitting soon to watch the movie clips and have a series of famous faces gush about the chance to work with Belinda Carson.

Drake shrugged in the direction of the flowers where Belinda's breathy little giggle could be heard rising above the crowd noise. "Quite a mother, your old lady."

Stephanie chuckled. "Don't ever say those two words in Belinda's presence if you want to save your skin," she advised, sipping at the sparkling liquid in her glass.

"Why don't you call her mother?"

Stephanie looked up, surprised at the protective tone of his voice. It was a new experience for her. It also ignited a sweet pleasure she'd never known. "Belinda?" She shrugged. "I don't know. It never seemed appropriate."

Drake scowled into his drink. "Well, that's probably the most honest thing I've heard tonight."

Before Drake could get a chance to question Stephanie further, one of the pop musicians Belinda had befriended had to tell her how grateful he was for the great lady's patronage. Wasn't she just a dear? She just was, Stephanie agreed, smiling back without agitation. It was about all Drake could stand.

"How many people in this room know she's your mother?"

Stephanie hesitated. "Just about everyone, I'd say. Why?"

"Why won't *she* admit it?"

That feeling of specialness grew in Stephanie with his words. Drake was actually angry for her. Angry at Belinda. In all her life that had never happened before.

"Don't be too hard on her," Stephanie begged, a hand on his arm. "It isn't her fault she's who she is. I told you. It wasn't all that bad."

Drake's eyes trapped her, surrounding her with their protection. He would be there for her, they said, no matter what. Stephanie stopped, her hand frozen where it lay, her heart quickening. Don't promise too much, my Galahad, she thought with desperate urgency as the sounds of the crowd filtered through to them. You can't know now what promises you'll be able to keep.

"Time to eat, kids," the MC announced as he slid up to them, his hand snaking across Stephanie's waist and edging toward the soft fullness of skirt that hid her bottom. Slipping away with deft grace, Stephanie smiled over at the world-famous actor and nodded. His eyes had an unholy light, one she was used to. His hand tried a return journey that she could have just as easily avoided. This time, though, Drake was there.

Moving with that cat's grace that made him such a great skier, Drake grabbed the offending arm in his left hand and squeezed. The man all but howled, his eyes popping in indignation and pain.

"Just who the hell are you?" the star demanded, the next breath undoubtedly ready to carry the word "lawyer" on it.

"Her fiancé," Drake said with a cold smile.

"You'll never work in this town again!" The actor's voice grated in rage and his skin was crimson all the way to his artfully disguised toupee.

"One more sleazy move like that," Drake challenged him, letting the man's hand go, "and you'll never walk in *any* town again."

"My fiancé?" Stephanie asked after the man had taken himself to the head table. Stephanie and Drake would be seated about halfway back in the room. Her eyes betrayed amusement at Drake's reaction.

"Seemed a good way to make a point."

Stephanie nodded, the laughter growing. The actor—the same man who sold insurance to pensioners and billeted a succession of young mistresses at the Bel Air Hotel—had taken the dais, slipping immediately into the character of the warm, loving family man.

"Aren't you worried?" she asked Drake.

"About what?"

She giggled now, a soft, earthy sound that snaked along Drake's skin. "Why, you'll never work in this town again. You heard the man."

Drake rolled his eyes. "Thank God for small favors."

Stephanie's delighted laughter turned heads.

"You don't think much of my life, do you?"

Stephanie sat alongside Drake on her terrace, the city below them blanketed in gems, the night sky shrouded. The limo had dropped them off an hour ago, leaving them to wander into the night with their drinks in hand. Seated at the edge of her precisely laid-out garden, Stephanie was a faint specter in midnight and moonlight, her necklace glittered like stars at her throat.

Looking over the quietly asked question, Drake shook his head. "It's not that," he argued. "Maybe I was just a little overwhelmed tonight."

"It is a bit much to get used to all at once," she allowed with a wry smile. "But then, so is your friend Chip."

Drake scowled. "Don't drop that burden in my lap. I had enough to deal with the last few days when he didn't win. The fact that I was laid up in a hospital seemed to cheer him somewhat, though."

"Don't." Stephanie's voice was harsh as the picture of the moment when she'd seen him fall relentlessly resurrected itself. "Will they really let you race?"

"Of course. Why shouldn't they?"

The dry reproach in her expression should have been answer enough. "How can you possibly concentrate on what you're doing on that course with everything that's going on?"

Drake shrugged. "A problem, I admit. But I can't just walk away because I'm afraid of falling. If I did, I never would have stepped on the hill in the first place."

Stephanie looked out over the city, her expression introspective and dark. After a moment, she could do no more than shake her head. "The way you race..." she whispered, as much of a plea as a statement.

"Edge of the world," Drake conceded. When Stephanie looked over in surprise, he elaborated. "That's where I ski. Right at the edge of the world. It's the only way you can play it when you stand at the top of a downhill course and look straight down into the shadows." He smiled at her puzzlement. "When I was first racing, I used to play a game. Maybe I'd just ski right off. Come off one of those hills and sail right off into space. Of course, the times I've come closest I usually end up looking like this," he admitted, indicating the swathe. His wry humor finally found its way to Stephanie, igniting a reluctant smile.

"And when you have to step back from the edge?" she asked quietly.

Drake leaned forward, resting his drink on his thigh, his eyes first focused on its dark liquid, then looking up to Stephanie. "When you first met me I would have said that I didn't know. That I'd do my best, I guess, and make do with what was left me. Since then, I've begun to discover that there's more than one way to walk the edge."

His words had quietly stolen Stephanie's breath. She got to her feet, afraid of the commitment in his eyes, of the admission she'd invited.

"Do you want to know why I didn't call after you'd been hurt?"

"I know why you haven't called. I understand."

Stephanie turned back to him, surprised. She was greeted by a smile so sweet that it set up a trembling in her. Fear took over.

"Why are you so all-fired understanding?" she demanded.

Drake got to his feet and approached, his gait easy. "Because you deserve it," he said, lifting gentle fingers to her cheek. "I'm going to understand you to death, if I have to, lady. I'm falling in love with you."

Stephanie straightened as if he'd slapped her, her eyes stricken, her posture rigid. "Please, don't...."

"Well, hello young lovers!"

The two of them whirled to find Corey draped over the upstairs balcony, a long chiffon scarf drifting from her hand like Rapunzel signaling for help. Stephanie's first reaction was to snap at her, until she realized that Corey could have had no way of knowing what had transpired beneath her bright gaze.

"I see you've found her!" the blonde giggled delightedly. "He absolutely beat down my door, darling!"

"You called *me*, Corey," Drake reminded her dryly.

"Don't spoil the romance, Drake my love, or I won't tell you how devastating you look in your tux. Doesn't he, Stephanie?"

Stephanie turned brittle eyes on her friend, unable to answer.

"Stephanie?"

"Yes!"

"Well, good. Well, my darlings, I'm off. Have a lovely time. And Drake?"

"Yes, Corey."

"Don't forget Stephanie's virtue."

"Her virtue?" he countered. "What about it?"

"It needs some serious ruin, darling. Do what you can."

Before either of them could so much as protest, Corey was gone. There was nothing left but to consider the incapacitated state of Drake's arm in the light of Corey's appeal. The idea broke the tension and set the two of them laughing.

"Do you want the couch or the bed?" Stephanie asked Drake.

"The couch," he conceded, wrapping an arm around her shoulder and leading her back into her glass house. "If you'll help me get this shirt off, that is."

Drake went to see his orthopedists while he was in town and began physical therapy to strengthen his shoulder. He walked along the steep streets of the Hollywood Hills and borrowed Jack's bike to ride, having learned the precarious talent of one-armed balance the first time he'd dislocated his shoulder. He even sat in on some of Stephanie's sessions until she told him he was distracting Fawn from her work. In the evening when Stephanie got home, the two of them would sit in the quiet house and talk or read, all the time observing a tense kind of truce.

He slept on a foldout bed in Jack's den, a room almost as big as Stephanie's living and dining room, and wondered just why it was that Jack inhabited the vast majority of the house that Stephanie owned. When he saw the four Oscars that sat on the bookshelves bracketing the great stucco fireplace, he began to understand.

The revelation did little for his frustration. He'd come to L.A. to get acquainted with Stephanie on her own turf and was now plagued by the feeling that he understood less and less as the days went on.

It took two days for Drake to become impatient, another three for him to start snapping at people. He was itching to get back on the slopes, to get away from the heavy pall of smog that blotted out the sun and turned the sky to nondescript gray on most days. And the longer he stayed around Stephanie the more desperately he wanted to have it out with her.

She was holding him at arm's length, dealing with their relationship by not dealing with it at all. The closest Drake could get to her was a Hollywood-like peck on the cheek. His patience never a strong suit, was wearing fast.

Drake woke on Sunday morning to find that Stephanie hadn't come home from work yet. Evidently that wasn't unusual when she was on a tight schedule. The fact that Jack hadn't made it home either shouldn't have bothered Drake but it did. That was when he knew that the situation had reached an impasse.

Drake was sitting on the terrace, gloomily considering the city below as he slowly worked his arm through its range of motions. He could actually taste the metallic poison of the pollution. Tomorrow would be the last appointment with the orthopedist, so he'd be technically free after that to return to skiing. The reopening of the Inn would take place in another week, and Christmas was three days after that. Instead of looking forward to it, he walked around with a vague sense of dread.

"There you are."

Drake turned to see Stephanie appear around the corner of the yard, her gait slow, her hair just that much mussed from lifting and resetting her glasses and earphones over the long night.

"Hi." He smiled though he didn't feel like it. "Did Fawn finally finish?"

"Fawn finished," she said. "We finished, and it's time for the next contestant to sign in." A healthy yawn escaped. "But not until tomorrow."

Slipping his arm back into the sling, Drake got to his feet.

"How's your arm?" Stephanie asked, leaning over to sip at his coffee.

"Smashing. The air stinks around here."

She arched her eyebrows. "It's not that bad. Besides, it usually clears up a little...." Stephanie stopped for a moment, turning toward the gray soup that hovered at the edge of her yard. "Yes—" she nodded slowly "—you're right. It does stink."

"I don't know how you stand it."

Stephanie didn't think Drake would want to hear that she'd never really considered it before—just as she'd never considered having a different kind of mother. It was just the way things were. Her mother was Belinda Carson, and the air over Los Angeles usually smelled of car exhaust. Why should that suddenly bother her?

"Would you like an afternoon of sunshine?" she asked, suddenly turning to him.

"Isn't that what you call this?"

She smiled. "Above the pollution."

Drake considered her skeptically. "You fly?"

But Stephanie would have none of it. "You go in and empty out the fridge. I'll get Jack."

"He's coming?" The distaste had slipped into Drake's voice quite by accident.

"Not likely. He has another date with Corey. I'm going to offer him the Jag."

Stephanie was halfway up to Jack's door before Drake, a fresh scowl on his face, thought to answer. "You haven't let *me* drive it!"

Stephanie wasn't just lending Jack the Jag. She was trading it for his four-wheel-drive truck. He'd never used it as a four-wheel-drive vehicle, of course. Jack had never found a great interest in the wilderness, but the vehicle looked so good. Stephanie didn't exactly tell him the truth about where she was taking it, so he let her have the keys with great glee.

"Mulholland?" Drake asked a while later as they turned off Beverly Glen Boulevard onto the famous stretch of road. Best view, best driving, most lethal except for freeways.

"It also turns into a four-wheel-drive road over the mountains," Stephanie informed him.

"You're supposed to be asleep," Drake retorted. "Why are you playing range rider?"

She considered that for a minute as she sped around a corner and up the next hill. Then she shrugged. "I need to get away. This is away."

Drake couldn't think of an answer for that.

The idea that Colorado's sky could be found over Los Angeles was too much for Drake to find credible. But they had no more than crossed over onto the dirt track that Mulholland Drive became than the hills climbed above the basin and its wreath of fog. The sky, that sharp cerulean that lured flyers and painters, soared straight up beyond the brilliant sun. Each time Stephanie turned, though, Los Angeles would reappear to their right, a congealed soup of smog and civilization to remind them that he wasn't so far away, after all.

Even so, Stephanie found a little spot that looked on the cleaner area to the northwest, where the hills stepped away in crisp succession toward the ocean. Spreading out a blanket among the scrub just out of sight of the road, they unpacked their food and opened a bottle of red wine. The wind swept up the hills, its bite no more than pleasantly chilly, the sun warm and fresh on their faces.

"Do you come up here often?" Drake asked, stretched out on the blanket, his good arm beneath his head and his wineglass in the other hand.

Stephanie paused from nibbling the fresh grapes she kept plucking from their stems. "This is one of the best benefits of living here. Year-round freshness. I can also drive down to the farmer's market on any given day and pick up fruit and vegetables. No frozen foods for me, thanks."

"The land of milk and honey," Drake commented dryly.

"When it's good out here," Stephanie answered, her eyes on a hawk that was slowly circling the sun, "there's nothing better."

"And when it's bad?"

She shrugged, wondering how different her life would have been if her parents had been successful in any other industry. Not much, she felt. "There aren't any Utopias, Drake. People have searched for them without luck as long as they've walked the earth."

"What's wrong with Colorado?"

Stephanie couldn't help but smile. "Have you ever flown into Denver? It's just as polluted as Los Angeles. L.A. has fresh fruit and the ocean, and Colorado has the Rockies and wildlife. Different tastes, that's all."

"Could you live without what you have here?"

She turned to see that his wineglass rested undisturbed on his chest while his eyes considered her calmly. The wind lifted his hair back from his forehead and set it to a slow dance that seduced her. His expression held a strength and sureness that silently spoke to her. Her own strength, Stephanie thought, had been manufactured as a protection for the soft places in her that could be hurt. Drake's had been inbred from the safe childhood that had crafted his personality. He could share that with her, bestowing his peace like a balm on the raw nerves that still troubled her.

At what cost to her? she wondered, her heart skipping faster at the soft invitation in his eyes. Would his intrusion into her life shatter her facade? Would he chip away her protection only to find that there was nothing to her after all? This was an afternoon for gentle conversation, not great revelations. But Stephanie had the unsettling feeling that she had set herself up for the latter.

"My concept of myself is here," she admitted at last. "What I do, the people I know. The industry that respects my work. I don't know that I have anything to replace that with."

"Being a partner in the Inn just isn't the same?"

Stephanie saw the humor in Drake's expression and was grateful. "No. It would be like my offering you a job in films to compensate for your losing your chance to race."

"Would you consider doing both?"

That forced her eyes away from him. She sought the hawk, still hovering far above the earth, silent in his effortless grace. Too much peace for the turmoil in her soul. In the end, fear answered with a quiet voice.

"I don't know."

"Stephanie."

She turned to him, the very sun on his face scattering pain through her. He was so vital and bright, like a harsh wind on a high mountain breathing life back into an flagging spirit. Stephanie yearned so fiercely for that life that it terrified her.

Drake sat up and faced her, reaching out his hand to the titian swirls of hair sweeping over her shoulder, his gaze giving her no rest. "I can't stay in Los Angeles much longer," he said, his eyes reflecting the weight of his words. "But I want you to know that I'm not letting you go. I'll come back and come back again if I have to. Before the Olympics, after the Olympics, as long as it takes. I love you."

Stephanie stiffened, wanting to protest. She didn't want his love, she wanted to say. She wanted her solitude, her isolation from the jealousies and quarrels of the human race. But how could she have known how addictive the savage exhilaration he awoke in her would become?

"Whatever else happens," Drake said, "I'll expect you at my house for Christmas."

"But the film—" she protested instinctively.

"I don't give a damn about the film. You'll be there. I'm going to be busy after that, so I want us to have a couple of uninterrupted days together to talk."

"We're talking now," Stephanie retorted, her voice even softer, dying against his attack.

Drake shook his head. "No, today we'll just have a picnic. We'll eat a little and you'll sleep out in the sun where it'll do you some good, and then we'll go back to the house.

We both have some thinking to do, and the time until Christmas will be the time for it. Okay?''

What did he want her to say? Okay, fine, she'd think it over and have a decision in ten days? Maybe Drake McDonald could put some sense in his life in that amount of time, but she doubted sincerely that she could. He asked the impossible, and Stephanie couldn't bring herself to tell him so.

"Fine." She nodded, wanting no more than to finish the discussion. "Christmas."

Knowing exactly what Stephanie had in mind, Drake smiled with satisfaction nonetheless and bent forward to kiss her. The lips he met were at first unyielding, their taste hesitant. He refused to be rebuffed. Curling gentle fingers into her hair, he pulled her closer and let his lips melt her resistance. As the hawk's cry finally drifted toward them on the wind, Stephanie lifted her hand to Drake's face and submitted.

The next day Stephanie returned home from work to find that Drake wasn't there. The note he left merely said that he had to leave sooner than planned but that he'd be seeing her. There was no mention of what they'd talked about, or the revelation he'd made. Stephanie looked blindly out over her city, the paper crumpled in her hand, and wondered just what Christmas would mean.

## Chapter 12

December twenty-third found Stephanie in her cutting room matching the sound track to film. She'd spent the weekend at the Inn, satisfying herself that Diane did, in fact, have everything well in hand, then returned to a rainy, cold city and a half-finished work load.

She hadn't heard from Drake, which was just as well. Stephanie still wasn't sure she was going to keep their date the morning after next.

It wasn't that she didn't want to spend Christmas with him. She did. And that was what frightened her. The only person Stephanie had ever felt safe with at such a sentimental time had been Jacques. He had never demanded more of her than she could give. Even Belinda insisted on overdoing the occasion, lavishing gifts and affection in indiscriminate proportions, then topping it off with an intimate dinner for fifty on Christmas night to show off her largesse and decorating taste.

Stephanie had successfully avoided those fetes until three years ago, when she finally gave in to Belinda's manipulation, only to spend the day cringing. This year she had planned to spend Christmas in the quiet of her own house, reading and feasting on the turkey and chestnut dressing she'd decided to prepare. She'd planned her Christmas for quiet recollection and suddenly found herself anticipating emotional upheaval.

Would Drake hope for too much from her on the occasion? Would he want the Christmas spirit, expecting to find her eyes to light up as if she were in a camera commercial while she unwrapped presents in her robe and stirred gravy in the kitchen? Making commitments and drowning in good fellowship and warmth? The idea sent her stomach plummeting.

But Stephanie couldn't quite dispel the picture of the two of them seated companionably before a fire, glasses of wine in hand, the sound of his blues filling the soft night, reaffirming the special closeness of the season.

She'd even bought him a present, a beautiful antique hutch that would hold his trophies so that he could bring them home. She'd found it over the weekend and stashed it at the Inn until she could give it to him. Now she wasn't even sure she had the nerve to show up.

"Excuse me, Ms. Fleming?"

Startled from her thoughts, Stephanie straightened at the sound of the voice. A young woman had edged through the door from the hallway, her stance aggressive, her smile assured and assessing.

"Please come in," Stephanie invited her, motioning to a chair. "Paula Evers, aren't you?"

She got a surprised nod from the woman. "Franklin said I might talk to you. Would you be interested in doing a little film cutting?"

Stephanie eased back in her chair, stretching the kinks she'd accumulated from hunching over her machine. "He must have told you that I'm committed for a couple of weeks."

Paula edged onto the other chair like a bird perched on a high wire in a breeze. "It's after that. Middle of February, to be exact. I'm looking for someone who might like to do a few weeks of location work for me, and he said that when you're not dialogue editing, you're just about the best cutter around."

Stephanie smiled. "Franklin does enjoy his moments of excess."

"The thing is, I'm doing a documentary on figure skating in America. The editor I've been working with just came down with hepatitis, so I'm short on options. Would you be interested in spending a couple of weeks at the Olympics?"

For a moment Stephanie could do no more than stare. It occurred to her that someone might have thought this a bad joke, but Paula Evers wasn't the kind of person who knew what a joke was. A bright and upcoming director, she attacked her art like a holy war. She would never waste her time on a frivolous mission.

"Would I have enough time to see a couple of the Alpine events?"

Stephanie couldn't believe she'd said it. She'd told Drake "No" straight out when he'd invited her. She couldn't imagine why she didn't do the same for Paula. But here she was clasping her hands in her lap like a schoolgirl waiting to be told if she were elected prom queen, the sudden ambivalence sharp in her chest.

"Sure, I don't mind. Set your own schedule, just as long as I can get dailies to go over."

It was decided as quickly as that. Paula left and Stephanie tried to go back to her moviola without much success. Her spur-of-the-moment decision sat like lye in her chest, eating at her patience and concentration.

What had made her do that? Stephanie wasn't even sure she was going to see Drake at Christmas. The idea was still too fraught with the idea of commitment. Why would she so quickly decide to follow him to the Olympics where all his dreams would be on the line?

Because his dreams had become important to her.

The realization had Stephanie back on her feet. She'd have to go find Paula and tell her that the Olympics were off. She had another commitment she'd forgotten, or a sick relative or something. Busy setting down her things, Stephanie didn't hear the door open behind her.

She'd almost made it halfway across the small room before she turned fully to find the door she was heading toward already blocked. She stopped. Lost her voice, her breath. Drake stood before her.

"Hello would be nice," he said at last, grinning at her open-mouthed astonishment.

She shut her mouth. "Hello."

Closing the door behind him, Drake strolled over to her, his hands stuffed in his jeans pockets. He had on a T-shirt and wheat-colored oversize linen jacket, and his hair was still damp from the rain. Stephanie felt that odd lightning strike her, just the sight of him stealing away her strength. She'd missed him.

"Who let you in this time?" she finally asked, willing her voice to remain calm.

"Old Sam the guard. He likes me." Edging nonchalantly past her, Drake lowered himself into an easy slouch on the same chair Paula had just vacated. "Especially after I told him that we were going to be married."

That broke through Stephanie's control. She turned on him, white with shock. "What!"

Drake shrugged agreeably. "Got me inside."

"What did he say?" she demanded, wondering just how she was going to explain this before it hit every tabloid in town.

Drake beamed. "Congratulations."

Stephanie couldn't manage the wherewithal to deal with it. Giving in to astonishment, she returned to her chair and sat down again. "But why are you in L.A.?" she asked. "I thought you were going to be in Telluride."

He nodded. "I am. Tomorrow. It's Christmas Eve tomorrow, you know."

Stephanie's eyes narrowed ever so slightly. "I know."

"Well, when I got to Telluride and found that you'd already been there and left, I decided to take definitive action."

Her stomach was sinking again. "What kind of definitive action?"

Dispatching another equable smile, Drake took a look at his watch. "The plane's standing by at Burbank."

"I was flying back tomorrow."

"I know. I decided not to chance fate." With a shrug, he got to his feet. "I mean, who knows? L.A. could have fog. There could be a blizzard, or tomorrow could be the day California finally slides off into the Pacific Ocean. I just decided I didn't want to take the chance. Ready to go?"

"Are you crazy?"

Drake leaned very close to her, his eyes alight. "In love." The way he said it, there didn't seem to be a whole lot of difference. "C'mon, Stephanie. We have enough time to throw some things together at your place and be up there before the pilot decides to take off without us."

"Drake, I . . ."

He smiled, his eyes alive with an unyielding determination that made mincemeat of Stephanie's objections. "I know. You're not used to being bullied. Well, this time you need it. Enjoy the attention, Ms. Fleming."

Stephanie looked around her as if the objections she needed would present themselves. There was no help to be found. Her frenzy of work had put her ahead of schedule, and there wasn't anyone scheduled to record again until the twenty-seventh. Nothing stood in the way of her leaving L.A. and taking the next few days off.

Drake saw the uncertainty in Stephanie's eyes and acted on it. Grabbing her purse, he lifted her out of the seat with one hand and turned her back toward the door.

"I still have to shut down," she protested.

He smiled, swinging the purse back and forth. "I'll wait."

They left the rain behind in California. Colorado was bright and cold and invigorating. Telluride bustled with holiday activity, its streets strewn with decorations and its shop windows overflowing. As Drake drove her along the town's length, Stephanie decided that deep down in her soul somewhere she must be a traditionalist. She'd always preferred a cold, white Christmas to the manufactured ones at home.

This year seemed to be no different. The minute she saw the snow, heard the familiar carols piped through an appropriate setting—as opposed to the lanes of a supermarket on La Brea—Stephanie recognized the stirring of all the old emotions. Anticipation, hesitation, hope. Maybe this year it would be different. Maybe this year they could all sit around together and sing carols and laugh as the snow trembled in the night air. Would she finally find that ideal Christmas she'd so longed for as a child, or would she be disappointed yet again?

Diane, her instincts as sharp as ever, met them at the door with a smile and a brace of Irish coffees to celebrate the reopening of the bar. The insurance company still hadn't coughed up any money because the police still listed the fire as an unsolved arson, but there hadn't been any new problems, and Nathan Ames hadn't thought to exacerbate any of the old ones. The clients were beginning to come back, and it looked as though it was going to be a rowdy, highspirited Christmas in the mountains.

"You just missed Chip," Diane said with a smile as a happy side note while dispatching the bellboy with Stephanie's luggage.

Both Stephanie and Drake looked up in surprise. "Here?"

Diane nodded. "He said that Stephanie had invited him for Christmas. I hadn't heard anything, but I figured you'd forgotten. If you don't mind staying in Jacques's old rooms, I put Chip in the room you had. The space is kind of limited...."

"It's okay." Stephanie waved her off with a wry smile, taking a too large sip of coffee and letting the whiskey bite at her throat.

"He's invited me to dinner tonight," the girl admitted, the blush on her features endearing.

Drake smiled affectionately. "He has better taste than I gave him credit for. Have a good time. And carry along a can of mace . . . just in case."

Diane's blush deepened and she went back to her duties.

* * *

Stephanie and Drake spent Christmas Eve catering to their guests. Eggnog was served and carols were sung before the roaring fire. Decorated in the old Victorian mode with ribbons, doves and imitation candles a twelve-foot blue spruce had been set up along the back wall of the great room, suffusing the air with the fresh scent of pine. Garlands stretched up the stair rail and across the short balcony to the second floor, and Diane had bordered the front desk with tiny white lights. Outside the moon glistened off the snow and paled the stars. The winter night was a perfect one, conjuring up traditions and legends of Christmases past.

For all that she had dreaded this holiday, Stephanie found herself almost grudgingly having a good time. She sat with children in her lap and listened to unspoiled hopes and dreams, feeding on the bright anticipation in young eyes as they wondered just how Santa could know to find them so far from home. It made her ache for the innocence she'd never had and smile at the wonder that never seemed to die.

When it came time for carols, Stephanie sang along for the first time since she'd been a child. After the children had been put to bed, she sat on the floor at Drake's feet sharing the quiet hours of the night with the young guests' parents. In the firelight and Christmas lights, the room and the special places in a person that are saved for just such a time softened. Stephanie laid her head against Drake's knee and accepted his gentle hand on her hair and savored the rare peace that filled her.

Stephanie never remembered falling asleep. When she awoke it was to find herself in Jacques's old four-poster, snug under acres of comforter as the sun struggled up in a leaden sky outside.

She sat up, trying to focus her thoughts. At least she should remember how she came to be in her nightgown, with her clothes from the evening before neatly folded over the old bureau next to the bed. She must have fallen asleep in front of the fire, the warmth and silence stealing over her like a hypnotic. And someone had gotten her upstairs and undressed. . . .

When Stephanie arrived at the desk in a green and gold sweater dress, Diane greeted her with a bright "Merry Christmas."

Stephanie smiled. "Merry Christmas." Diane was wearing a red sweater dress. The two of them looked like mannequins in one of the store windows in town. "How was your dinner date last night?"

Diane's smile broadened considerably. "Really nice. Chip bought me a Christmas present." She pulled her hair back a little to reveal small emerald and diamond earrings. Stephanie nodded, trying to think of something to say that wouldn't include warnings. It wasn't that she suspected Chip of having an ulterior motive. It was just that Chip wouldn't think anything of giving a gift like that. It didn't necessarily mean what Diane wanted it to.

"They're beautiful," she finally agreed with a slightly reluctant smile.

"I came over to show them to you last night," the girl continued, "but you were already asleep. Drake said he'd just taken you upstairs."

Drake. Wonderful. The very idea resurrected vivid sensations of his hands against Stephanie's skin. Her skin, her entire body, responded with alacrity. She turned away a moment so that Diane wouldn't see the sudden color in her cheeks.

"You're not going to spend all day here," Stephanie asked as she nodded a greeting to a family that drifted into breakfast, "are you?"

"No," Diane admitted. "Dinner at my sister's in town tonight. I just wanted to check on a couple of things before I went. How 'bout you?"

Stephanie turned to her, wondering if Drake had let anything slip. "I'll be in touch with everything here," she confirmed. "That way you can take a night off without worrying about business."

Chip wandered by as Stephanie was checking room status with Diane.

"Wow, you two are knockouts!" He whistled, slipping an arm around either waist.

Diane blushed all over again. Stephanie smiled and edged out of reach. If Chip felt offended, he didn't show it.

"It's too nice a Christmas for you two lovely ladies to be working. Did you know it's snowing out?"

Stephanie looked up to see that the first flakes were floating by the big windows. A white Christmas, just like the ones the songwriters invoked. Her ambivalence toward expectations that were growing too great to be met was increasing steadily. The best way to ensure disappointment.

"Stephanie, good, you're ready."

Drake strode in, his hair sprinkled with newly fallen snow and his smile bright as Christmas cheer. He wore a jacket and tie. The savage beauty of his features was not at all tamed by his civilized attire.

"Ready?" she echoed, not wanting to say too much in front of the good Mr. Markinson. He'd have a great time with her uncertainties.

"For church." Drake nodded. "We have about fifteen minutes to get there." Dropping a quick kiss on her forehead, he turned to take in everybody. "Merry Christmas, all."

Church? Stephanie hadn't been inside a church, especially at Christmas, in too many years to count. Another odd legacy from her parents; one hadn't cared, and the other had cared so much that he'd felt betrayed by a God who'd taken away his dreams. It had never really occurred to him that he'd been given other dreams, but Stephanie had only been exposed to the venom.

Chip wrinkled his nose. "Have a good time, you two. I'll keep the home fires burning."

"Home fires—" Drake grinned easily "—or hellfires?"

Chip laughed. "Jealous, old son. It doesn't become you. Of course, now that I'm preparing to take your Olympic laurels from you, you might as well get used to it."

"Speaking of hell," Drake retorted in the same easy tone, "you know what they say about that cold day, Markinson."

Stephanie decided this had gone far enough. "I'll get my coat," she told Drake with a smile.

It wasn't so much the songs of hope or the message of love and rebirth that affected Stephanie that morning. It was the feel of Drake's hand around hers, his quiet, sure presence next to her that so touched her. He never presumed or demanded, seeming to sense when Stephanie felt the most uncertain and holding her just a little more tightly there.

He sang with a sweet baritone and was clearly comfortable with the service. And when it was over and the strains of "Joy to the World" fairly thundered through the small church, Drake turned bright, animated eyes on Stephanie and gathered her into his happiness like a father would take a lost child into his strong arms.

Caught by his sweet gray gaze, Stephanie struggled to retain her composure. She felt as if she'd stepped into another world, one where she didn't quite know the landmarks, where her experience and discipline didn't apply. Could it really be this easy? Could love really grow without the monumental battles and hysteria she'd so remembered from childhood? Fear grew alongside the hope, churning up a bright headiness in her that colored her cheeks and settled in the depths of her eyes. Anyone but Stephanie would have known in an instant what that special glow was that transformed her features. But then, Stephanie had never let herself fall in love before.

Stephanie's emotions took another tumble when Drake ushered her into his house. Not only had he put up a Christmas tree, but the mouth-watering aroma of turkey and chestnut dressing filled the air. Stephanie even noticed that the Spartan living conditions had been subtly modified—an afghan here, a plant or two there. An area rug in Navajo geometrics had appeared before the fire. It was beginning to look as if someone really lived here instead of just slept here on stopovers.

Then she noticed the biggest addition to the room.

"How did that get here?" she demanded as surprise changed to disappointment.

Drake grinned at her. "Couple of the maintenance guys from the Inn delivered it yesterday. The message that came along with it was 'Merry Christmas from Stephanie. Maybe now you'll get all those trophies out of the Inn.'"

Stephanie turned on him, aghast. "That was *not*..."

It didn't seem to matter. Drake swung her into his arms, laughing at the outrage in her eyes and the delicious humor in the jumbled salutations.

"It's a beautiful gift," he assured her, planting a kiss on her forehead. "Just what I've been looking for. So I could get all those trophies out of the Inn."

"But I didn't mean that they didn't belong there," Stephanie insisted.

He nodded. "You meant that they belonged here, in my home. Until I met you, though, I didn't think of this place as a home."

Stephanie squirmed at his words. Don't ask too much. Don't expect too much. She saw frustration touch his eyes and wanted to apologize.

"Please understand," she said, doing her best to stay still within his embrace, the anxiety at his assumptions setting her heart off at a race. "I'm not used to this. I'm not...Christmas just isn't the same for me as it is for everyone else."

"I know." Drake nodded, not easing his grip at all. "It's why I'm trying to be so patient. But Stephanie, I'm not by nature a patient man."

She grinned. "I know."

"Help me with dinner?" he asked as the atmosphere eased between them. "Then I'll give you your present."

Stephanie couldn't have asked for more from the meal, the day or the company. As time passed and they settled into the comfortable quiet of his house, sharing a delicious meal and trading holiday toasts Stephanie had never been able to mean before, she felt the dread in her weaken and finally begin to crumble.

It was the Christmas she'd always wanted. She spent it with Drake, laughing over dinner, quiet before the fire, the scent of the tree perfuming the air, the snow outside trembling in the moonlight. They drank their wine, toasted with champagne and then sat on the couch with cups of coffee in hand. There Drake gave Stephanie her present.

Stephanie looked down at the rectangular package in her hands, knowing what it was simply by association. Why was another question. She slowly opened the paper, a quizzical expression on her features. Drake watched with undisguised anticipation.

"How did you know?" she asked a moment later, her tremulous smile revealing her uncertainty. Should she be excited or betrayed? He'd delved into her soul and picked out a secret not even a handful of people knew—the fallacy of the Stephanie Fleming poise.

"I looked," he admitted. "It didn't take much to discover your weakness, my dear, Ms. Fleming."

"But why?"

Drake smiled, his expression almost possessive. "Because it struck me that I've never heard you really laugh. Let loose. You're always so in control that I wanted to find out what it would take to break through it."

You did, she almost said. What a sweet, silly thing to do. Stephanie couldn't imagine anyone else in her life who would have gone to the trouble to seek out her nonsensical side and then indulge it. Then again, how could she tell anyone that the one thing in life sure to send her into helpless giggles was good old-fashioned slapstick? The Three Stooges, Laurel and Hardy, the Marx Brothers. Drake had discovered her secret cache of tapes and then presented her with three more to enjoy. It wasn't the tapes that were special. Stephanie could go out and get them anywhere. It was the gesture.

"Want to watch?" Drake asked.

She looked around to reassure herself that there wasn't a TV in the room, much less a VCR.

His grin grew somewhat rakish. "In the bedroom."

Stephanie lifted an eyebrow at him. "Lure me into your bedroom and then make sure I'm helpless?"

Drake smiled without remorse. "Something like that."

Stephanie leaned forward to brush her lips against his. "You sure know how to seduce a girl."

Drake had hoped he would be able to see another side of Stephanie. He hadn't realized that he'd see a complete metamorphosis. From the first pratfall, she quickly dissolved into a bright, happy nymph, the last shreds of serene control scattered like fall leaves before her peals of laughter. They watched the Marx Brothers and then Abbott and Costello. At first they sat propped side by side in the big bed but soon Stephanie ended up in Drake's arms, their shared laughter waking memories in the old house and chasing away the ghosts.

It was within that laughter that Drake found his greatest delight in Stephanie and his greatest desire. She instinctively nestled closer, the silliness indeed leveling her defenses, provoking the first tears Drake had ever seen her spill, tears of mirth and pleasure.

He had loved her before. He had begun to understand her more in the last few days. But tonight he adored her.

When Drake finally clicked off the set a few hours later, Stephanie turned to him with bright eyes and a brighter smile. "You've given me the best Christmas I've ever had," she admitted softly.

"The best is yet to be," he warned, a finger to the top of her chin, his gaze snaring her before she had time to rearm against his touch.

Drake let his finger stray along her mouth, sketching the outline of her lips and dipping between them. Stephanie's eyes widened, the brown dark like smoke on a winter day, her attention on his gaze rather than the finger that was reconnoitering the territory he obviously planned to plunder.

When he stroked the soft line where her lips met, she let them open, tasting the tip of his finger with her tongue. Drake's breath caught in his chest. He felt the hard knot of desire lodge in his belly, the languid fire in Stephanie's gaze provoking harsh tremors.

Stephanie saw Drake's eyes go dark and recognized the passion he'd curbed. She also saw the commitment he would demand if they went any further. Even though she could still see the laughter that lingered in him, she knew he was absolutely serious about this moment.

The soft caress of Drake's finger along her lip and nothing more kindled a fierce joy in Stephanie she'd never known. She felt at once vital and tremulous, the anticipation of his touch sapping the strength from her limbs. Knowing there was no turning back, she still wanted to go forward.

"I love you, Stephanie," he said softly, anticipating her. "I can't keep my distance any longer. Tell me if I should stay or just disappear from your life."

Stephanie looked up at Drake, the possibility of losing him sharp in her. A knife, a slow death away from the wonderful passion in those eyes. Would he understand half measures? she wondered. Could she give him as much as he was able, knowing that it wasn't everything he wanted?

"No," she managed to whisper, her voice strained, her hand up to his chest. "Don't go. I want to try. I'm just not . . . good at this. I don't know how to expect a lifelong commitment."

"You don't expect it," he said. "You work for it."

Suddenly the light in Stephanie's eyes blossomed, a siren song of humor that completed her capture of his heart. "Work...how?" she asked, sliding her hand along his chest. He'd long since abandoned the tie, and his shirt was open to reveal the lean lines of his chest, the soft dark hair that curled there. Stephanie's fingers roamed over it with impunity.

"I'm warning you," Drake growled, his control tested, Stephanie's slow forays along his skin maddening him. "You don't get another chance to walk away."

Stephanie lifted her uncertain gaze to him, her smile as hesitant as it was delighted. "I couldn't walk away right now if I wanted. Teach me how to hope, Drake. Please."

Her words shattered his reserve. Drawing her into his arms, Drake consumed those soft, sweet lips as if he'd waited his whole life to taste them. He curled his hands into the thick wool of her dress and the dense silk of her hair, her body crushed close to his yet impossibly apart. He felt her hands at him, clutching, caressing, tasted her soft whimpers. Drake pulled her to him and drank of the dark honey that was her taste and scent.

He'd dreamed of Stephanie during those long days they'd been apart, the time in Europe he'd spent purging the song of her voice from him with grueling work and brutal speed. During the days in the hospital when he'd had nothing to keep the dream of her away.

Every waking hour since he'd been back Drake had thought of Stephanie in his arms, of the fiery core of passion that simmered beneath her cool facade, the delicious dance of her body beneath his. How he'd wanted this moment. To find his way back again to where the real Stephanie Fleming existed. To taste the passion in her cries and the seduction of her touch.

Her long, sleek legs, her hips, her belly, the soft pleasure of her breasts. Drake discovered them one by one, his hands impatient against her. He kissed the velvet of her ear, the silk of her breast and then returned to savor the pleasures of her mouth where the darkest, most intoxicating sensations awaited.

Drake felt her writhe in his arms, felt the bite of her nails as they gently raked his back, met the hungry insistence of her tongue with his own, and knew what a drowning man felt like. He was drowning in her, and sought only to sink deeper.

Stephanie had never had a chance. Desire had gathered in her, easing her into the beautiful fireworks that shimmered through her body. The minute Drake's lips had touched hers, she'd been racked by explosion after explosion. The passion she'd so long kept dormant leaped to life beneath his hands, searing her with its brilliance. It drove her body to rhythms she had never known in intimate choreography against the harsh angles of Drake's. It fueled her hands to desperation, consuming the sleek muscle and sinew like a starving man his first meal.

Stephanie couldn't get close enough or have her fill of the feel of the deliciously coarse expanse of Drake's chest, the steely pressure of his thighs against the creamy smoothness of hers. They were a symphony of differences, soft against sharp, rough against smooth, a banquet of sensations with the thrill of discovery and the sweet comfort of familiarity.

The light was in Stephanie's eyes, far away and beyond the wild darkness of Drake's head. But it paled against the light that he'd ignited in her, kindled with his hands and his mouth. He swept a hand up her thighs, coaxing them open. Bending to her breast, his mouth closing so gently around the aching flesh, he laid his hand flat against her, cajoling her hips to begin their dance. His fingers slipped toward the suddenly hot core of the light, sweetening it within her until she was gasping, her hands on his shoulders, in the wild tangle of his hair. Stephanie felt her body begin its slow undulations against him, against the vortex of heat that was beginning to spread its fierce fire throughout her.

Drake suckled and caressed, the delicate taste of Stephanie maddening him. He trembled with the effort of control the ache for her savage in him. Lifting his head, he found her wide-eyed beneath him, her hair tumbled in sunset curls over the snowy pillow, her skin flushed with his attentions, her nipples stiff and moist from his kisses. She was whimpering, her lips open and inviting, her body arching in hot hunger at his touch.

"I've waited so long," he whispered, bending to taste the sweet nectar of her mouth again. "So long, my beautiful Stephanie."

Stephanie heard his words like a song on the wind. His eyes smoldered, scorching her with their intensity. His hands stole her sanity. She was desperate for him, for the fulfillment of union. Her body wanted and her mind reeled.

"You don't have to wait any longer." She smiled, her hand to his cheek, her body throbbing with the cost of the words. She couldn't breathe, couldn't rest. Please, her mind shrilled, please don't torture me.

He heard her. They moved together, instinctively wrapping around each other, their arms tight, their mouths together, trapping the light between them. Their dance once again gathered momentum, stoking the sweet, white heat until it consumed them both, shattering the silence of the house with their breathless cries and brightening the soft night with their smiles. Drake saw new tears on Stephanie's cheeks and knew their worth, because they were for him. Capturing one with a gentle finger, he paid her back with the gift he thought she would value most.

"You're never getting rid of me," he promised as he gathered her into his arms once more. "I plan to be sitting out on that porch with you when we're both eighty."

For a brief moment, there was silence. "You don't have to make promises," Stephanie finally said, her voice uncharacteristically small.

Drake heard the voice of a child in those words. He knew more now than she thought he did, and smiled, stroking the silken confusion of her hair. "I told you there was no turning back," he warned. "This is what I meant."

Stephanie stiffened in his grip. "Drake—"

"Right here."

"How about if we walk before we run?"

He chuckled against her. "I think we just did run. At least my heart's still beating like it."

Stephanie raised herself on an elbow, her hair settling over her shoulders in a soft glow. "I just can't go as fast as you want to, Drake. Can you understand that?"

Drake saw the pain in her eyes, the trepidation that was so at odds with the lingering smoke of lovemaking that still darkened them. His frustration crested quickly, stiffening his arms a little against her and forcing him to look away for a moment. He just couldn't go on like this with no end in sight. Once he'd realized that he was falling in love with her, Drake wanted Stephanie there, waiting for him. Wanting him. It was disconcerting to see that traumatized child peek out of her so unexpectedly.

Not without reason, he knew. He knew what her parents had put her through. With an effort, he pushed his frustration away.

"I do have to go back on the road again in a couple of days," he admitted. "I'd be happy to work hard at this while we're here and then give it a good breather while I'm away. Time to think?"

"Do you think you can just walk away and pay attention to your skiing like you should?" she asked.

His expression darkened even more. "Better than if I left before we made some kind of commitment."

Stephanie didn't move, held by the intensity of Drake's gaze, trapped by his need and her fear. He had been so wonderful to her, anticipating her needs and respecting her fears, his words as gentle as his hands. Yet all she was doing was waiting for him to turn. Strike out. Hurt. It was the pattern she knew, and the fact that she expected it again disheartened her.

"A commitment to try," Drake elaborated, a hand up to her hair again, her cheek. "I think I can manage with that."

"You think?" Stephanie demanded. "You can't just think when you're standing up in the gate waiting your turn at the hill. You have to know, one way or the other, or you're going to end up right back in the hospital with your Olympic hopes right down the tubes."

"If I think I have you in my corner—" Drake smiled purposefully "—I can't miss. Nothing else will matter after that."

Stephanie was already so torn that she couldn't know whether to believe him or not. Her body still sang with the sweet afterglow of Drake's love. Her soul still rejoiced at the unexpected union. How could she make a rational decision about the future when she felt like this? Right now, there was nothing in the world she wanted more than to believe Drake. And her relentless mind told her that right now was the last logical moment she should.

"You mean to tell me you can forget the Inn and Ames and Chip if I just tell you that I'll be here waiting when you come back?" she asked, grinning tremulously.

"I vow it," he said. "There isn't anything more important than knowing you'll give us a good, solid try."

The comfort of Drake's touch was stealing away her resolve. Stephanie had to deny herself his embrace before she could answer. Pulling away, she swung out of bed and faced him. It didn't occur to either of them how incongruous she looked standing there naked. There was steel in her expression, directed not at Drake, but herself.

"When you get back," she said, her voice trembling only a little, "I'll be here. I'll try. I..." A smile bloomed, a soft, shy flower that was bewitching on such a commanding figure. "I love you, too. I don't want to lose you."

With a swiftness that left Stephanie a little breathless, Drake was on his feet and holding her. "In that case—" he laughed, bestowing a kiss that robbed Stephanie's legs of strength "—nothing can stand in my way. My worries are all past."

Stephanie almost told him about the shiver his words generated. She had a feeling of dread, as if Drake had challenged fate with his words. Stephanie remembered it all that night as they made love again and fell asleep in each other's arms in the peace of a silent house. She remembered her superstition the next day when she returned to find the Inn busy and threatened only with impending prosperity. But then she drove away in Drake's Jeep to check with a nearby blacksmith about some grillwork he was doing for the Inn, and she forgot. She shouldn't have. As she was heading over the pass into Silverton, Stephanie's steering gave out and she lost control of the Jeep.

# Chapter 13

Slow down," Chip warned, a hand out to the door to steady himself around a sharp corner. "You're not going to do her any good by ending up in a ravine yourself."

"She could have been killed!" Drake snapped, the anguish keen in his voice. "Damn it, why did I let her go off by herself?"

"Because you didn't know the steering would go out.... Damn, McDonald, you're real close to wiping out America's Olympic hopes!"

"I'm in perfect control."

Chip watched another sudden precipice pass within inches of his window and closed his eyes. "Well, I'm in danger of losing lunch."

Drake pulled to a sudden stop in the emergency driveway of the hospital that almost sent his teammate through the windshield. He never heard the fresh protests. He was already out the door and running in to search for Stephanie.

She was sitting on an exam table watching the nurse tape a swathe of gauze around her arm when Drake burst through the door. The nurse jumped a foot. Stephanie turned deceptively calm eyes on Drake, an absolutely illogical joy blooming in her chest at the frantic worry in his eyes.

"I'm fine," she insisted even before he could ask. "I wanted to call you, but the police said you were already on your way in."

Drake was examining her as if expecting to find missing parts, gaping holes. The fact that there were none didn't seem to comfort him.

"Your head," he said, eyes on the Technicolor patch just below her hairline. "Are you okay? What happened?"

Stephanie smiled. "I veered the right way. Hit the mountain instead of five hundred feet of air."

She'd been trying to lighten the situation. Her words only reignited the pain on Drake's face. Giving the nurse minimal time to clear the area, he strode up to pull Stephanie into his arms, oblivious of the cotton patient gown she wore and the disheveled state of the rest of her. Chip appeared behind him.

"Nice to see you in one piece." He grinned rakishly.

"Nice to be in one piece," Stephanie assured him, involuntarily wrapping her arms around Drake's back. She felt like warm pudding, the adrenaline still racing heedlessly through her, the terror of those eternal minutes of uncontrolled velocity still vivid. Drake felt so strong and vital against her. So solid. She laid her head against his shoulder and gave way to the tremors that had been threatening all along.

"You're ready to go," the nurse assured her. "I think the sheriff wanted to talk to you first, though."

Stephanie nodded against Drake, her eyes closed. It seemed to be enough for the nurse, who backed out of the room. Since she was a petite blonde with big blue eyes, Chip followed.

"Excuse me, Miss Fleming."

The new voice at the door carried some authority, so Stephanie dragged her head back up.

"Yes?"

Drake turned with her, his arm around her. He wasn't about to let her face any of this alone.

"That your Jeep?"

"My Jeep," Drake said. "She was borrowing it."

The sheriff turned his attention to Drake. "It's over at the San Juan Standard station down the street. Your lady friend here was real lucky. She missed three other cars and a steep first step down. Had that Jeep looked at lately?"

Drake shook his head, more in confusion than answer. "Not more than two weeks ago."

The man nodded, making a note. "Well, might have a talk with the boy who checked it. The steering went completely out, just like the young lady here said, and that just doesn't happen overnight."

Stephanie felt Drake tense at the sheriff's words. He had a look on his face like a deer sensing an intruder—careful, wary. She wondered what he was thinking.

"Well," the sheriff concluded, pocketing his notebook and handing Stephanie back her license. "I guess that's about it for me. I'll get in touch if I hear anything else."

Drake had hardly let the sheriff out the door before he turned on Stephanie, his hand tight on her sound arm. "Would you mind waiting a minute for me to get back? I have to check something out."

"Something what?" she asked, not at all liking the peculiar fire in his eyes. Stephanie saw indignation and fury, suspicion that darkened the gray into dead ash. The sudden terror that still raced through her precluded any rational puzzle solving, so she couldn't quite decide why Drake was so upset. It didn't matter. She knew that she didn't like him taking off looking like that.

"Just something," he said dryly, anticipating the questions he had no intention of answering. Dropping a kiss on Stephanie's nose, he turned in time to catch Chip coming in the door.

"Stay here with Stephanie till I get back, will you?" Drake asked, and walked out.

Chip spent a moment watching the empty door before answering. "Glad to, Drake. Anything for a pal."

"Where is he going?" Stephanie asked, looking in the same direction.

Chip swung toward her with a big grin. "Knowing McDonald, it could be anything from chewing out the guy who services his Jeep to driving up to see what happened himself. He was just a wee bit upset on the way out here."

Stephanie saw the truth behind his banter and felt both better and worse for it. "I was, too." She smiled, attempting a bit of humor of her own. It didn't help her a bit.

"Yeah," Chip retorted, wagging a finger, "but you aren't in love with you. He is. And he thought he was going to have to bring you home in a black bag."

Stephanie proffered a grimace, not secure enough to enjoy the implications of Chip's offhand statement. "I could do without the graphic allusions, thanks. And now, if you don't mind, I have to get dressed."

Chip's eyes lit like jack-o'-lanterns. "I don't mind at all."

"At which time—" she continued unfazed "—you will have to wait outside. In the hallway." Still he didn't move. "Where the nurse probably is."

That produced not only a wider smile but some action. Chip slipped out, and Stephanie did her best to struggle back into her blouse and slacks. Not only were her arm and head hurting from where they'd slammed against the side of the Jeep, but the muscles she'd instinctively tensed against the impact were beginning to tighten up. She was going to be one sore lady by morning. Stephanie still felt shaky on her feet, the tremors of surprise and violence still racing through her. It would be nice to get back to the quiet of the Inn and a bit of rest.

No one seemed to want to cooperate.

Stephanie stepped out of the room to find Chip in head-to-head contact with the pretty young nurse, feeding on her coy smile like a plant feeds on sunlight. Drake was still gone, and the activity of the hospital went on around her. Stephanie was no longer a patient, therefore she lost her place in their concern. Easing into an uncomfortable waiting-room chair, she waited.

"You're looking a little peaked, lady," Chip commented a little while later as he took an adjoining chair. The arm he

settled around her shoulders was companionable, supportive.

"I feel a little peaked," Stephanie admitted with a wan
smile. "I wish Drake would get back. I don't trust him."

"Aw, he won't do anything rash. Maybe punch the me-
chanic out or something. Any more than that, and he'd have
to miss a race."

"Ebnat-Kappel isn't for another two weeks."

"True, but Garmisch-Partenkirchen isn't. McDonald's
decided to go for another downhill before Olympic time."

Stephanie found herself closing her eyes, the image of that
bright, tumbling form once again replaying like a news clip.
Let's just watch it one more time to get that feel of outrage
and shock. Let's remember just how far and fast he fell, and
then watch him do it again.

"It's too soon," she protested ineffectually. "His arm..."

"He's skied with that arm before. Nothing bothers the
great McDonald when he's on a run. Nothing except losing."

Stephanie heard bitterness creep into Chip's voice and
knew how keenly he felt the ruthless intent of Drake's competition. Chip spoke not only of the man he so wanted to
beat out there, but for himself. For anyone who drove
themselves to challenge an icy, unforgiving mountain at
ninety miles an hour just for the honor of winning.

"And losing doesn't bother you at all," she couldn't help
but answer, her voice sounding more weary than challeng-
ing.

"Not at all," Chip assured her just a little too brightly.
"Especially since I don't do it anymore."

"Uh-huh."

"We're ready to go."

The two of them looked up to see Drake stride up, hands
jammed into pockets, brow furrowed with suppressed fury.
Mistaking the intent, Chip pulled his arm back and stood.

"A little brotherly concern," he offered equably.

"What's wrong?" Stephanie asked.

"Nothing. Let's go."

For all the tight anger in his voice, the hand Drake offered was surprisingly gentle. He helped Stephanie to her feet and guided her out the door. Chip followed, his expression losing some of its sunniness.

"So, who have you been abusing?" he asked. When he didn't get any reaction, Chip asked again. It wasn't until they'd made it back to the Inn that he finally got his answer.

"I'd appreciate it if you'd stay here with Stephanie until I get back from the police station," Drake told him as they walked up to Jacques's dormer.

"You sure assume a lot, McDonald," Chip snapped a bit testily.

"Just do it, damn it," Drake snapped back, his eyes darker than ever.

"Why are you going back to the police?" Stephanie asked. "And why do you suddenly think I need a baby-sitter?"

Drake opened the door and guided her in. When he had her seated in one of the chairs, he told her.

"Because your accident wasn't an accident," he said, his hand in hers and his eyes fierce. "Somebody cut the steering cables."

Stephanie was sure that she should have said something. She should have protested, held him back or laughed at such an absurd idea. She couldn't. While Stephanie sat in a stunned silence, Drake leaned forward to kiss her goodbye and got to his feet.

"Who could have done that?" she asked at last as Drake turned to receive Chip's assurance that he would, in fact, watch over Stephanie for the time being.

"Who, Drake?"

But she knew who he thought it was. It wasn't until Drake was already out the door that Stephanie realized something else. If it had been Ames who had sabotaged the Jeep, it wasn't her he'd been after. It was Drake. A deathlike chill filled her as she reflected that Chip was by several measures much too unruffled by the whole incident for her taste.

* * *

It was close to sundown before Drake came back. By then Diane had come and gone, and Chip had fallen asleep on the couch by the window. Stephanie had kept her vigil in the same chair, not interested in eating or sleeping until she knew that Drake would return in one piece. The minute she heard him slam Chip's rental car to a stop in the driveway, she slumped with a sigh that verged on weary tears. When Drake arrived to kick out an unrepentant Chip, Stephanie forced a smile.

"Are you sure you're all right?" Drake asked for the third time as he hovered over Stephanie's new position on the couch.

"Would you feel better if I said no?" she asked, eyes closed. Her head was throbbing steadily, but not badly, and the fresh stitches on her arm were sore. Stephanie could name several new muscle groups she'd never known she possessed, and the fleeting image of that endless, awful abyss to the left of her wheels kept replaying like a broken film clip before a stretched-out brain. All in all, she felt a bit like frayed electrical cord, set to shock at the wrong touch.

Drake gave up asking and settled next to her, his arms slipping around her shoulders. "You scared the hell out of me, damn it." His voice sounded even worse than hers, his cheek possessively against her hair. "I kept imagining..."

Stephanie giggled shrilly. "So did I. I kept seeing myself scraped up by a stamp collector somewhere on the bottom of that ravine."

Her words only served to make him hold her closer. "Don't even joke about it. Somebody tried to kill you."

"Or you." That realization didn't make Stephanie feel any better. In fact, it set up a new wave of trembling. She squeezed her eyes more tightly shut and burrowed into the comfort of Drake's arms, soaking in his energy, his strength, his life. The thought of him spread over that ravine terrified her even more than her own misfortune. Death happened. But to be so suddenly and violently alone, just after Drake had planted the first seeds of the future in her—Stephanie didn't think she could bear it.

"You didn't go see Ames, did you?"

"No. I decided to let the authorities do that. Besides, he's out of town."

Stephanie looked up, startled.

"He left about an hour ago." Drake smiled without humor.

"What did the police say?"

Drake rewarded her with a new smile, his eyes dry. "That they'd been laboring under the misconception that we were behind all the Inn's bad luck."

Stephanie shook her head. "What about now?"

He chuckled. "They seemed duly impressed with my outrage. Considering that if you were trying to kill me you'd hardly go off in the defective Jeep yourself."

"You could have sabotaged it to get me," she reminded him.

"I convinced them that that would be unlikely."

Stephanie looked up at him. "How?"

"I told them I was hardly going to kill the woman I was about to marry."

"There you go again..." she began—then saw his eyes. This time he was serious. The terror lingered, the sudden, harrowing realization that he'd almost lost her. For that immutable moment, Stephanie lay trapped before the truth in Drake's eyes, the overwhelming meaning for them both.

"Did that trick work as well as it did at MGM?" she asked finally, turning away. Her first reaction to his words was to pull back, to get clear of the emotional entanglement she'd so neatly worked her way into. She was beginning to expect too much, hope too dearly. How long could it last? Just the feel of his arms around her was so poignantly sweet that Stephanie felt tears catch in her like a searing fire.

His answer was delivered quietly. "They've pulled the Jeep in and decided to go back over all the other problems we've had with a more finely toothed comb."

"And while they do?"

Drake drew her a little closer. Each of them had their eyes fixed on the distant hills, safely hidden from the other. "While they do, we'll be very careful."

"When is Garmisch?" Stephanie asked softly, her hand splayed across Drake's chest, seeking the vital reassurance of his heartbeat and breath.

He didn't seem all that surprised that she knew. "This weekend. I decided to go since I'll be back in form." Somehow he made the words sound like consolation instead of expectation.

"Will you be careful?"

Stephanie knew he was smiling just by the way he stroked her hair. "Everywhere but on the course."

Don't ask for much more, the tone of his voice said. Stephanie didn't, but Drake's words cut deeper than the attempt on her life. He would be so vulnerable. Would Nathan Ames follow him that far? Would he take the war away from Telluride?

"Maybe if the two of us stayed away from Colorado for a while, things would settle down," she suggested.

"I've thought of that." Drake nodded against her. "I'm not sure if it's that or a matter of timing so that we just start to feel secure—to throw us off balance."

"Can you hold out until the Olympics?"

Drake took a moment to answer her. "As long as I know you're all right."

"What about the Inn?" Stephanie asked, eyes still closed. "What if something else happens and we can't stop it?"

Pulling away just a little, Drake forced her to face him. "Then we'll just rebuild. However many times it takes."

Her gaze lost within Drake's, Stephanie nodded with a tremulous smile. "As long as you're all right," she agreed.

"I've got Chip watching over me." He grinned. "He doesn't just want to win, he wants to beat me. Wouldn't be the same if I weren't in one piece."

Stephanie found herself laughing. "Now if that isn't the most warped logic system I've heard, I don't know what is."

Drake shrugged. "I did the same thing. The new gun can't prove himself unless it's against the old gun."

She scowled. "How quaint. I can't wait to see it."

Drake straightened a little. "You're planning to watch?"

Seeing the hesitant hope in his eyes, Stephanie thought of the last race she'd watched, thought of the wild fear in his eyes when he'd stormed in on her that afternoon, and of her promise to be at the Olympics. For better or worse, she decided that she couldn't tell him just yet that she might be there to see him race. After all, she still hadn't decided. There would just be too much hope and pain to face.

"Probably," she finally said with a poker face. "I'm sure Corey will want to pull her six-foot screen out again."

A little of the light went out of Drake's eyes. "Oh. Yeah, probably."

Stephanie's first reaction was to recant. She suddenly couldn't bear the disappointment in his eyes, the stiffening of his posture. Her words had put a distance between them that once would have made her feel safer, but now only served to stir a new pain, a loneliness she'd never allowed herself before.

"Are you going back tomorrow?" she asked quietly, easing back into his embrace. Drake's hold was a little less sure, but she found herself savoring it all the same.

He nodded, a hand instinctively lifting to indulge itself in the texture of her hair. "It's going to be a solid run from here to Calgary from now on."

"So this is our last night together for a while."

Stephanie felt his hand stop, hover uncertainly at the unexpected invitation in her words. A sudden hesitation took hold of her, a sweet anticipation that nothing would quell. It was the excitement of possibility, of uncertainty. Stephanie wasn't sure if she'd meant her words as an invitation. Lately what she wanted and what she knew was best seemed to collide without successful resolution, as first one side spoke up and then the other without her being able to quite control the situation. She very much wanted to immerse herself in the fierce comfort of Drake's touch, to give him a sense of sweet unity, so that when he had to face his mountain he would no longer do it alone. Stephanie knew she should back away now, before what was given and received became too dear to forfeit—before she deprived herself of the chance to return in peace to her glass haven on the hill. The opposites battled in her, neither winning, neither letting go. Her heart raced and her palms grew damp.

Stephanie remembered what it was like to stand in that gate with the timer beeping away the seconds, staring straight down into eternity. Her race was about to begin now, and she couldn't make up her mind whether to push off or run away. And the timer continued to count those ruthless seconds, giving no quarter.

Drake lifted her face with a gentle hand. His expression held the same hesitation, as if he, too, knew what it was like to have hoped for too much.

"You should be in bed," he said, dropping a sympathetic kiss on the bruise that now colored the right side of Stephanie's forehead.

"That's just where I intend to be," she assured him with a smile that was at once tremulous and triumphant. It was the same smile she'd worn when she'd first felt the earth slip away beneath her skis. Equal parts exhilaration and fear; the thrill of risk.

"But the accident . . ." His voice spoke of warning. The line of his jaw grew taut, and Stephanie could feel his heart accelerate alongside hers.

"Needs to be forgotten."

For a moment, Drake couldn't move. Even more than her words, Stephanie's expression held him. In it he saw the sweet uncertainty that colored her excitement. Lord, how he'd wanted her to want him, to look at him with expectation, with longing. He couldn't keep doing this dance, though, one step up and two back. Its unpredictability was killing him. He'd given her the chance to back away. He'd given himself the lectures about patience. But he wanted nothing to do with either when it came to Stephanie Fleming.

Knowing full well that he was probably setting himself up for another game of hide-and-seek, Drake kissed her. Stephanie's immediate response drove out all objections. She melted against him, her lips pliant and welcoming. He heard a raw groan and realized that it had been born in his own throat, as the savage pain of desire swept him like a sudden brushfire. Drake gathered her into his arms, trying his best to remember restraint for the hurt she'd suffered, and deepened his kiss, the weeks ahead of him suddenly stretching out unbearably without her.

Stephanie closed her eyes at the caress of his lips across hers, the taste on her cheeks, her eyes, her throat. Each awakened to life, transforming the pain of solitude into a sweeter joy of union. Drake's hands sought her hair, her arms, her throat, to trace the pulse there and search out the tender skin below her ear. Each place his fingers touched began to glow, the soreness lifting, the weariness changed to delight. Was it the discovery of his hungry touch that so pleased her, or the quickening pulse of his pleasure?

Stephanie sought him equally, her hands savoring the sinewy grace of his body, the steel-hard shoulders and sleek, hair-roughened chest, delighting in the sensations of crisp cotton and fluid muscle. Just the feel of him sharpened her arousal, its tight coil slowly unwinding in her belly in a hard, sweet ache that brightened with Drake's smile and his soft words of promise.

"Give yourself to me," he whispered, letting his hands calm the tremors of uncertainty that still persisted, even as Stephanie felt her blouse fall away in a whisper of silk. "I'll take care of you, Stephanie. I promise."

Stephanie couldn't answer, knowing that he spoke of more than just the moment, knowing that he meant forever. She couldn't see forever, couldn't relish it as he could. She still expected betrayal.

Drake brushed Stephanie's hair back over her shoulders and dipped to taste the soft, sweet flesh there, igniting new, different tremors. Stephanie's ragged breathing brushed his ear. Her hands clutched at his back as if to keep her from falling. It was Drake who was falling, though. Inexorably, fatally, willingly, pulled down by the green apple smell of Stephanie's hair and the tenuous hold she kept on happiness.

Drake raised her face once more, snaring her attention with eyes the color of dove wings. "What do you want me to tell you? How do I convince you that I'm serious? I want to marry you. I want to come home to you every day, to have children and grow old together." He traced a tear with his finger, shaken by the immense upheaval he was effecting in her. He saw yearning in her eyes, love, a fledgling joy that set up a like joy in him. She made him want to laugh, to shout, to conquer. She had such a hold on him and didn't even understand it. God how he loved her.

Stephanie tried to remain still. She wanted Drake's hands on her, wanted to join with him in solace and ecstasy, sure that she could always count on him to be there for her, to be her shield, her buffer, her savior in a world that for too long had been hostile. She wanted so much to believe in him enough to try. He asked so much, and she wanted nothing more than to be able to give it to him. She loved him more fiercely than her own life. But how that love frightened her.

"How can I promise anything?" she asked, her voice no more than a whisper. "A promise only lasts as long as it's convenient."

"Not in my world," Drake said, pulling her closer to kiss her again, her indecision an agony. "I promise forever, Stephanie. I promise that I'll always love you and be there for you. I promise that I'll never make you suffer the way you've suffered already. I'd kill anyone who hurt you."

Stephanie tried to smile away her terror. "I don't think I'd ask that," she demurred, dropping her gaze to his chest, the warm, strong plane that hid his heart and protected her with his strength. She wavered, suddenly desperate for the future his words promised. Not for the domesticity, the happy plans of a married couple. For the sure power of Drake's love, the sweet pleasure of having someone to share her triumphs. It would have been so lovely to have had someone else there to hold that Oscar up for. Someone who didn't resent the success or perceive it as profit. Stephanie wanted another Christmas like the one she'd just had, filled with the peace of belonging that she'd never known with her parents. Drake was offering her just that.

"Take a chance," he urged, his eyes alight, their heat drawing her back. "For once, just get out there and go for it. Edge of the world, Stephanie, right there between the earth and the sky. There's no place like it. But you'll never know unless you try."

His eyes were so sweet, so soft, so beguiling. How could Stephanie doubt him? How could she deny him?

The clock on the wall ticked away the passing seconds. A low wind tested the windows and slid in under the eaves. Beyond their warm room the sun had died, leaving the sky to the moon and night stars. The world was soft and quiet, waiting, patient. Stephanie's heart pounded with the fear of commitment. She saw her father screaming at her mother, throwing whatever was handy just to hurt her after he'd made the same promises, offered the same commitment.

Suddenly the silence was shattered. Someone was pounding at the door in a hurry. Drake jumped and cursed. Stephanie shied away as if she'd been hit.

"It's not time to be playing footsie!" Chip yelled from the hallway, his voice as impatient as his hand.

"Damn it, Markinson," Drake snarled, letting go of Stephanie and turning for the door. "This is too much!"

Stephanie hurriedly pulled her blouse back on, the surprise still pounding in her chest.

"You'll thank me when you're in a better mood," came the voice. "But get down to the phone first. The coach has been trying to get ahold of you. You might be ineligible for the Olympics."

Stephanie was glad she'd managed to pull herself together. Once Drake heard that, he had the door open without another thought.

"What the hell are you talking about?"

Chip shrugged, looking for once sincerely outraged. "Just how am I supposed to beat you if you're not there? Those stuffed shirts have no sense."

Drake's patience disappeared in a frightening hurry. Stephanie couldn't remember ever seeing him so angry. "How could I be disqualified?"

"Your trust, old man. There's a report out that you tapped into it to renovate the Inn, which, as we know, would disqualify you. If you don't get back and straighten it out, you'll be watching from the stands."

"But I have to go to Germany," Drake protested, dragging a hand through his hair. "It's the only chance I'll get at a downhill before the Olympics."

"Aren't you listening?" Chip demanded. "Unless you get to Colorado Springs, you're not even going to downhill at the Olympics. You didn't really use that money to spiff this place up, did you?"

Stephanie felt her heart skid for Drake. The rules were that any moneys paid him for promotion while he skied for the U.S. team would be put into a trust for when he had finished competing as an amateur. Any use of those funds now would be interpreted as payment for his skiing, making him a professional, disqualified from competing in the amateur Olympics.

"Don't be an idiot," Drake snapped blackly. "Of course I didn't. It's just some screwup. Get down there. Tell him I'm on my way."

"Okay." Chip shrugged heading for the stairs.

For a moment Drake couldn't even speak. He shook his head with a stunned, bewildered look in his eyes. Stephanie saw the new desperation take hold, the fear that he wouldn't after all be able to finish his career the way he wanted. The sudden possibility that someone had carelessly taken his last gold from him.

"What else?" he raged. "What else can they do to me?"

Stephanie stepped forward, a tentative hand reaching out to him, more torn than he, the stricken light in his eyes searing her with memory and understanding. No! her father had cried when he'd really been drinking. No, they can't take that away! It's my life, my life, damn it! And then he'd begun to break things.

Her hand had barely made contact with his arm when Drake swung on her. "No!" he howled, rage and disbelief blinding him.

Instinct met his action, and Stephanie fell, arms up, mouth open in a child's silent cry. Drake might have had no intention of hitting her, but she couldn't know. She cowered, her stricken eyes staring into his, his one frustrated act shattering her hope as brutally as a hammer to glass.

"Oh, God, Stephanie!" Drake stretched his arms to her, the fury still in him. Just as her father had done so many times. Stephanie stood and backed away, struggling mightily to keep her composure. All she wanted to do was crawl off to safety as she'd done when she'd been a child.

"You'd better...answer that call," she said, her voice unrecognizable in its desolation.

"I'll be right back," he offered, hesitating beyond her reach. "We can talk then."

But she wasn't there when he returned. Drake didn't know where she'd gone, and didn't follow. He'd known the minute he'd seen those stark, silent eyes that he'd lost her. Whatever he'd inadvertently done had ruined that careful wall of trust he'd been building over the last few weeks.

Drake circled the low, warm rooms a couple of times, trying to work off some of the frustration, but it only went on building. He'd have to wait to go to her, to explain and apologize. He'd have to wait until he'd finished with the Olympic committee and attended his races. Only then could he think clearly enough to make Stephanie understand and accept. Until that time he'd have to survive. But without her quiet, sweet support, he wasn't sure all of a sudden that he could do it.

When he finished walking, Drake began throwing. First pillows, then breakables, and finally the trophies that still remained in the room. And when he had finished he still didn't feel any better.

# *Chapter 14*

Stephanie had never thought she'd find herself at the opening ceremonies of the Olympics. Even as she sat huddled in one of Corey's furs, watching the splendid pageantry of nations coming together to compete, she couldn't help but wonder how she'd gotten herself into this.

She hadn't, in the end, been able to back out on Paula Evers. Stephanie had always been a person of her word, and once it was given, she felt loath to take it back. She had spent hour upon hour debating the matter only to finally come to the conclusion she'd known she would reach all along. She was going to have to spend February at the Olympic Games.

The crowd cheered, waving thousands of small flags and banners to salute the games and their participants. Rich, martial music rose into the afternoon sky as group after group of athletes appeared from the far archway to make their way around the stadium. Their fresh faces brimmed with enthusiasm, with the thrill that would carry them through the years to the time when they could tell their children and grandchildren of the cold February day when they'd marched behind their flag into the Olympic Stadium.

Stephanie watched the parade pass. Austria, Canada with its great exultant roar from the stands, France, Japan. She sensed the elation that swirled around her and felt only fear. Drake was down there, waiting his turn, counting down the last hours of his career, psyching himself for the fierce competition he would face. Stephanie hadn't seen him since that night in Colorado, hadn't even talked to him. Corey had told her of his second in Garmisch-Partenkirchen, and his fifth at Ebnat-Kappel where the announcers had said that he hadn't seemed like the same old Drake McDonald. Diane had told her about the results of the inquiry into his finances. Drake had, it seemed, been the victim of computer tampering. Instead of pulling funds out of his personal savings to rebuild the Inn, the computer had withdrawn them from the trust account. Somehow the numbers had been switched. It had taken a private investigator and two weeks of trouble to unravel the whole mess, and had cost Drake his calculated edge in skiing.

Drake hadn't been able to concentrate enough to follow that special course he carved between earth and sky that took everyone's breath away and won him medals. Stephanie, growing more miserable each day she was apart from him, couldn't gather the courage to show her support.

She had spent those weeks secluded in her house and studio desperately trying to reassemble her peace of mind. Stephanie had seen what Drake's kind of intensity could do to a relationship. She'd seen what it did to a person, driving him so relentlessly that when he lost his goal he turned in on himself and the people he loved until there was nothing left. There was simply too much pain, too much conflict. Having spent so much of her life caught in that kind of turmoil, she wanted nothing more now than peace.

The United States. Another cheer went up as the phalanx of athletes stepped out into the sunshine with the flag snapping to life at its lead. Stephanie's heart skidded. Drake was carrying the flag. How had she not known that he had been selected? His teammates would have voted for him, the honor being the best they could give. Tears stung her eyes as she saw the familiar stride, the straight, proud posture of someone who knew the worth of the gift.

He marched past the reviewing stand, the flag steady. The American flag was never dipped in salute. On any other occasion it might have seemed a gesture of arrogance. Drake made of it a symbol of pride. Stephanie watched him and thought she could see the sun glance off the sharp planes of his face. A shaft of sudden loneliness penetrated her.

Suddenly, she couldn't understand why she'd kept herself from him for so long. Her life had been dry and lifeless without him, just as it had been until she'd met him. Could the possible pain be worth the bright life in his eyes? Was there a way to construct some kind of protection against the traumas that still kept her so isolated?

Just that day she'd heard from the investigator that her father had made some progress toward health. Stephanie didn't know how long it would take or how long it would last, but didn't it offer her a little hope that life wasn't as inevitable as she'd always thought?

Around her people were cheering and waving as the team drew abreast of them. Some of the athletes waved in response. Not knowing why, Stephanie waved along.

Even though it was Drake's third Olympics, his reaction hadn't changed. The pride of representing his country still filled him. The splendor of the pageant still awed him. The minute he stepped into that stadium to meet the surge of emotion from the spectators, a wave of sound that swept over the brimming, exultant stadium, unexpected tears pricked at his eyes.

The last time. This was going to be his finale, capping a career he was rightfully proud of. And he had to admit that he couldn't think of a better way of ending it. If only Stephanie had been here to share it with him, it would have been complete. Battling against a sudden, illogical sense of loneliness, Drake smiled up to the waving, cheering crowd and imagined that she waved back.

\* \* \*

"Diane, slow down. I can't understand you." Pulling out an earring, Stephanie shifted the phone to her other shoulder and finished taping her splice. Out of the four hours of filming Paula had done at the opening ceremonies, she would probably end up with about a minute or two spliced into the finished film.

"The police were here. They said that they had tried to get ahold of you, but you weren't home."

"I know I wasn't." Stephanie smiled easily. "I was here."

"Well, that's what I told them. But they said you'd want to know."

"Diane—" Stephanie tried again, since she'd heard the setup four times without the delivery "—know what?"

"That they've arrested Mr. Ames."

Stephanie suddenly forgot her tape. "What?"

"They found the Inn's insurance policy in his office, just where Drake said it would probably be."

"Gloating?" she asked instinctively.

"I guess. They also found a set of duplicate security keys for his building."

"Where the insurance company is." Stephanie grinned, suddenly feeling the weight of the world off her shoulders. "I knew it. Ames was at that computer. Have they been able to connect him with the accident or the fire?"

"Or Drake's bank problems, since that's computer-related, too? No. They're still trying. And of course Ames is denying it all. It seems as though it's over, though. The insurance company is even helping in the investigation now."

Stephanie sat a moment, taking up her pencil and tapping it. Thinking. The first runs of the grand slalom were this morning, and she'd planned to go. She'd have to now, to let Drake know that it was all over, that he could ski without anything left to interfere with his battle against that new gun. Well, she amended to herself, wishing she didn't feel so suffocated by the thought, almost.

"I'll tell Drake today," she finally told Diane, her fear feeling too much like anticipation to suit her. "Thanks."

"Anytime," the girl answered happily. "Cheer Drake on for us."

Cheer Drake on. Stephanie was going to have to see him before he raced. She'd actually tried to talk to him already, but he'd been out on Mount Allen, doing practice runs for the slaloms. If she weren't still so afraid of what she felt for him, she would have tried harder.

Stephanie had managed to see Chip, and had come away fascinated in the change in her bright boy. The light had hardened to steel, the happy disregard tempered to competitive zeal. He still threw off his breezy banter, but beneath it he was all business. And all of his energies were zeroed in on Drake. Stephanie couldn't imagine how Drake could put up with him so well when the younger skier had an eye on his back like Bob Ford on Jesse James—the young gun going after the old gun.

Checking her watch, Stephanie decided that she had just enough time to get out and talk to Drake before he headed up for his runs. Paula would just have to wait for her dailies.

The drive out from the city was a pretty one, from the wide, windy prairie to the tumble of the Canadian Rockies. At any other time Stephanie might have enjoyed it. Now she was prepared to forgo the pleasure of a late winter afternoon in the mountains and the traffic that accompanied Olympic events for the preoccupation of just what she was going to say to Drake when—and if—she finally got to him.

She could just tell him about Ames and back off. She could tell him that she'd come to see him race because of her job and nothing more. Or she could tell him the truth. That she hadn't had a decent night's sleep since she'd walked away from him, that she'd watched each of his races a dozen times, aching for the wild flight he'd lost because of the troubles that had beset him. She'd admit it was destroying her to think her own indecision might deprive him of that determination to take that breathtaking risk that set him so far apart from his competitors.

She could tell him she loved him and she wanted to believe that nothing else mattered. But it did matter, and that was what had kept her away from the phone all these weeks.

It was easier to get to him than she'd thought. Flashing the credentials she'd borrowed from the cinematographer and brandishing his light meter, Stephanie had walked right up to the area where the athletes gathered before breaching the hill. They were all in little clusters, outfitted like sleek, tropical birds in their bright bodysuits as they collected at the foot of the lift. Above them the hill waited, pristine in the morning sunlight, the gate flags flapping in an uncertain breeze, the crowd scattered along the route like brightly colored confetti.

The athletes watched that hill, chattering, scanning the weather, the crowd, the competition. Support and the camaraderie of competitions small universe were given in a dozen languages.

Stephanie spotted Drake at the edge of the U.S. knot, talking with a middle-aged gentleman who didn't seem to know how to smile. Walking up, she stationed herself just out of earshot until they were finished.

They finished, it seemed, the minute Drake looked over to the hill for a quick update and spotted her instead.

It took him a full minute to comprehend. As he did, Stephanie smiled as bright a greeting as she could, trying to ignore the sudden staccato of her heart and the heat that rushed to her cheeks.

"You came."

The gentleman seemed even less happy as Drake walked away without a word of explanation.

Stephanie nodded, wishing there were some way to say more. "I came. I brought you some good news."

"The fact that you're here is good enough for me. Stephanie, I..."

She held up a hand. "You have a race to win, Mr. McDonald. Everything else can wait. Except this." Then she smiled again, thinking how incongruous it was for her to be delivering such news to a man who was hugging skis. She couldn't even see his beautiful hair for the futuristic helmet that topped his suit.

"Ames was caught red-handed," she said. "Insurance policy in office. Not only the police, but the insurance company are continuing to investigate. The Sundance Inn and her partners appear to once again have a future."

For a moment, Drake could do no more than stand there. Two shocks so close together were too hard to assimilate. The sun danced in Stephanie's hair and settled along the dramatic angles of her cheeks. She'd pushed her sunglasses up so that she squinted a little, sharpening the brown of her eyes and luring him with it's sweet familiarity. Suddenly so close to her, all Drake wanted to do was pull her back into his arms and force her to return to him. The hill didn't even seem to matter as much.

"What about you?" he asked.

Stephanie arched an eyebrow. "I thought you'd at least enjoy a little well-deserved sense of satisfaction at the news."

Drake nodded, reaching out to her. "I'm glad. Relieved. But I'm not going to be any good on that hill until I get the chance to talk to you."

"Don't blackmail me," she warned, stiffening instinctively.

"I just have to know," he said. "One way or another."

Stephanie's eyes widened, suspiciously moist in the dry mountain air. "But what if I don't know?"

"Hi there, gorgeous!" Chip grinned brightly as he appeared from the edge of the crowd. "We're going up, McDonald. Make your goodbyes short and sweet."

Stephanie ignored him. All she could see was the fire she'd ignited in Drake's eyes, the life that had not been there when she'd first seen him. She had done that by simply showing up. To mean so much to him, make such a difference unnerved her. She meant more than skiing, his expression told her. More than anything now.

How could he frighten her so much down there where the old uncertainties lived, and yet have her wanting nothing more than to be here with him? Could taking that kind of chance really be worth it?

Edge of the world, he'd said. Take that one big chance that would set you between earth and sky. Go for it. Stephanie wasn't at all sure about that. She just knew that she was suddenly sorry she hadn't given him the chance to explain that night in Telluride.

"Go win your race," she told Drake with a brightening smile, the consequence of her decision bringing new vitality to her eyes. "I'll be here when you come back."

"Will you be here when he doesn't win?" Chip asked with that almost maniacal gleam in his eyes.

"I won't have to find out," Stephanie assured him with an even gaze.

She didn't. Assuming her position in the crowd right along the finish line, she watched as the skiers swept down in slick, swift succession, her heart climbing successively higher until she saw first Chip and then Drake take the hill.

From her first sighting of him, high up on the mountain, Stephanie knew that the edge was back. Drake attacked the gates with the precision of a surgeon and skimmed the snow as if he did in fact have wings. After two runs, he outdistanced Chip to his first gold medal by a margin of only a few hundredths of a second. The crowd cheered. The announcers clustered around Drake, keeping Stephanie away. Off at the corner of the crowd, Chip watched with precarious patience.

Two days later, it happened again. Since Drake was living in the Olympic village and Stephanie still had a job to do, they didn't have the time they wanted to talk about their future. All they could do was meet for some of the meals and smile in the face of the publicity that insisted on tagging Drake's attempts with the word epic.

"The greatest triple threat skier since the legendary Jean-Claude Killy, Drake McDonald must fight off a pack of hungry youngsters for his gold. Vermiller, Schmidt, LeVallier, and most of all Markinson have their sights set on preventing the great skier from the triple gold he plans to take home from these Olympics."

Standing next to the announcer at the bottom of the slalom run, Stephanie squinted up into the blinding white of the snow to see the tiny figures clustered at the top of the mountain. Two more, she thought, clenching and unclenching her hands in anticipation. Just two more medals.

Drake was hurting from his runs, his knees stiffening up from the tremendous strain, his back tight and his shoulder aching. Stephanie saw his pain in the way he walked, in his tight smile. It made her hurt, too. Would he be limber enough to take the fighter course? Or would those tired knees give out and send him tumbling again? And to think that he still had to get through the downhill after this.

Thank God she hadn't known him since the beginning of his career. She never would have lasted.

But once again, he flew. Around Stephanie the crowd was left gasping, urging Drake on with their bodies and their cries as the seconds ticked away and he zigzagged with frightening abandon.

"Oh, my God!" somebody gasped behind her as Drake came perilously close to the sky, teetering precariously on a wide turn. "How does he keep from falling?"

"You think this is exciting," another answered. "Wait till you see him downhill."

Stephanie came close to shutting her eyes, wishing she could think of a way to stay away from that downhill. Drake would keep himself far too close to the edge in that race to suit her. A cheer went up and Drake swept across the finish line, a full eight-tenths of a second faster than his nearest competitor.

Later as he stood on that highest platform watching the flag rise to the strains of the "Star-Spangled Banner," Drake seemed to be the most vibrant, essential person Stephanie had ever known. She couldn't imagine ever loving him more. Her eyes filled with tears at the pride and triumph in his as he accepted the praise of fan and fellow-competitor alike.

Looking over, though, she saw that the silver medalist wasn't wearing the same animated smile as his co-competitors or even his audience. Chip looked out beyond the crowd and the cameras as if he were seeing something else. Stephanie saw the hard glint in his bright blue eyes and thought of a warrior in battle. He only had one more chance to best Drake, and she had the feeling that any pretenses of friendship would die in the attempt.

When the ceremony ended and Drake offered his hand, Chip took a moment to accept. In that moment, Stephanie saw the challenge spark between the two men, and knew that Drake wasn't in the least deceived by the bright-boy exterior. He understood quite well what lay behind it. No more than a few weeks earlier, that exchange of looks would have set Stephanie shivering. Now she was beginning to accept it.

Stephanie spent that evening in her cutting room, trying to catch up on the film that hung like drying spaghetti all over the place. Drake was holed up in the village, pacing away the night before the downhill in seclusion, his entire energies concentrated on the upcoming race.

Stephanie wished he was there with her. She jealously wanted to be the one to ease his prerace tension, to walk the course with him in the morning and stand at the top of that mountain looking out and down over the world he sought to conquer. Having spent her entire adult life shunning the arena of competitive skiing, she suddenly felt left out of it.

Bent over the moviola and scenes of gliding, whirling skaters, Stephanie smiled at her own vacillation. She felt as unsure as an ancient explorer braving the unknown oceans, wondering whether it would come to falling off the edge of the world or being swallowed by great monsters. Just as those explorers did, though, she recognized the thrill of the gamble and the joy of discovery. For the first time in her life, Stephanie reveled in taking a chance.

Pulling out a length of film taken during the school figures, the test of control and precision in skating, she spliced it to a scene of the finished freestyle. The crosscutting emphasized the solid groundwork that went into the beautiful artistry of figure skating, while the careful concentration balanced the smiling exuberance of performance. Stephanie liked the results. So, she thought, would Paula. It would prove that Stephanie was paying attention to more than the Alpine standings this week.

Stephanie raised her head at the knock on her door. Her room was at the back of the space the TV crews rented for the Olympics in Calgary. After eight, she didn't even have access to a phone.

"Yes?"

"You had a phone call," the evening secretary informed her. "A Drake McDonald. He'd like you to meet him for breakfast in the morning. He said to meet him at that little greasy spoon just past the village on the side of the highway."

Stephanie thought back. She remembered seeing a little diner, the kind truckers and teens frequented. Not the greatest food around, but far enough out of the limelight to suit their purpose.

"Thanks." She nodded, scanning her watch and thinking that she'd have to get in touch with Drake. She was supposed to meet with Paula in the morning. Maybe she could put off breakfast with Drake a half hour and fit them both in.

Stephanie called, but Drake had already gone back to his pacing. She left the message with one of his teammates, who promised to let Drake know that Stephanie would meet him at the little diner at eight-thirty instead of eight. She went to sleep a while later feeling better than she had in a long while.

Snow clouds had gathered by morning. Stephanie first saw them from the restaurant window at her hotel where she sat discussing the revised shooting schedule with Paula over coffee. She drove into it a little while later as she tried to keep her appointment with Drake. She'd taken care dressing this morning, wearing a soft gray jersey dress and boots. With her Irish shawl thrown around her shoulders, she turned heads wherever she walked.

It didn't take much to find the diner. The breakfast crowd was there, men in work clothes bent over coffee and donuts, and tourists shifting impatiently for take-out orders to carry away to the games. The parking lot was nearly filled, the only open spot around on the far side. Stephanie pulled into it and took one last look in the mirror.

It occurred to her that she was acting suspiciously like a teen with her first crush. She checked her makeup and straightened her hair to make a good impression. Her heart was fluttering just a little at the thought of a few minutes alone with the man she loved. It was straight out of a movie romance, Stephanie thought. Maybe fate had decided already that she would attend the Olympics. It seemed that her subconscious had made decisions that her mind knew nothing about.

Laughing at the scared look on her face, she opened the door and stepped out onto the parking lot.

"I'm glad you could make it, gorgeous."

Wheeling at the sound of the voice, Stephanie came to a shuddering halt. Her first instinct was to be irritated. She wasn't in the mood for Chip Markinson's games. It was his tone, the cocky greeting betraying the fact that *he* had made that call the night before.

But before Stephanie could get out a word about childish pranks, she caught sight of Chip and fell silent. A gun. He was smiling and pointing a gun at her. In broad daylight.

"For a while last night," he said easily," I wasn't sure you'd come. McDonald's been eating his guts out over the fact that you can't seem to make a commitment. But here you are. He'll be glad to know."

Stephanie couldn't drag her eyes away from the gun. "What are you doing?"

Chip's laugh was chilling. "Going for the gold. Same thing I've been doing all along."

That got her to face him. The little-boy light had finally died, leaving only emptiness, like a vast, lonely desert. Chip Markinson's facade had collapsed and there was no soul to be found behind it. Only obsession.

"What do you mean, 'all along'?" Stephanie demanded.

Chip shrugged. "Ames is hungry," he admitted. "But he's not imaginative. He played the paperwork games. When I saw what that did to McDonald's concentration, to have the precious Inn at stake, I just took it all a few steps further. Even without Diane's unsuspecting help it would have been painfully simple. She ended up providing me with keys to the office, access to the computer and an opportunity to play with the Jeep.''

''You tried to kill Drake?'' Stephanie asked, too stunned to attempt escape. She simply couldn't comprehend the magnitude of what she was hearing.

Chip was shaking his head. ''Not him. If I killed him, I'd defeat my purpose. No, I tried to kill you. I found out after a while that where the Inn wouldn't interfere with Mc-Donald's racing, you would.''

''But it doesn't make sense....''

''Doesn't it?'' he demanded. ''Do you really think so? You think McDonald would stop at anything to win those medals? Not likely he wouldn't. This is my last chance. My last chance to finally put an end to all the comparisons, all the exceptions. You know, 'Chip Markinson's good, but he never beat the great Drake McDonald.' Well, I'm going to beat him today. And you're going to help me.''

Chip had taken her by the arm and she hadn't even realized it. Fighting the terror his words bred, Stephanie tried desperately to put some kind of order into her thoughts. She should be able to handle an irrational person. God knows she'd dealt with them before. She'd cut her teeth with her father, his words had sounded painfully similar to the precarious logic of Chip's plans. Stephanie ought to be able to get the better of him. They were on a parking lot, for God's sake, in the middle of the morning! Somebody had to see what was going on. Somebody eventually had to come out of the diner.

''Step back into the car,'' Chip instructed her, motioning with the gun. ''You'll drive, and I'll guide. We're going someplace where we can be alone. Someplace the police can find you before Drake goes up on that hill this afternoon.''

''Chip, please don't do this to yourself. Somebody will find out....''

He stepped close to her, shoving the gun into her ribs. "Don't be my friend, Stephanie. Just get in the car. We're late already."

Chip backed away enough to guide her toward the passenger's side. She would slide all the way over, covered by the unwavering gun, and then he would get in. There had to be a way, she thought, fingering the car keys like rosary beads. There had to be some way of getting away from him.

"I wouldn't try it." He smiled sharply, anticipating her. "I want this enough to shoot you right here."

Stephanie didn't goad him any further. Hands up a little, she worked her way around to the passenger seat and opened the door to slide in. Chip stepped in close to her so that the door of the car was between the gun and any witnesses. Stephanie concentrated on getting across the seat.

"Go ahead and put the keys—"

Suddenly Chip's words were cut off. Stephanie turned to see a look of surprise blossom on his face, then rage. He swung the gun away from her. Stephanie saw a blur of movement just beyond the car. As he whirled to face his attacker Chip slammed back against the door.

Someone from the restaurant, Stephanie thought with relief. She caught sight of a body bent low to the ground, someone who had wanted to stay just out of sight until Chip was at his most vulnerable. Then Chip slammed against the car again, the gun clanking against the metal. His head cracked against the roof. He spun away and the door was forced shut, leaving him out in the driveway.

Stephanie's first reaction was to start the engine and escape. She was still too close to that madman. But her rescuer was alone, matched against an enraged Chip and the gun he wielded. She didn't know what she could do, but she had to help.

Then she saw who her rescuer was.

Straightening from a crouch, Drake propelled himself at Chip a third time. Stephanie recognized him and still didn't believe it. By the time it had sunk in that Drake was risking his life, Chip had regained his balance. The two men struggled with a silent ferocity, lurching between the parked cars in a kind of obscene dance. Stephanie saw a few patrons from the diner finally take notice, and hoped one of them would think to call the police. She looked around, trying to find something that could help Drake.

There was a savage fury in Chip's eyes. His voice escaped in a keening howl that echoed the frustration and passion he'd brought to this moment. Drake was the sum of everything that had kept him from his goal. Drake had stolen the medals from him, taking even the special glory of the World Cup away from Chip by not competing. Drawing closer and closer to the brink over these last months, Chip had slipped over the edge when Drake had showed up yet again to steal his glory. The obsession that had so long served him in his quest for championship had finally turned against him. If he couldn't win, he would kill.

Stephanie slid down in the seat and moved closer to the passenger door, closer to where Drake and Chip traded blows in their attempts to gain control of the gun. They were now in front of the car, Drake's back pressed against the hood as Chip briefly got the upper hand. Drake was in Olympic form, but Chip possessed the power generated by madness and rage. It couldn't be an even match. They were grunting with the exertion, their arms outstretched against each other, their legs straining for balance. Just as Stephanie reached the door, thinking she could swing it against Chip, he pulled out of Drake's grasp.

Turning back on Drake, Chip swung the gun like a club. Stephanie saw Drake spin away from the impact. He didn't move quickly enough. The gun caught him behind the right ear. Stumbling, he grunted with the pain. Blood stained his shirt. Chip swung again, this time for Drake's bad shoulder. It brought Drake down. Her heart in her throat, Stephanie reached for the door handle and pushed the door open.

She wasn't in time. Before she could force Chip off balance, he aimed the gun straight down to the spot where Drake had fallen and fired.

# Chapter 15

Drake considered himself lucky. If he hadn't started to roll, the bullet Chip fired would have ended up right where it was aimed, about a millimeter above his left eye. As it was, he felt a dull thud in his arm as he hurled himself at Chip's legs and sent him flying. The gun clanked away somewhere on the asphalt. Chip came down all arms and legs, still struggling.

Drake did his best to hold him off. He had only one useful arm. The one Chip had hit was numb from the shoulder down, it's movements slow and uncertain. The parking lot spun dizzily away from him as he moved, the sharp pain from the back of his head shooting down his neck. He felt Chip's hands close around his throat and knew that he didn't have the strength to stop him.

"Chip, let him go! I'll shoot!"

Drake heard Stephanie's shrill voice. He didn't think Chip did. His eyes were glassy and wide, their focus on Drake's face. Drake brought up a hand, wedging it between Chip's hands and his throat, trying to take off some of that brutal pressure, trying to keep from blacking out. He kicked and clawed as wildly as Chip did.

Drake's lungs screamed for air. He was blacking out. In desperation, he rolled, pinning Chip beneath him on the cold, black asphalt. Chip never loosened his grip. Drake got his other hand up, forced it to work and methodically began to slam Chip's head against the ground. He was seeing sparks, the sun dimming to redness. Chip's eyes never wavered. His strength didn't ebb. Desperate now for air, Drake kept on fighting.

Stephanie stood impotently by, gun in hand, knowing that her threats had landed on deaf ears. Chip was past caring about a gun or retribution. He'd lost again, and Drake was going to pay. She couldn't believe it.

When she saw that Chip really might kill Drake, she couldn't wait any longer. A crowd had begun to gather, a few of the tourists and workers, standing back at a careful distance. They wouldn't help either. The police would be too late.

Stephanie ran forward, gun in hand, not sure what she could do. Chip was still moaning, that strange howl that seemed to rise from his chest like a wounded animal. Drake, deathly silent, fought for his life. She thought maybe she could hit Chip, maybe help pry those deadly fingers loose.

She'd just gotten to the two of them when Chip's hands suddenly loosened. His eyes rolled. The mad howl died and his hold on Drake slackened, as if the passion, the fuel that had propelled him this far, had suddenly been cut off. He dropped to the ground, unconscious, his arms thrown out at his sides.

Trying to get away, Drake fell forward. His back heaved with the effort to breathe. His hand went to his throat, where the marks of Chip's fingers showed in livid slashes. Blood trickled down his neck and his left arm. His eyes were wide with surprise and relief.

"He had...a helluva grip," he gasped with a feeble smile as Stephanie reached him. The first keening of sirens could be heard in the morning air, and a few of the crowd had come closer. Stephanie took hold of Drake and pulled him against her.

"You're a mess," she whispered, hot tears coursing down her cheeks.

"At least my arm's beginning to hurt," he retorted more easily, his face against her throat. "I couldn't even feel it before."

Drake should have felt ludicrous, shaking and gasping in a disheveled pile on a parking lot. He smelled the spring in Stephanie's hair, felt her hand against his head and knew nothing more than sweet comfort.

It had been too close; the shock of discovery still pounded through him, the terror of sudden madness was still sharp. Drake had never seen someone crash through the barriers of sanity that fast or that impressively before. Like sudden lightning, striking without warning. Drake knew he'd eventually feel sorry for what had become of Chip.

"Are you okay?" he asked, bringing his hand up to Stephanie's face, holding her just as close.

"I'm fine," she whispered, eyes squeezed shut, hands trembling against him. "I still can't believe it."

"I know. What set him off so fast?"

Stephanie lifted her face, her eyes still ravaged by what she'd been through. "It wasn't so fast. He's been behind most of what's been going on at the Inn all winter. To distract you from your racing." She sighed a little. It sounded as crazy as Chip's self-justification. "He just got desperate when he realized that he only had one medal left to win from you. He was going to . . . I think he was going to kill me."

Drake brushed the tears from her cheek. "It's all over now," he murmured, the bile in his throat belying his calm words. The crowd had found them now, a few recognizing his face from the TV coverage. They hadn't yet made the connection with Chip. A squad car swung into the parking lot and braked to a swift stop just beyond. It was time to get on with things.

"Let's go and talk to the police," Drake suggested. "The quicker we get on with this, the quicker I can be ready to ski."

Stephanie stiffened as if she'd been shot. Before she had the chance to voice a protest, Drake ran a quick finger along the line of her cheek.

"No, you can't talk me out of it," he said with a steely smile. "It's my last chance, too, you know."

He helped Stephanie to her feet, only to find that the parking lot dropped away from him as he rose. It was all he could do to keep from falling right back on his nose as the world tilted and swayed. For a moment he thought he was going to be sick. Chip must have had some muscle behind that swing. Drake had had concussions before, and this had all the earmarks.

"You can't really expect to race downhill today," Stephanie protested. "You'll end up right back in traction."

"Then I'll end up in traction," he retorted, using all his energies to keep from stumbling. The dizziness would pass, just like the headache and the nausea. Drake could only hope they'd pass quickly enough. "I'm not missing my last chance at a downhill win."

"And what do you plan to do about the bullet hole in your arm?" Stephanie demanded, really frightened now. She hadn't had the chance to worry about what would happen to Drake when he'd jumped Chip. She did now, with the race still another two hours away. There would be far too much time for her to replay Drake's fall in her mind as she relentlessly catalogued the injuries Chip had inflicted.

"It's just a scratch," Drake assured her. He didn't tell her that it felt as though his collarbone was cracked. That would just set her off again.

Stephanie scowled. "I should just tell your coach and be done with it."

Drake's reaction almost frightened her anew. His features froze, the expression in his eyes becoming flat and hard. What Stephanie had meant as a throwaway complaint had been perceived as a real threat. A threat that jeopardized their relation on a level so basic that Drake couldn't verbalize it.

That Stephanie would interfere with the fulcrum by which Drake balanced his entire future seemed inconceivable. If she knew only one thing about him, it had to be that nothing was going to keep him from the slopes today. If Chip had shot him in the chest, he would have done his best to postpone dying until he'd made his try for the gold.

"That's what I *should* do." Stephanie smiled dryly, linking her hand unobtrusively to Drake's to assist his balance before he had to face the police. "I didn't say that it was what I was going to do."

"This is what it all comes down to on this bright, windy day in Canada. Left without the fierce competition of Chip Markinson since that skier's surprise withdrawal from the race, Drake McDonald suddenly finds just as worthy an opponent in the Swiss great, Mueller. It's going to be difficult to beat the incredible time Mueller put in on this course, especially since the snow's beginning to get soft...."

Stephanie rocked from one foot to the other, trying to ignore the cold that steadily seeped through her clothes. The person next to her held a small TV, so that they could see the televised racing. From the vantage point of the finish line, only the last twenty percent of the course was visible. Besides, Stephanie decided with steadily mounting anxiety, the races seemed so much more precarious with the breathless exclamations of the commentators.

One of the Austrians was just coming into view, a near fall up top putting him completely out of the standings. The crowd cheered his effort and then turned their attention to the next racer, Drake McDonald. One of the greatest American skiers, the epic warrior who was making his final bid for immortality. A little slower than he once was, a little less spectacular. Still, he was the holder of seventy separate World Cup medals and two all-around World Cups, a bevy of gold and silver medals from three Olympics and the hushed respect of every announcer who had ever covered skiing in the last decade.

Frans Mueller had forced Drake's hand by racing an unbelievable two seconds faster down the roller coaster course than the nearest competitor. One second thirty faster than anyone had ever done the course. And McDonald, older, at the end of his career, beaten up from the tumbles he'd taken over the years and still recovering from the one he'd taken that fall, was going to try and catch him.

And that, Stephanie thought with a solid lump of fear in her throat, didn't even take into account the goose egg hidden beneath the helmet and the bandaged arm covered by his bodysuit. More than his reputation would be on the line out there. His life would be on the line.

Three... Drake rocked back on his heels, forcing the pain away. Two... He watched the rutted, sheer mountain at his feet. One... Imagined the finish line....

"And McDonald is on his way," the announcer cried, his voice already brimming with excitement. "Look at him push off on that first steep slope! He's not taking any chances on this course. He's going to go all the way for this win."

Stephanie's eyes strayed to the tiny screen where Drake could be seen going into his crouch, his body looking as lithe as ever. He tucked his arms in and his head down and rode the mountain like a comet.

"Look at him hold those corners.... Then into the bumps, taking a little air. It's going to be a wild ride. I don't think even Klammer attacked a course with as much reckless abandon as McDonald. You're sure he's going to just sail right off it any minute... Oh, look out! He almost lost it on that bump, windmilling to regain his balance...."

Stephanie turned away. Drake was hurtling down the hill, so close to the edge of control that she couldn't bear to watch. The crowd around her gasped, then gasped again, the announcer's voice growing progressively louder.

"He's picking up time! Look at that! He's shaved off six-hundredths of a second and he's going even faster. McDonald just pours himself down this mountain!"

"There he is!" somebody cried. The heads went up to discover the bright red blur speed out of the turn and sail straight down the mountain. Stephanie looked up, too, her attention drawn inexorably to the brilliance of Drake's performance. She'd never seen anything so graceful or breathtaking. One moment her heart was in her mouth for fear he'd fall. Then she laughed at the thrill of his risks. Drake was skiing for all of them, for everyone who wanted to throw caution to the wind and take a hill as if he owned it.

"I can't believe it, he's still picking up speed! I've never seen skiing like this! He's all over that course. I can't believe he hasn't fallen all the way down. His speeds are in excess of ninety miles an hour! Oh, look out!"

Stephanie saw Drake's arms rise, yanking precarious balance out of thin air. Then he swept across the finish line like a bullet. The announcer's breathless cries were lost in the roar of the crowd.

Microphones bristled, spectators surged forward as Drake McDonald slid out of his skis, his body trembling and heaving from the exertion. But before anyone could get to him, a tall figure separated itself from the crowd and hurtled into his arms. No one could see that she was the force that kept him upright during all the interviewing and congratulating, her arm around his right shoulder to keep people from pummeling that side, her eyes knowing and shining with a dry humor that only McDonald seemed to understand. The two appeared to share the moment with a rare empathy, their joy combined and translated into a delicious enthusiasm that made copy on just about every front page in America.

"You look like you were hit by a bus," Stephanie observed a few days later. She and Drake had celebrated at the Inn, and then gone to L.A. where he could see his orthopedists and she could be with him.

The schedule had worked out fine. By the time they got to Stephanie's, the majority of Drake's injuries had progressed from the unbearable stage to the merely uncomfortable. He wore a clavicle strap for the collarbone, and a new knee splint for the wear and tear he'd taken on the hills those last few days. The stitches had been removed from his head and arm, and the bruises had faded to less virulent shades of brown and purple. All in all he still looked dramatic, but healthier.

Stephanie knelt at Drake's feet, her hand on the stiff material that covered his knee. He brushed a gentle hand through her hair, relishing the quiet evening and their isolation.

"Bloodied but unbowed." He smiled, his eyes the color of contentment. There was a new softness to him, a stillness Stephanie had not seen before. Drake had always been driven toward something. Now that he had achieved his goal, and the three medals encased in his Telluride home, he faced the future with a new peace. Stephanie savored the change. She could spend hours, days, watching the new Drake McDonald begin to take shape within the old one. She could have sat just as she was for the rest of her life.

"What are you doing?" he asked without as much suspicion as the words might have warranted.

Stephanie just smiled, not bothering to look up as she worked buckle and Velcro. "Setting you free."

"Set me free from that splint and I might just fall on my face," he warned lightly, his fingers weaving sharp chills along the length of her hair.

"Just as long as you end up next to me," she agreed with a private smile, opening the brace and sliding it free. Bending to the still swollen knee, Stephanie kissed it, running swift fingers over Drake's skin. "I thought you'd want me to make the hurts feel a little better.... Does it hurt here?"

"Mmm."

She kissed his thigh where it met the hem of his shorts, her hand sliding farther along.

"Let's see, seems to me you hurt your arm."

"That's right."

Stephanie scooted up next to him, her long torso deliberately snaking along the territory her hand had breached. Drake's reaction was predictable and swift, brightening the smile Stephanie offered. With slow movements, she worked his buttons free to get to the shoulder and arm that needed her ministrations.

"Poor shoulder...."

Drake seemed to be doing his own ministering, his hands sliding their way up beneath the cotton crop top Stephanie wore over her own shorts. He spanned her waist and searched out his own fasteners, sparking delicious tremors down the length of Stephanie's body.

Stephanie let her lips linger over the old bruises, the feel of Drake's skin provoking her. She searched out the sinew at shoulder and chest and taunted him with her deliberation.

"I don't suppose you can take off that strap," she murmured, kissing the still livid scar along his deltoid muscle.

"Think of it as a challenge," he replied, easing her more closely into his grasp and dipping his face toward the silken allure of her hair.

"That's the way I think of *you*." She was surprised by the quick tremor of response beneath her lips. "Does that feel better?"

His answer was a harsh laugh as he let his hands search her body with greater equanimity.

"What about here?" Drake motioned to the slashes of color that had yet to fade from his throat. Shivering at the memory they ignited, Stephanie met them with tentative lips, offering comfort rather than stimulation. Drake had been through so much, come so close to sacrificing the end of his dreams for her. He had come so close to dying that Stephanie couldn't think of it without shuddering. What would she have done? Would her life have been better because she had been so wise as to refuse a commitment to him?

Her hands at his shoulders, Stephanie nuzzled against him, soaking in his vibrance, his passion. Passion was all right, she decided, as long as its owner knew just what to do with it.

Drake pulled her tightly to him, asserting his dominance in the most traditional of ways. He had his arms around her and his lips on her forehead, beginning a slow foray down toward her mouth. Stephanie sighed with her own contentment and settled into his embrace, welcoming the fires he stirred and seeking to stir her own.

"What else can I make feel better?" she murmured just before he found her lips.

Drake's chuckle provoked new shivers, quicksilver racing through her at his touch, at the sweep of his breath against her skin, the delicious suggestion in his voice.

"You didn't hurt that," she giggled breathlessly, pressing against the hand that fitted her waist so neatly, urging it on.

"You didn't say anything about being hurt," he reminded her, edging around to tease at her ear. She shuddered with the sharp stab of delight he ignited. "You just wanted to know if you could make it feel better."

"In that case..."

Drake's fingers swept the underside of her breast, eliciting new sighs, new sensations of urgency and languor. Stephanie closed her eyes, accepting the deep exploration of his kiss and savoring the heady reaction to his touch. She sought and gave pleasure, testing the textures of fabric and skin, tracing the unyielding line of muscle and tendon, searching out points of pleasure that could provoke Drake to those surprised little shudders of delight.

Stephanie had never known a man who responded to her touch in such an intoxicating way, telegraphing his mounting excitement, sharing his exultation with her like a gift. She had never felt more a part of another person than she did with Drake.

"Are you sure your neighbor isn't going to be doing any more surprise gardening?" Drake asked.

Stephanie opened her eyes to the gathering dusk outside her wide windows. The blanket of lights flickered below them in the night breeze and massing clouds concealed the distant ocean. It would rain by morning. Stephanie thought how much she wanted to lie in bed with Drake and watch it, sharing the world below them like distant gods.

"Jack's in Palm Springs with Corey," she assured him quietly, closing her eyes again. Somewhere below a car horn sounded and another answered. A jet threaded its way through the back of Stephanie's consciousness and faded. All that mattered in the world right now was the man who held her in his arms.

Drake smiled against her, his fingers at the buttons of her blouse. "I've always wanted to make love in front of a view of a city." Freeing the buttons, he spread the material with the flat of his hand, following the contour of Stephanie's breast. "It's almost as nice as making love in the mountains."

Stephanie felt the rasp of his callused hands on her skin and arched, wanting more. Her breasts ached, sharp and full for the feel of him. "We could enjoy both, if you'd like," she suggested with a slow smile.

Her words brought Drake to a halt. He straightened a little, his hand laid against her skin as if seeking the heart of her.

"Not if you don't marry me, we can't," he said, his expression suddenly intense. "I can't go on without some kind of commitment."

Stephanie knew he felt the way her heart skipped at his words. She couldn't keep the sudden fear from her eyes, the latent distrust that leaped out unbidden when the future opened up too brightly to believe. This time, though, she pushed that old logic away. Drake held her in his arms, and he promised forever. They rested intertwined, their bodies as familiar and exciting as daybreak or summer storms. Her body sang and her soul soared. No one had ever given her that, and she knew without a doubt that she couldn't live without it, any more than she could live without the new sense of security Drake had given her. She needed him. She wanted him. And he, passionate, stubborn man that he was, wanted her. Who was she to say no?

Lifting a hand to the handsome angles of his face, Stephanie smiled, the entire content of her heart in her eyes. "Are you asking?"

Drake's answering smile was surprised, as if he hadn't quite thought of it that way himself. "I guess I am. Marry me, Stephanie. Share my life and my friends, and be there when I wake up in the morning."

"I still have my work," she reminded him, her eyes unexpectedly brimming with happy tears. The longer she knew

Drake McDonald, the more she cried—and the more she enjoyed it.

He kissed her, the command of his mouth equal to the certainty in his voice. "Nothing like a little travel to spice up a marriage."

Stephanie set her hands against his chest, whether to caution or stabilize, she couldn't tell. She just knew that his kisses were dangerously leaching the strength from her limbs, from any of the convictions that could keep her from him.

"I still won't ski."

Another kiss, longer and sweeter, the outside world dimming between them.

"And I won't go to any more benefits for your mother."

Stephanie chuckled, her voice husky and sensuous. Drake felt its vibrations with his fingers, and thought how delicious the sound and feel of her voice were. How he would never tire of it, ripening into lush music as she got older.

Basking in the sweet glow of Drake's eyes, Stephanie offered him a smile that held more than any words could. And then she gave him the words as well. "I've been so afraid of you. From the moment I first set eyes on you. All the time that I was telling myself that I refused to fall in love with anyone and put up with that kind of nonsense, I was falling in love with you." She brought her hand up once again, seeking the planes of Drake's face as if there resided the true spirit of him, the harsh, passionate soul that took him to the tops of mountains and gentled the fears of a lonely woman. His cheeks felt rough against her fingers. His eyes, those jewels that captured her with their hypnotic fire, were infinitely tender. Stephanie felt cherished and trembled at her discovery.

"I love you, Drake. If you hadn't asked me to marry you, I would have asked you."

Giving a whoop of victory, Drake pulled her tight against him. "It's about damn time, lady! My next plan was kidnapping."

Stephanie laughed again, her hands once again left to the lazy exploration of his chest. "Kidnapping sounds like fun."

She'd no more than said it than Drake had her in his arms as he got to his feet.

"Your knee..." she instinctively protested.

He gave her a resounding kiss. "Will be fine as long as we don't exceed eighty miles an hour or hit any bumps. I think it will last as long as it takes me to get you to bed."

Her bed with its pink and green comforter served them well, nestling them like a field of wildflowers on a summer's evening. Drake turned off the lights and let the city and the night sky light their way.

The room darkened into starlight and shadows, softening contours and granting grace in movement. Stephanie saw Drake settle over her, felt his hands remove her clothes and wondered at the beautiful dreamlike quality of the actions.

It felt as if she were floating, surrounded in an ocean of sensation that lapped at her, swirling along her legs and across her belly. Drake agitated the waters with his hands, those hands that knew her now so well and yet couldn't seem to satiate themselves. Those hands she craved like sunlight against her skin.

She could see his body, naked now in the soft, flickering light, and it enticed her. So strong, so sleek, seething with a power that was just slightly dangerous, a passion that was barely kept in check. Stephanie let her hands play along his body as if it were an undiscovered terrain, stoking her own arousal with the heat of his skin.

"You're so beautiful," Drake whispered, his breath sweeping her throat as he traced little kisses along it. "So delicious, like honey and sunlight...."

Stephanie tangled a hand in the wild darkness of his hair as he bent to her breast. She arched her back, the desire centering, settling into the depth of her belly, just above the juncture of her thighs. It tightened, pulling her head back and her arms up to him, drawing him closer against her. Begging him to take her with his hands and mouth, to awaken each nerve ending and set it to unbearable light, her hands blindly reached for him, seeking the union, the communion that could quench the ache he'd ignited.

She heard a low whimper and recognized her own voice as if from a distance. Drake had a hand to her breast, cupping it to him, rasping its sensitive underside as his tongue flickered against the nipple. His other hand sought her center, fingers swift and sure against the slick satin.

The tide that washed over her became light, pulsating along her limbs in a thousand brightening hues. She could do no more than roll her head from side to side, her body beginning its rocking, the rhythm as ancient as the act. She clutched at Drake, pulling him to her, begging him to enter, to fill her, to shatter the walls she'd built and bring her to life.

"Please," she whimpered, her hands at his back, at the firm shape of his buttocks, urging him closer. "I need you.... Don't wait any longer...."

Drake brushed the damp ringlets back from Stephanie's forehead and smiled, the effort of control turning his jaw to steel. "I love you, Stephanie." Bending to kiss her once more, he eased himself over her. Stephanie instinctively wrapped herself around him, drawing him home, sobbing now with hunger and need. She felt him slip in, then leave, easing his way into her, teasing and satisfying. Again, a little deeper until she begged, her eyes wild, her fingers raking his back. Then, when he'd driven her to the brink where reason and control failed her, he answered her plea.

Pulling her to him, he plunged into her, driven deeper and deeper by the honeyed warmth of her, the musky scent of her skin, the breathless cries he tore from her. His world dissolved, whirling into color and light, brightening, dazzling, shattering into sunlight as he lost himself in her and fell, spent and satisfied into her arms.

Stephanie ran a lazy hand through Drake's hair, her eyes on the night outside and her heart content. The glow of his attentions still coursed through her. Stephanie couldn't yet get her breathing to slow or her heart to quit its mad pace. Drake lay against her, his weight intimate, his peace gratifying. Somewhere deep in her insecurities, a small voice still questioned her judgment. Was she wise to commit herself? Shouldn't she know better than to make the kind of promises that had never succeeded in her life? No, she decided, sleep stealing away the force of her hesitation. I think I'll enjoy this particular promise. I think I'll look forward to sharing again what I had tonight.

The next morning Stephanie was in the kitchen fixing breakfast when the doorbell rang. She hurried over, hoping not to wake Drake who still lay haphazardly across the bed where she'd left him. They had made love again the night before, more slowly, more carefully, and then fallen asleep in each other's arms. Stephanie had never known a peace like she had when she'd woken to the warmth of a man next to her, the sight of a tousled head that would always be there when she woke. You never miss it until you have it.

"Yes...."

She swung the door open without thinking, expecting perhaps a salesman or one of the neighborhood missionaries. Instead an older man stood on her doorstep. Waiting there in the light rain that fell, he looked dissipated, his skin that putty color that betrays abuse, his clothes clean but old. A cardigan sweater hung loosely over a polyester shirt and work slacks. He held a hat in his hands as if he'd come to beg, and his eyes sought Stephanie's carefully.

At first Stephanie could do no more than stare. "Daddy?"

"I should have called." He smiled hesitantly, the fierce light in his eyes now no more than supplication. Stephanie thought her heart would break at the change in him. "Could I come in?"

She didn't show him in. Unable to stop the tears that filled her eyes or give voice to the thousand conflicting emotions that choked her, Stephanie stepped up and took the older man into her arms.

"He suggested I come," he was saying, his arms around her as well. "Said it was about time I apologized. I told him I didn't think you'd want to see me, you know. I'd hurt you enough."

"I've been looking for you for three years," she managed to say, straightening so she could feast her eyes on him as she finally thought to bring him in.

"And driving my car, I see." He smiled with some of the old fire.

Stephanie shrugged uncomfortably, closing the door behind them. "I didn't want to sell it. I was waiting...."

Edward Fleming nodded, looking at his grown daughter as a man looks on his salvation. "I know. He told me."

"Who, Daddy, Jacques?"

"No. Fella named McDonald."

Stephanie froze.

"Nice to see you again, sir."

Stephanie whirled to find Drake dressed and on his feet next to her, his eyes on her father.

"The last time I was here," Drake said, finally turning to her. "Before Christmas." His expression bore no apology. "The detectives called, so I found out where your father was. I went down to have a little talk with him."

"I didn't want you to see me yet," Edward Fleming admitted. "Not till I'd kept a few promises."

Promises. He was sober and quiet, the rage missing from the suddenly frail blue eyes. Maybe he'd had to spend these years away. Maybe he could actually rebuild his life so that he could at last find peace. Stephanie looked from her father to Drake and back again. Within the space of a day, her entire life had been turned around. She had a future, a past and a chance for real happiness. Turning to Drake, she found nothing but love in his eyes, the support that she was going to need to take the next steps forward.

Whatever, he said in silence, I'll be there with you. Forever.

"Come on, Daddy." Stephanie smiled, linking her arms with both men. "Breakfast is ready, and I want to tell you about the plans Drake and I are making. We're getting married. And you—" she smiled, feeling suddenly whole and full of anticipation "—got here just in time to give me away."

\* \* \* \* \*

*. . . and now an exciting short story
from Silhouette Books.*

\*

**HEATHER GRAHAM POZZESSERE**

## Shadows on the Nile

### CHAPTER 4

Jillian had no idea how long the car careened through the twisting streets of Cairo. She was nearly unconscious by the time that it stopped; the exhaust fumes had penetrated to the trunk, and she felt cramped and nauseated.

She tried desperately to free herself from the blanket, but she accomplished nothing. Then rough hands dragged her from the car. She was carried—wriggling and screaming—for an unknown distance, and then things became worse. She was slung over the back of a creature that she identified by its scent and sound as a camel, and her misery grew. She could barely breathe, and every awkward step of the camel slammed into her anew. Once again she had no concept of time, nor could she comprehend any of the Arabic being spoken around her.

At long last the beast came to a halt. At a shouted command it fell to one knee, and again rough hands grabbed her. Still in her cocoon, she was tossed over someone's shoulder.

Suddenly she was cast to the ground, where she freed herself from the loathsome blanket. At last she could see! She was in a tent, but it was a tent unlike anything she could have imagined. It was beautifully appointed with silken draperies and pillows and exotic palm frond decorations. There was a low mosaic table upon which sat an exquisite coffee urn made of copper and brass, along with trays of dates and nuts and fruits.

"Welcome, Miss Jacoby."

Jillian gasped. Seated upon an ebony chair was the man with the scarred face. He was staring at her with an unpleasant smile, his teeth very white against the darkness of his features.

Jillian struggled to her feet. Who in God's name was he, and what did he want from her?

"Welcome," he repeated, and his smile deepened in a way that chilled her to her bones as he stood and came toward her. It was a ruthless smile, and Jillian turned to run.

She stopped quickly. The entryway was blocked by two very large men with evil expressions, and long swords belted to their waists. She heard the laughter of the man with the scarred face behind her, and she swung around, praying for courage.

"This is kidnapping!" she snapped, trying to appear confident. "I don't know what you want from me, but I'm an American citizen, and you can't get away with this."

"Fine. Thank you for the warning. Now where is it, Miss Jacoby?"

"Where is what?" she demanded in genuine exasperation.

"The film. The film for Achmed Jabbar."

She stared at him blankly. "I don't have any film. Not for any Achmed Jabbar or anyone else! I don't even know what you're talking about!" She forced a smile. "Honest to God. I'd give you your film if I had it, but I don't. So please, if you'll just get your goons to move away, I'll leave. No hard feelings. I'll just forget the whole thing. Now—oh!"

She broke off, screaming in sudden fear and pain. He had caught her elbow and twisted it cruelly behind her back. His menacing whisper just reached her ear.

"I can make you more cooperative, Miss Jacoby, and I can enjoy every minute of it. You're a very beautiful woman. All that blond hair and soft white skin." He released her suddenly, shoving her away from him with such force that she landed on the blanket. He smiled, stepping over to her again, pulling his switchblade from a fold of his burnoose. "It's American, too," he told her, indicating the blade. He turned it in his hands and smiled. "It can leave the most delicate ribbon of blood against your flesh—"

He broke off, because there was a sudden commotion at the entryway. He turned away from her, his burning gaze falling on the nervous newcomer, a short, squat man who spoke very anxiously and quickly. The man with the scarred face started to leave, then turned back to Jillian.

"Excuse me. I promise I'll return as quickly as I can," he said with cold menace. Then he left the tent, his guards behind him. Jillian quickly ran to the entrance, only to discover that the guards had not gone far. They greeted her effort with amusement, then took her arms and deposited her less than graciously on the blanket again.

Time passed slowly. Jillian alternately swore to herself and fought the tears of panic that rose to her eyes. She also ranted against Alex Montgomery. Somehow this was all his fault—she was sure of it.

Then she wished desperately that he were with her.

Darkness fell. There was no light in the tent, only whatever moonlight filtered through the translucent walls. Desolate and despairing, Jillian curled against one of the silken pillows, trying not to think of what might happen when her captor returned.

She was so exhausted that she started to doze, but then a slight flicker of movement caught her attention. She looked up. Silhouetted against the walls of the tent was the shadow of a man rising behind her. A scream caught in her throat, and she spun around, ready to do battle. Someone was coming toward her. Someone clothed in black from head to toe, moving silently, stealthily, toward her.

Suddenly he leaped forward and caught her, his hand swiftly covering her mouth.

"For God's sake, don't scream," a familiar voice whispered. "It's me!"

"Alex!"

"The same."

"Alex, you son of a—" she began, but her words faded away as she saw the relief—and the tenderness—in his eyes.

He smiled ruefully in the pale light. His thumbs brushed caressingly over her cheeks, and he asked tensely, "Did he hurt you?"

"No."

He lowered his head until his cheek rested against hers, then inhaled sharply. "I was so frightened for you. I'm going to kill that son of a bitch this time. If he had touched you ..."

His voice trailed away, and he stared at her again with an emotion so intense that she felt as if she were melting. And then his lips met hers, and he kissed her with such passion that she actually forgot she'd been dragged into the desert and threatened with torture, and all because of some ridiculous roll of film she didn't even have. All she knew was the fever of his lips on hers, the sensual, sweeping stroke of his tongue, the hunger with which he touched her, and the sweet, desperate need he roused in her. She wanted him so badly. Her arms curled around his neck, and she wove her fingers through the hair at his nape, then felt the wonderful hot fusion of their bodies melding together. She felt ridiculously safe and secure, and deep in the recesses of her heart, she knew she was falling in love.

Love? How could she think about love? She was in this mess because of him.

Jillian twisted away from him, furious. "Damn you, Alex Montgomery! What in God's name is going on here?"

"I can't tell you now. We've got to get out of here. There's no time for explanations."

"Alex..."

But he was on his feet, as swift and agile as a black panther in the darkness. He laced his fingers through hers and pulled her along to the rear of the tent, where he had slashed an opening.

"You're no Egyptologist!" she whispered furiously.

"Yes, I am," he whispered back. "Now go!"

He shoved her through the opening, then followed close behind. She came out to a night alive with stars and a cooling breeze. In the distance she heard music and laughter, and she could see soft firelight outside a huge tent. She could hear camels braying and the snorts of horses, and smell the odors of sheep and goats.

"Let's go." Alex tugged on her hand. "Run. Now!"

She ran by his side, and together they reached a horse, a prancing, chestnut Arabian.

"Can you ride?" he asked.

"No!"

"Well, you're about to learn!" He swung her up, tossing her easily astride, then followed.

"Montgomery!"

The man with the scar was running toward them. But Alex didn't answer. Instead he dug his heels into the horse's flanks, and the Arabian reared, then galloped into the night.

Jillian turned to look behind them. Her hair flew across her face in the wind, nearly blinding her, and only Alex's embrace kept her on the horse, but she could see enough to be afraid. Scarface was now mounted, along with three others. And they were racing after Alex—after her—as they fled into the dark, never-ending void of the desert

\* \* \* \* \*

*To be continued . . .*
*Join us next month, only in Silhouette Intimate*
*Moments, for the next exciting installment of*
*SHADOWS ON THE NILE.*

# FOUR UNIQUE SERIES
# FOR EVERY WOMAN YOU ARE..

## *Silhouette Romance*

Love, at its most tender, provocative,
emotional . . . in stories that will make you laugh and
cry while bringing you the magic of falling in love.

6 titles
per month

## *Silhouette Special Edition*

Sophisticated, substantial and packed with
emotion, these powerful novels of life and love will
capture your imagination and steal your heart.

6 titles
per month

## *Silhouette Desire*

Open the door to romance and passion. Humorous,
emotional, compelling—yet always a believable
and sensuous story—Silhouette Desire never
fails to deliver on the promise of love.

6 titles
per month

## *Silhouette Intimate Moments*

Enter a world of excitement, of romance
heightened by suspense, adventure and the
passions every woman dreams of. Let us
sweep you away.

4 titles
per month

SILG-1R

# Take 4 Silhouette Special Edition novels and a surprise gift
# FREE

Then preview 6 brand-new books—delivered to your door as soon as they come off the presses! If you decide to keep them, you pay just $2.49 each*—a 9% saving off the retail price, *with no additional charges for postage and handling!*

Romance is alive, well and flourishing in the moving love stories of Silhouette Special Edition novels. They'll awaken your desires, enliven your senses and leave you tingling all over with excitement.

Start with 4 Silhouette Special Edition novels and a surprise gift absolutely FREE. They're yours to keep without obligation.  You can always return a shipment and cancel at any time.

Simply fill out and return the coupon today!

\* Plus 69¢ postage and handling per shipment in Canada.

## *Silhouette Special Edition*®

# Silhouette Intimate Moments

# COMING
# NEXT MONTH

## #225 STRANGERS IN PARADISE
### —Heather Graham Pozzessere

Alexi came to Florida looking for peace and quiet. Instead, she found a house haunted by nighttime intruders. Her neighbor, Rex Morrow, was sure she needed protection, and her mind agreed, though her heart knew it would be much safer without Rex than with him.

## #226 FANTASY MAN—Paula Detmer Riggs

Marshal Tatum Summers was falling in love with handsome Dan Kendall when she discovered he might not be as law-abiding as he seemed. She started investigating, determined to prove his innocence to the world, and just as determined to prove to him that they could have a future—together.

## #227 WINDS OF FEAR—Margaret Malkind

Celine Conway had come to England on business, but she immediately found herself caught up in a whirlwind of adventure, intrigue and danger. Only Ian Evans seemed to know what was going on, but Celine wasn't sure she trusted him—though she knew she could easily love him.

## #228 WHATEVER IT TAKES
### —Patricia Gardner Evans

Sarah Harland thought Matthew Weston was her children's imaginary playmate, a substitute for the father they had lost. But Matthew was very real, as real as his love for Sarah—and as real as the dangerous secret he was keeping.

---

## AVAILABLE THIS MONTH:

# Silhouette Romance™
# Legendary Lovers Trilogy

## BY DEBBIE MACOMBER....

**ONCE UPON A TIME,** in a land not so far away, there lived a girl, Debbie Macomber, who grew up dreaming of castles, white knights and princes on fiery steeds. Her family was an ordinary one with a mother and father and one wicked brother, who sold copies of her diary to all the boys in her junior high class.

One day, when Debbie was only nineteen, a handsome electrician drove by in a shiny black convertible. Now Debbie knew a prince when she saw one, and before long they lived in a two-bedroom cottage surrounded by a white picket fence.

As often happens when a damsel fair meets her prince charming, children followed, and soon the two-bedroom cottage became a four-bedroom castle. The kingdom flourished and prospered, and between soccer games and car pools, ballet classes and clarinet lessons, Debbie thought about love and enchantment and the magic of romance.

One day Debbie said, "What this country needs is a good fairy tale." She remembered how well her diary had sold and she dreamed again of castles, white knights and princes on fiery steeds. And so the stories of Cinderella, Beauty and the Beast, and Snow White were reborn....

---

Look for Debbie Macomber's *Legendary Lovers* trilogy from Silhouette Romance: *Cindy and the Prince* (January, 1988); *Some Kind of Wonderful* (March, 1988); *Almost Paradise* (May, 1988). Don't miss them!

SRT-1